STAR WARS™

HYPERSPACE STORIES

LIGHT AND SHADOW

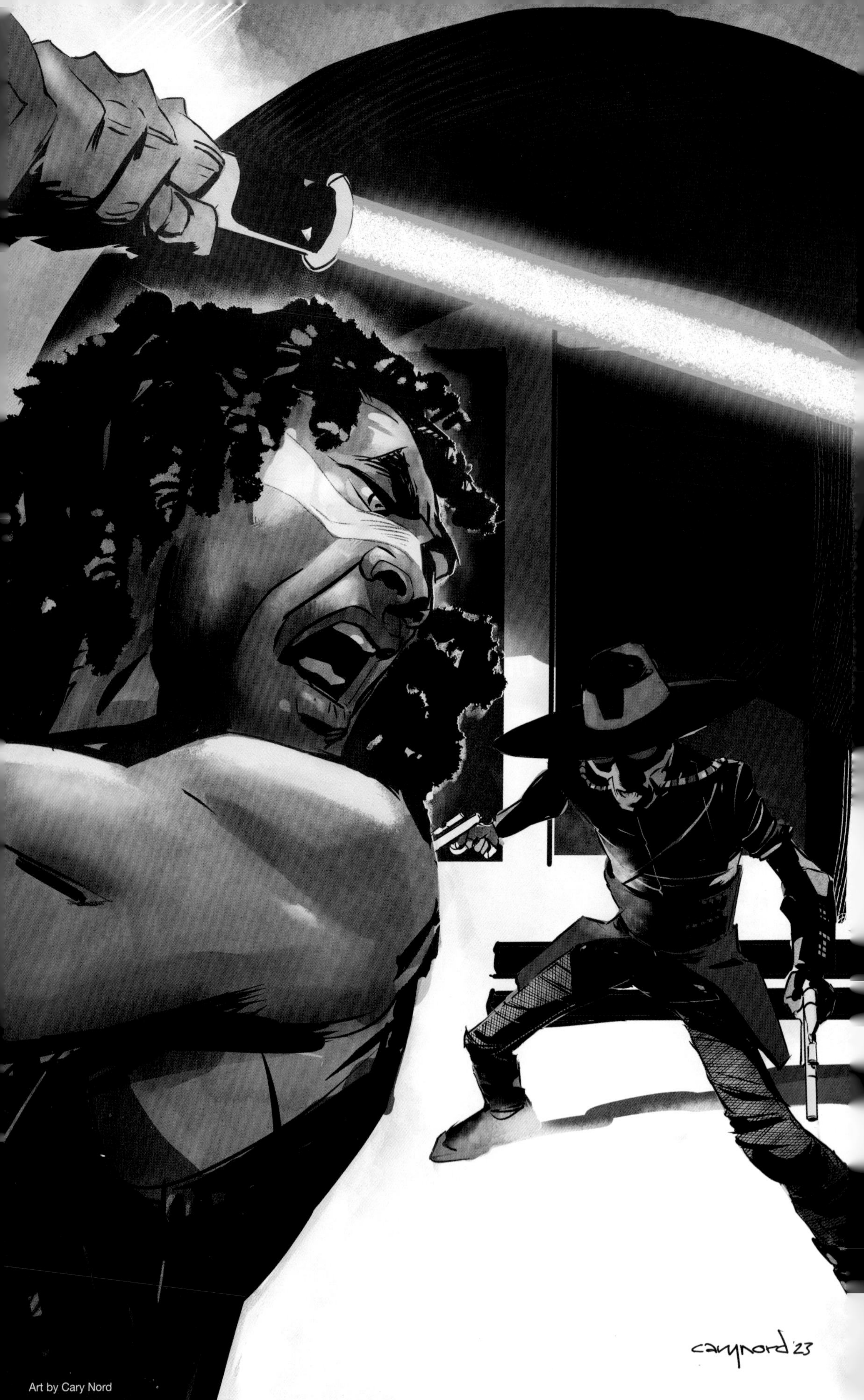
carynord '23

Art by Cary Nord

STAR WARS™

HYPERSPACE STORIES

LIGHT AND SHADOW

written by
MICHAEL MORECI
AMANDA DEIBERT
CECIL CASTELLUCCI

illustrated by
NICK BROKENSHIRE
RICCARDO FACCINI
MEGAN HUANG
LUCAS MARANGON

colors by
DAVID KENNEDY
NICOLA RIGHI
MEGAN HUANG
MICHAEL ATIYEH

letters by
COMICRAFT'S TYLER SMITH and
JIMMY BETANCOURT

additional art by
TOM FOWLER with **BILL CRABTREE**
CARY NORD
RICCARDO FACCINI with **NICOLA RIGHI**
LUCAS MARANGON

cover art by
CARY NORD

 •  Dark Horse Books

President & Publisher . . . . Mike Richardson

Editors. . . . . Spencer Cushing, Matt Dryer

Assistant Editors . . . . . Joe Cavanagh, Freddye Miller

Designer . . . . Hannah Noble

Digital Art Technician . . . . Joey Weaver

FOR LUCASFILM
Creative Director: Michael Siglain
Senior Editor: Robert Simpson
Associate Editor: Grace Orriss
Art Director: Troy Alders
Lucasfilm Story Group: Matt Martin, Pablo Hidalgo, and Emily Shkoukani
Creative Art Manager: Phil Szostak

DARK HORSE COMICS
Neil Hankerson, Executive Vice President • Tom Weddle, Chief Financial Officer • Dale LaFountain,
Chief Information Officer • Tim Wiesch, Vice President of Licensing • Vanessa Todd-Holmes,
Vice President of Production and Scheduling • Mark Bernardi , Vice President of Book Trade
and Digital Sales • Randy Lahrman, Vice President of Product Development and Sales • Cara
O'Neil, Vice President of Marketing • Dave Marshall, Editor in Chief • Davey Estrada, Editorial
Director • Chris Warner, Senior Books Editor • Cary Grazzini, Director of Specialty Projects • Lia
Ribacchi, Creative Director • Michael Gombos, Senior Director of Licensed Publications • Kari
Yadro, Director of Custom Programs • Kari Torson, Director of International Licensing • Christina
Niece, Director of Scheduling

Published by Dark Horse Books
A division of Dark Horse Comics LLC.
10956 SE Main Street
Milwaukie, OR 97222

StarWars.com
DarkHorse.com

First edition: June 2024
Ebook ISBN 978-1-50673-291-6
Trade paperback ISBN 978-1-50673-288-6

1 3 5 7 9 10 8 6 4 2
Printed in China

This volume collects issues #9–#12 of the Dark Horse comic book series Star Wars: Hyperspace
Stories, published September, November, and December 2023.

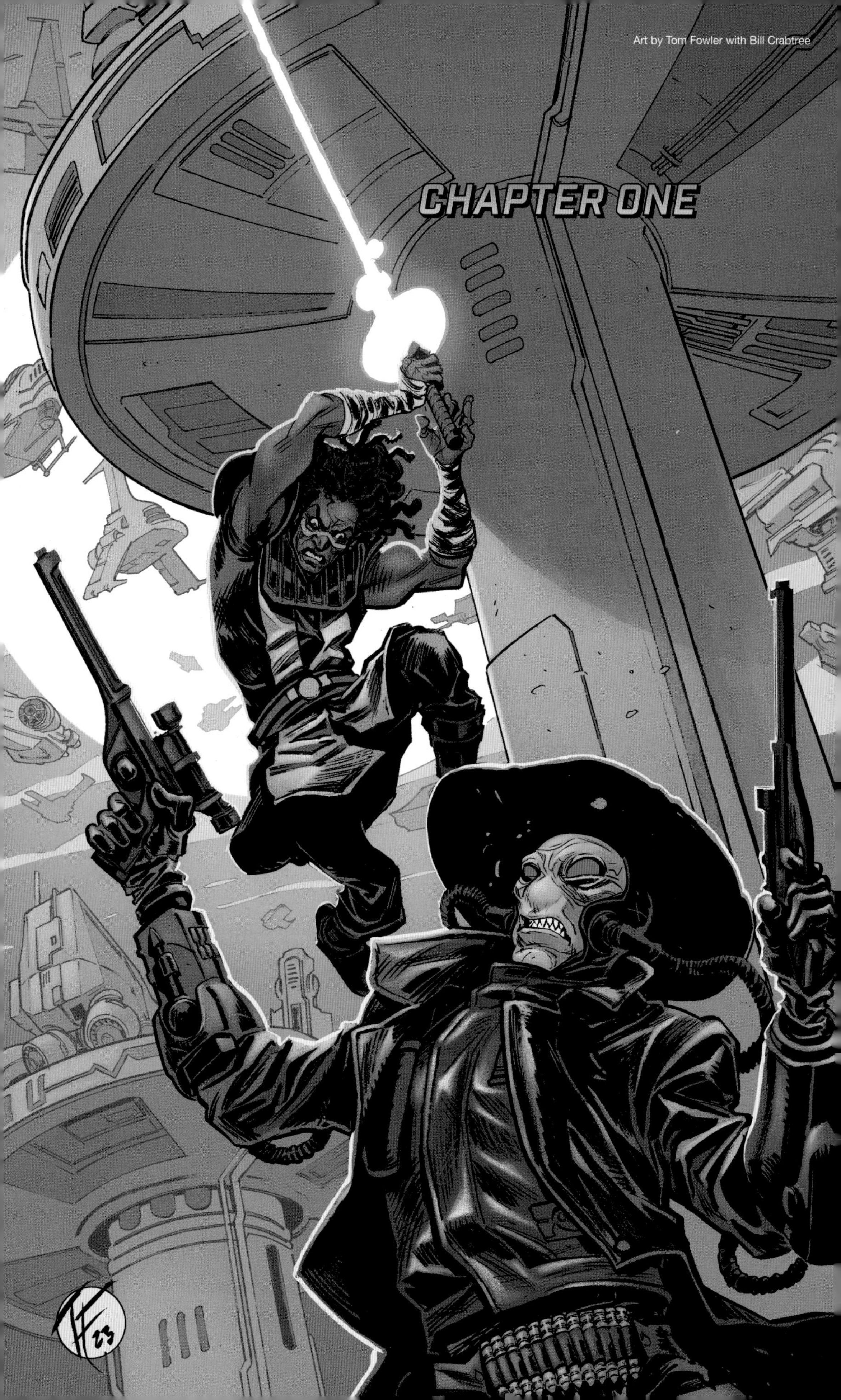
CHAPTER ONE

Art by Tom Fowler with Bill Crabtree

Art by Cary No

CHAPTER ONE: WHO'S THE VOS?

written by
MICHAEL MORECI

pencils and inks by
NICK BROKENSHIRE

colors by
DAVID KENNEDY

letters by
COMICRAFT'S TYLER SMITH and JIMMY BETANCOURT

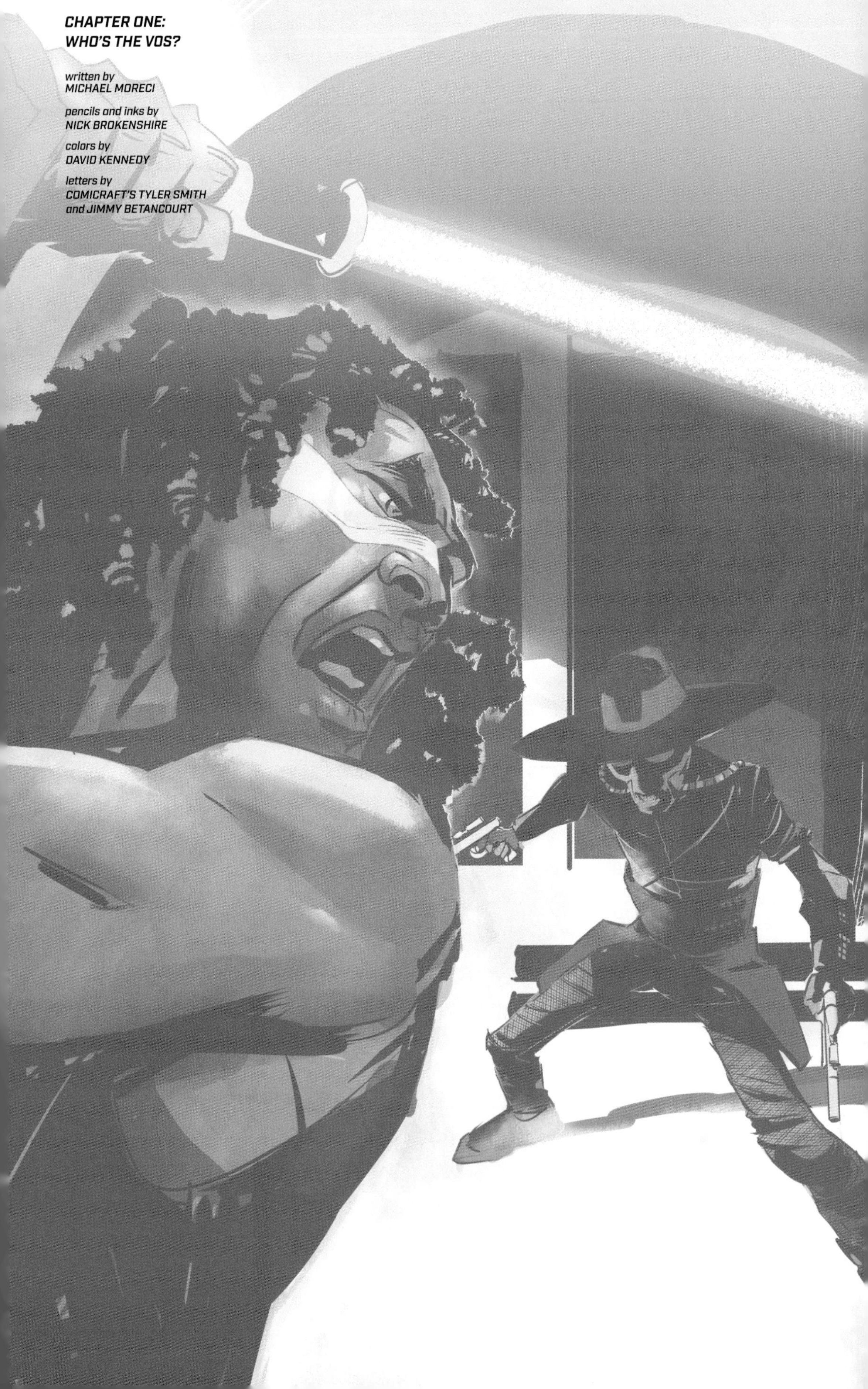

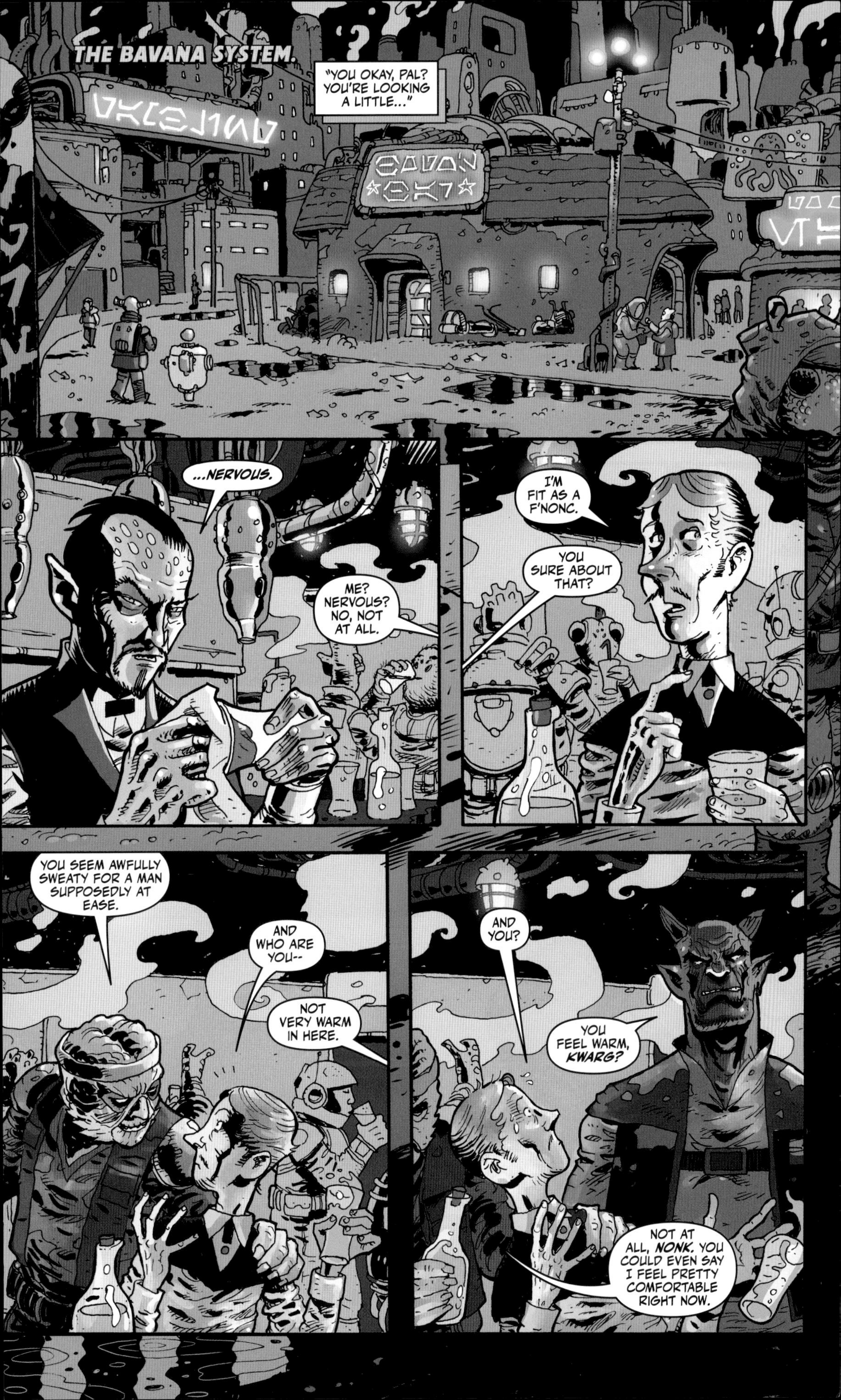
THE BAVANA SYSTEM.
"YOU OKAY, PAL? YOU'RE LOOKING A LITTLE..."
...NERVOUS.
ME? NERVOUS? NO, NOT AT ALL.
I'M FIT AS A F'NONC.
YOU SURE ABOUT THAT?
YOU SEEM AWFULLY SWEATY FOR A MAN SUPPOSEDLY AT EASE.
AND WHO ARE YOU--
NOT VERY WARM IN HERE.
AND YOU?
YOU FEEL WARM, KWARG?
NOT AT ALL, NONK. YOU COULD EVEN SAY I FEEL PRETTY COMFORTABLE RIGHT NOW.

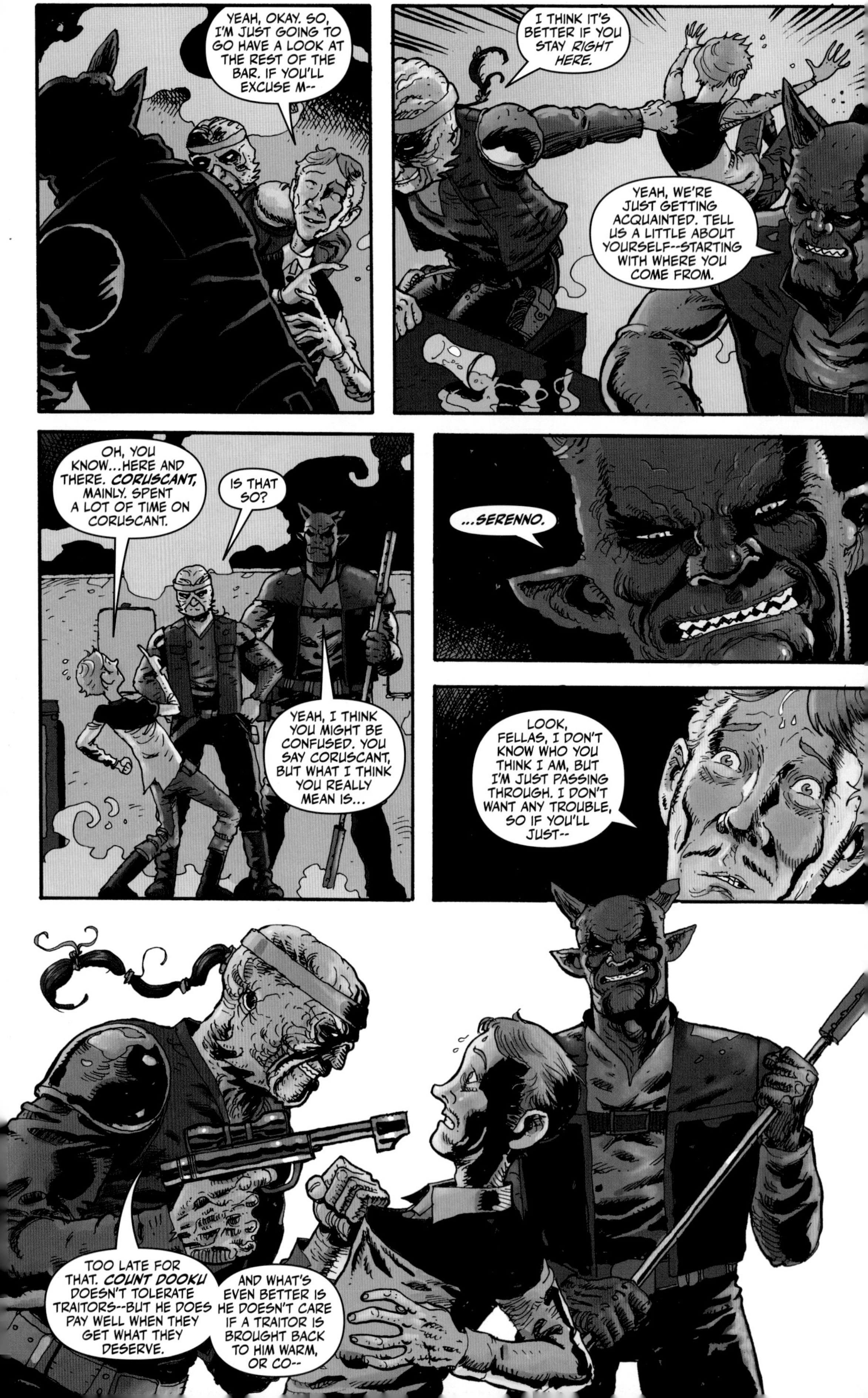
YEAH, OKAY. SO, I'M JUST GOING TO GO HAVE A LOOK AT THE REST OF THE BAR. IF YOU'LL EXCUSE M--
I THINK IT'S BETTER IF YOU STAY *RIGHT HERE.*
YEAH, WE'RE JUST GETTING ACQUAINTED. TELL US A LITTLE ABOUT YOURSELF--STARTING WITH WHERE YOU COME FROM.
OH, YOU KNOW...HERE AND THERE. ***CORUSCANT,*** MAINLY. SPENT A LOT OF TIME ON CORUSCANT.
IS THAT SO?
YEAH, I THINK YOU MIGHT BE CONFUSED. YOU SAY CORUSCANT, BUT WHAT I THINK YOU REALLY MEAN IS...
...SERENNO.
LOOK, FELLAS, I DON'T KNOW WHO YOU THINK I AM, BUT I'M JUST PASSING THROUGH. I DON'T WANT ANY TROUBLE, SO IF YOU'LL JUST--
TOO LATE FOR THAT. ***COUNT DOOKU*** DOESN'T TOLERATE TRAITORS--BUT HE DOES PAY WELL WHEN THEY GET WHAT THEY DESERVE.
AND WHAT'S EVEN BETTER IS HE DOESN'T CARE IF A TRAITOR IS BROUGHT BACK TO HIM WARM, OR CO--

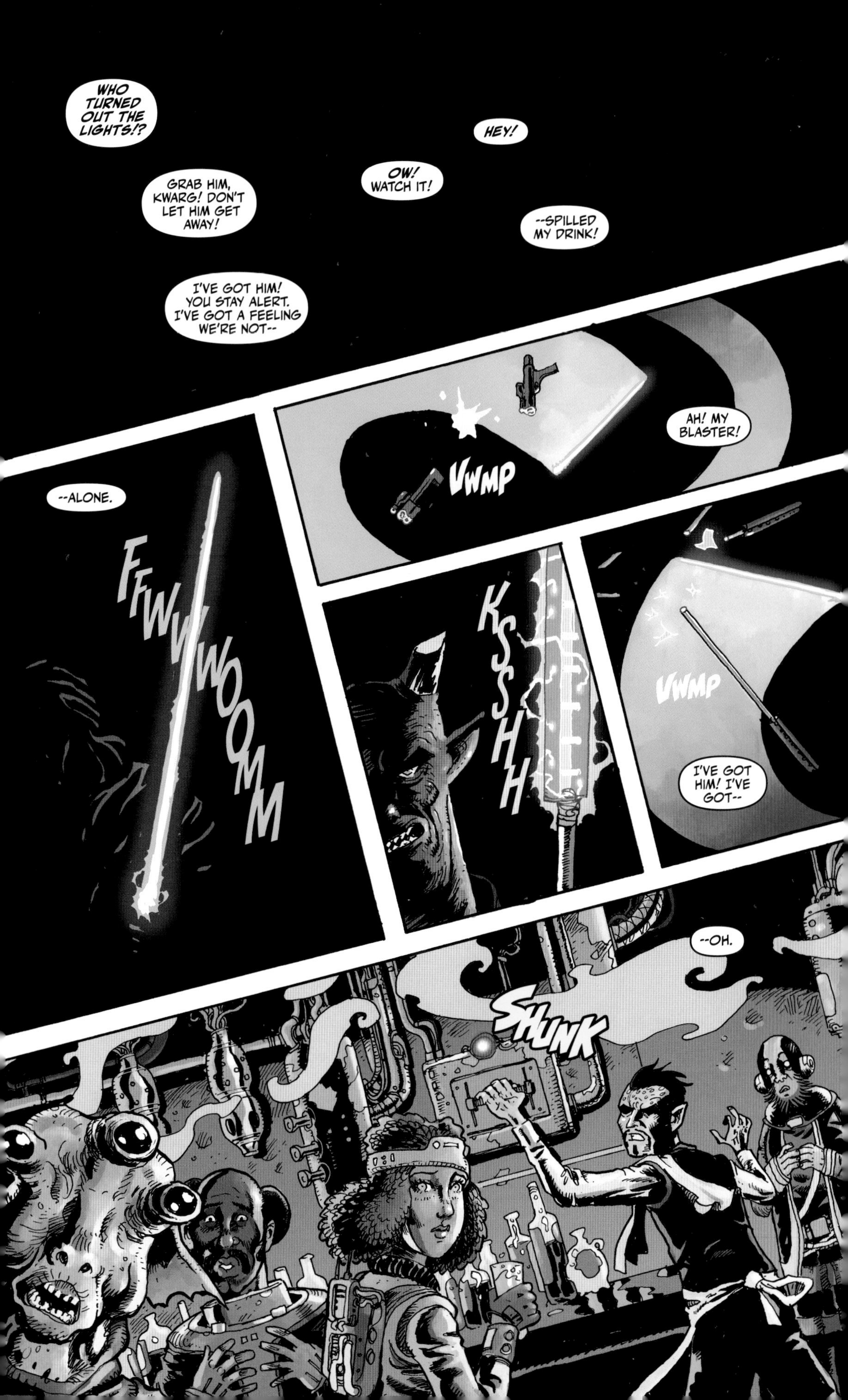
WHO TURNED OUT THE LIGHTS!?
HEY!
GRAB HIM, KWARG! DON'T LET HIM GET AWAY!
OW! WATCH IT!
--SPILLED MY DRINK!
I'VE GOT HIM! YOU STAY ALERT. I'VE GOT A FEELING WE'RE NOT--
--ALONE.
FFWWWWOOMM
UWMP
AH! MY BLASTER!
KSSHH
UWMP
I'VE GOT HIM! I'VE GOT--
--OH.
SHUNK

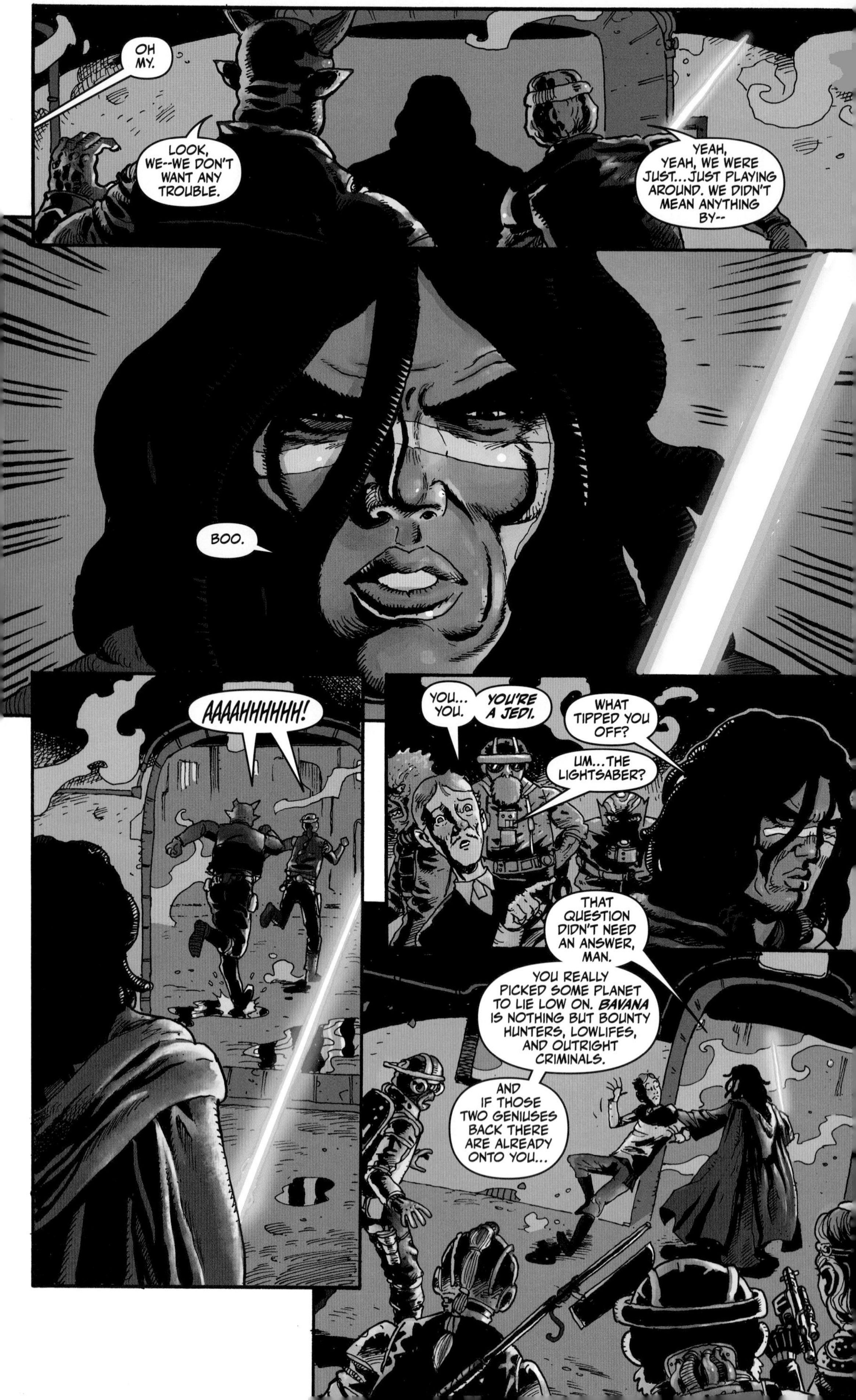
OH MY.
LOOK, WE--WE DON'T WANT ANY TROUBLE.
YEAH, YEAH, WE WERE JUST...JUST PLAYING AROUND. WE DIDN'T MEAN ANYTHING BY--
BOO.
AAAAHHHHHH!
YOU... YOU. YOU'RE A JEDI.
WHAT TIPPED YOU OFF?
UM...THE LIGHTSABER?
THAT QUESTION DIDN'T NEED AN ANSWER, MAN.
YOU REALLY PICKED SOME PLANET TO LIE LOW ON. BAVANA IS NOTHING BUT BOUNTY HUNTERS, LOWLIFES, AND OUTRIGHT CRIMINALS.
AND IF THOSE TWO GENIUSES BACK THERE ARE ALREADY ONTO YOU...

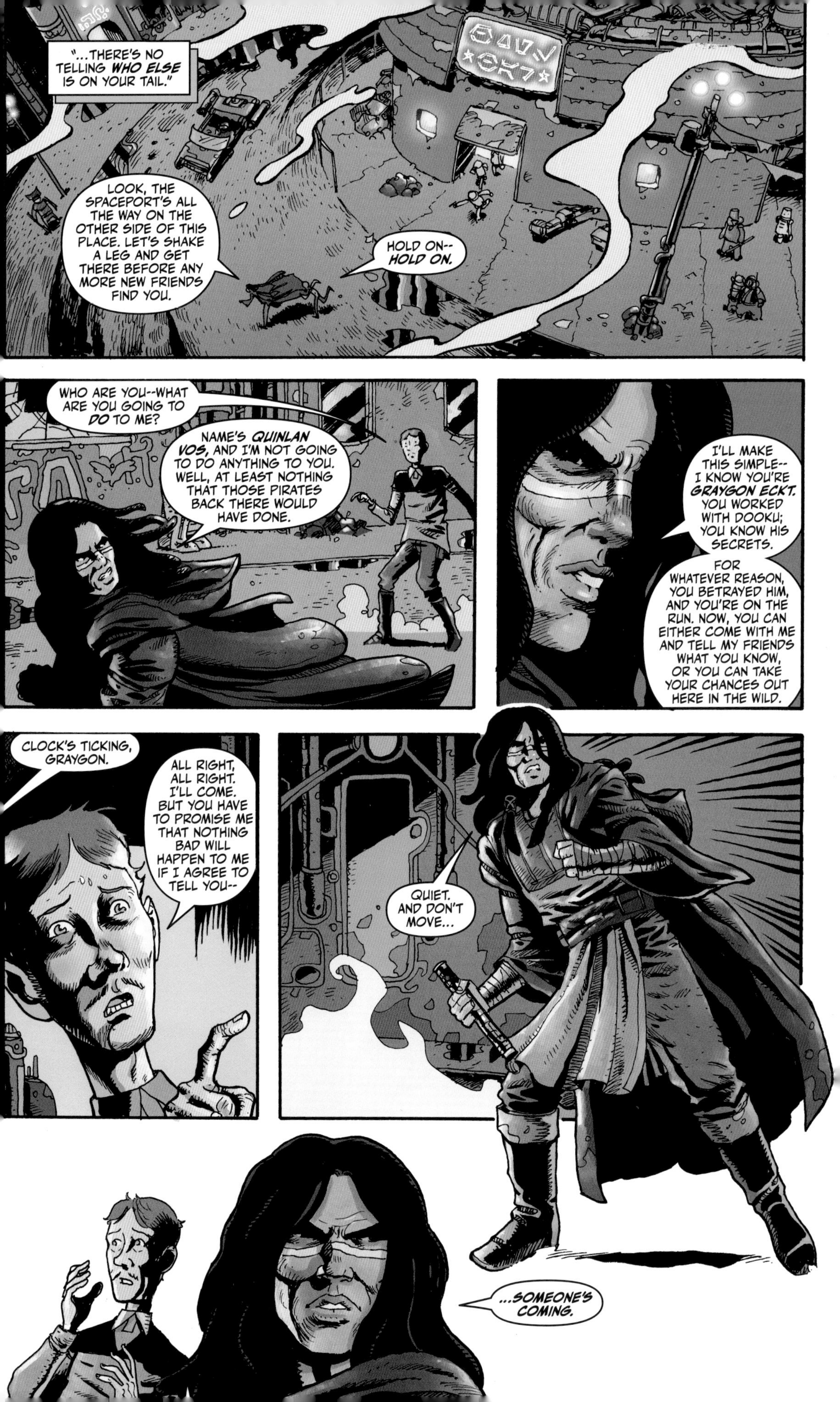
"...THERE'S NO TELLING WHO ELSE IS ON YOUR TAIL."
LOOK, THE SPACEPORT'S ALL THE WAY ON THE OTHER SIDE OF THIS PLACE. LET'S SHAKE A LEG AND GET THERE BEFORE ANY MORE NEW FRIENDS FIND YOU.
HOLD ON-- HOLD ON.
WHO ARE YOU--WHAT ARE YOU GOING TO DO TO ME?
NAME'S QUINLAN VOS, AND I'M NOT GOING TO DO ANYTHING TO YOU. WELL, AT LEAST NOTHING THAT THOSE PIRATES BACK THERE WOULD HAVE DONE.
I'LL MAKE THIS SIMPLE-- I KNOW YOU'RE GRAYGON ECKT. YOU WORKED WITH DOOKU; YOU KNOW HIS SECRETS.
FOR WHATEVER REASON, YOU BETRAYED HIM, AND YOU'RE ON THE RUN. NOW, YOU CAN EITHER COME WITH ME AND TELL MY FRIENDS WHAT YOU KNOW, OR YOU CAN TAKE YOUR CHANCES OUT HERE IN THE WILD.
CLOCK'S TICKING, GRAYGON.
ALL RIGHT, ALL RIGHT. I'LL COME. BUT YOU HAVE TO PROMISE ME THAT NOTHING BAD WILL HAPPEN TO ME IF I AGREE TO TELL YOU--
QUIET. AND DON'T MOVE...
...SOMEONE'S COMING.

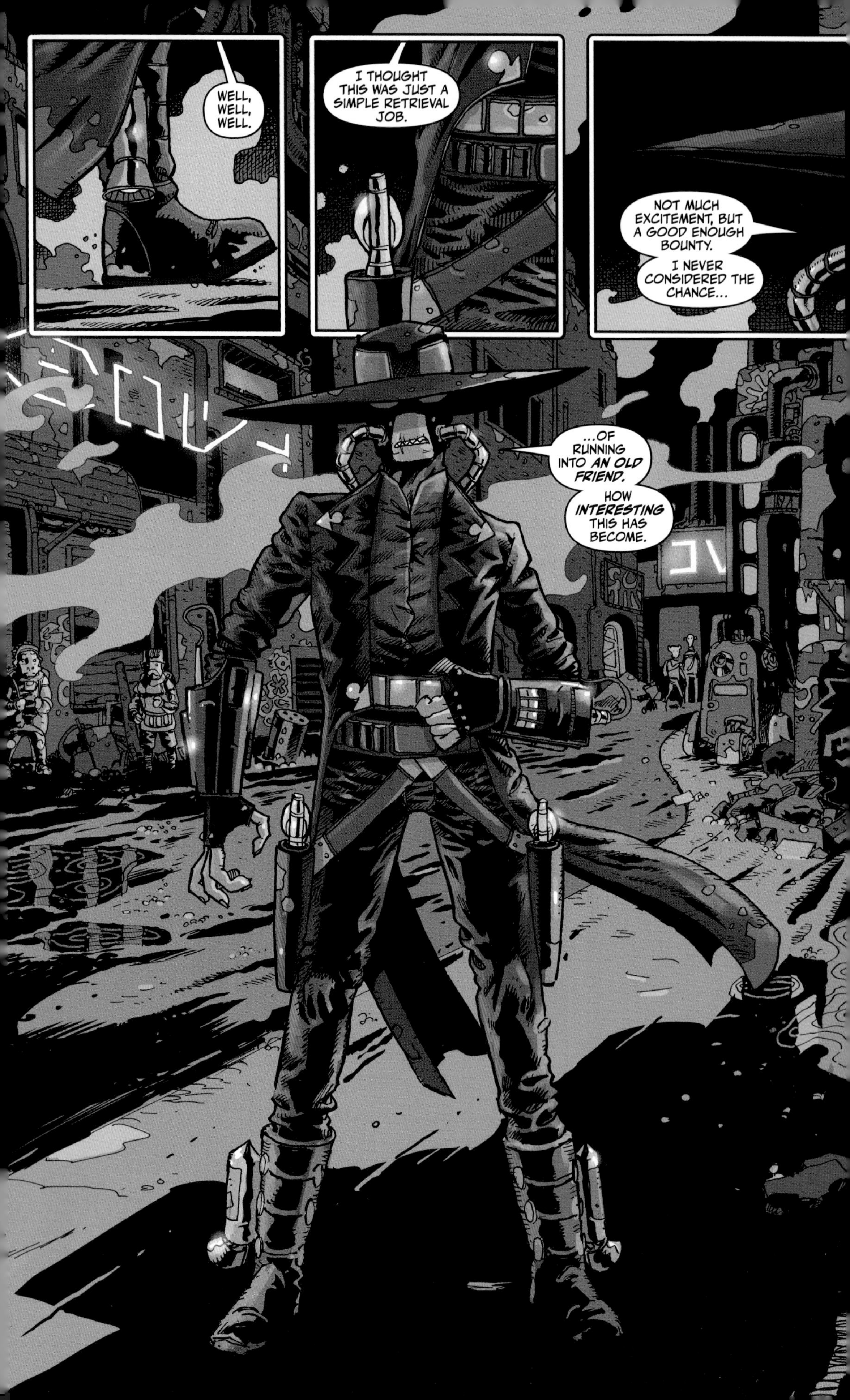
WELL, WELL, WELL.
I THOUGHT THIS WAS JUST A SIMPLE RETRIEVAL JOB.
NOT MUCH EXCITEMENT, BUT A GOOD ENOUGH BOUNTY.
I NEVER CONSIDERED THE CHANCE...
...OF RUNNING INTO *AN OLD FRIEND.*
HOW *INTERESTING* THIS HAS BECOME.

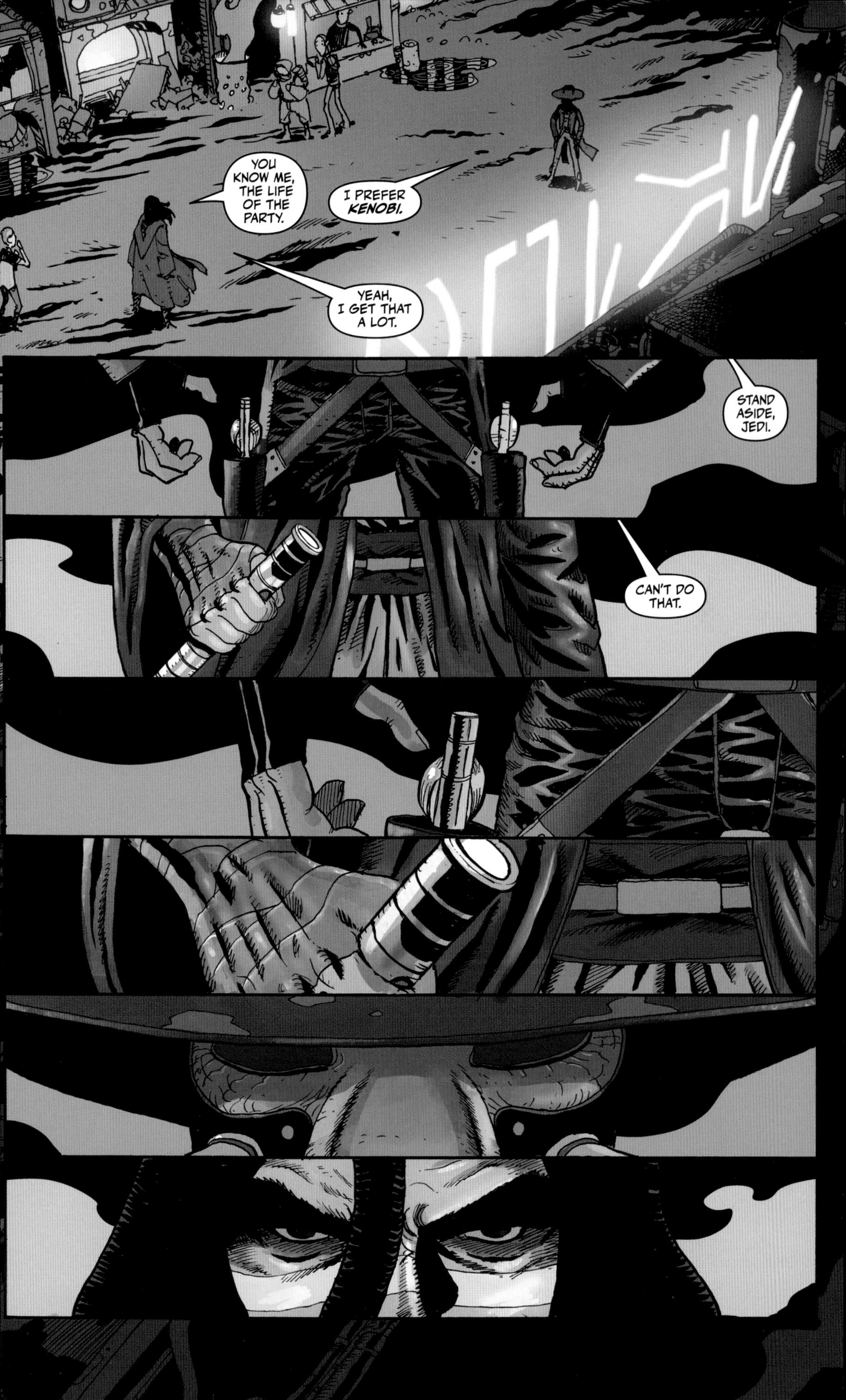
YOU KNOW ME, THE LIFE OF THE PARTY.
I PREFER KENOBI.
YEAH, I GET THAT A LOT.
STAND ASIDE, JEDI.
CAN'T DO THAT.

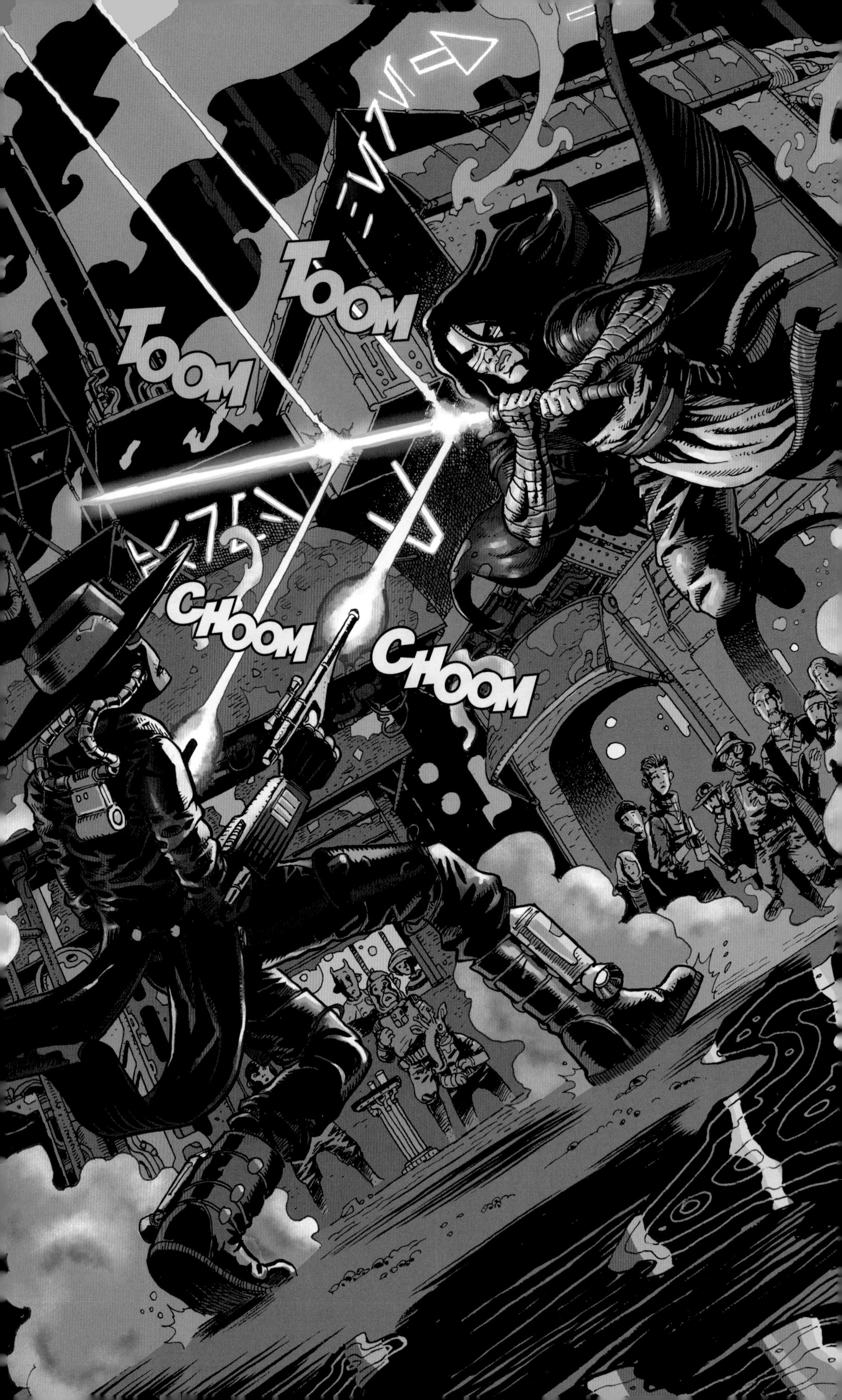
TOOM
TOOM
CHOOM
CHOOM

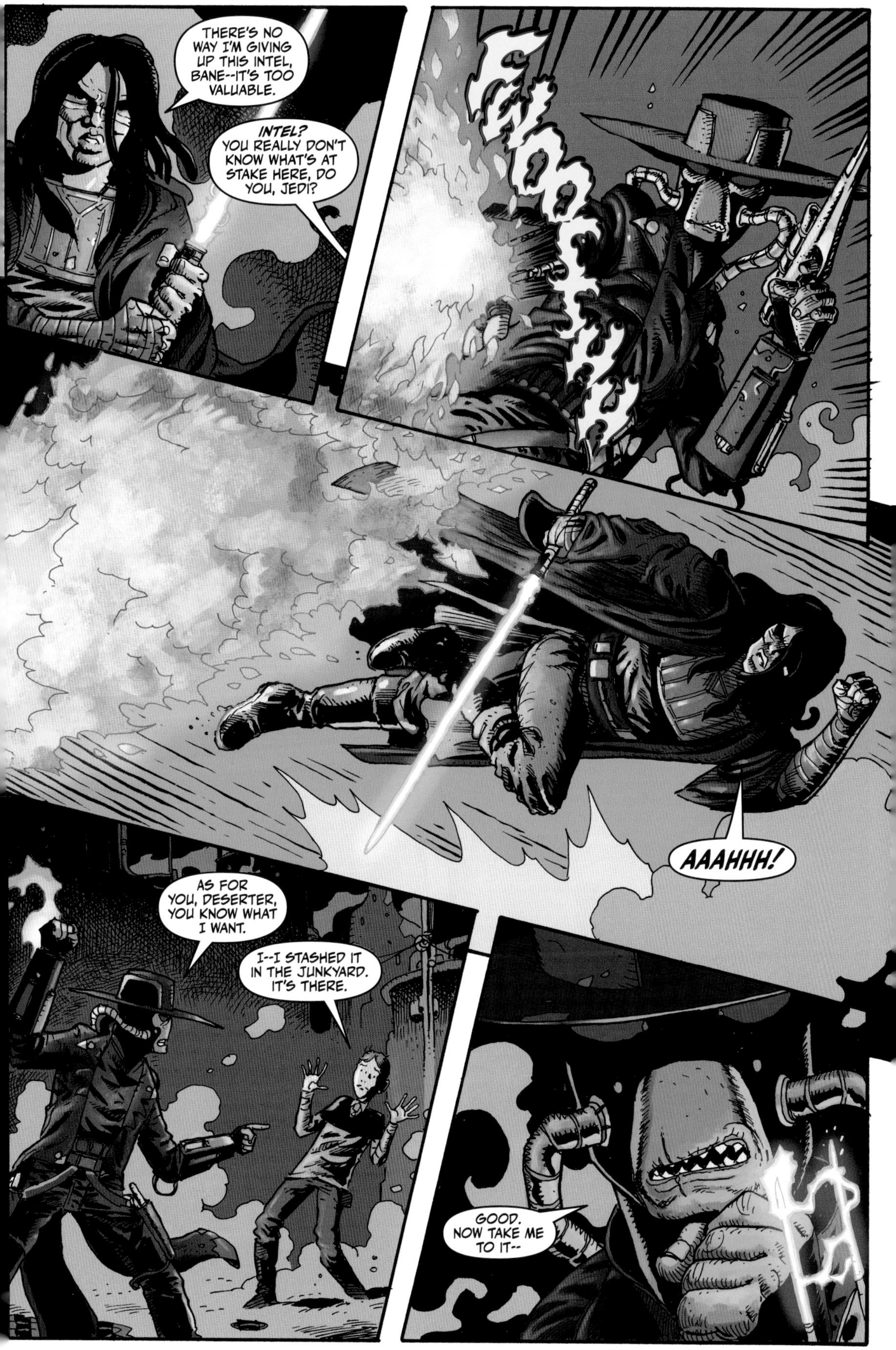

THERE'S NO WAY I'M GIVING UP THIS INTEL, BANE--IT'S TOO VALUABLE.
INTEL? YOU REALLY DON'T KNOW WHAT'S AT STAKE HERE, DO YOU, JEDI?
AAAHHH!
AS FOR YOU, DESERTER, YOU KNOW WHAT I WANT.
I--I STASHED IT IN THE JUNKYARD. IT'S THERE.
GOOD. NOW TAKE ME TO IT--

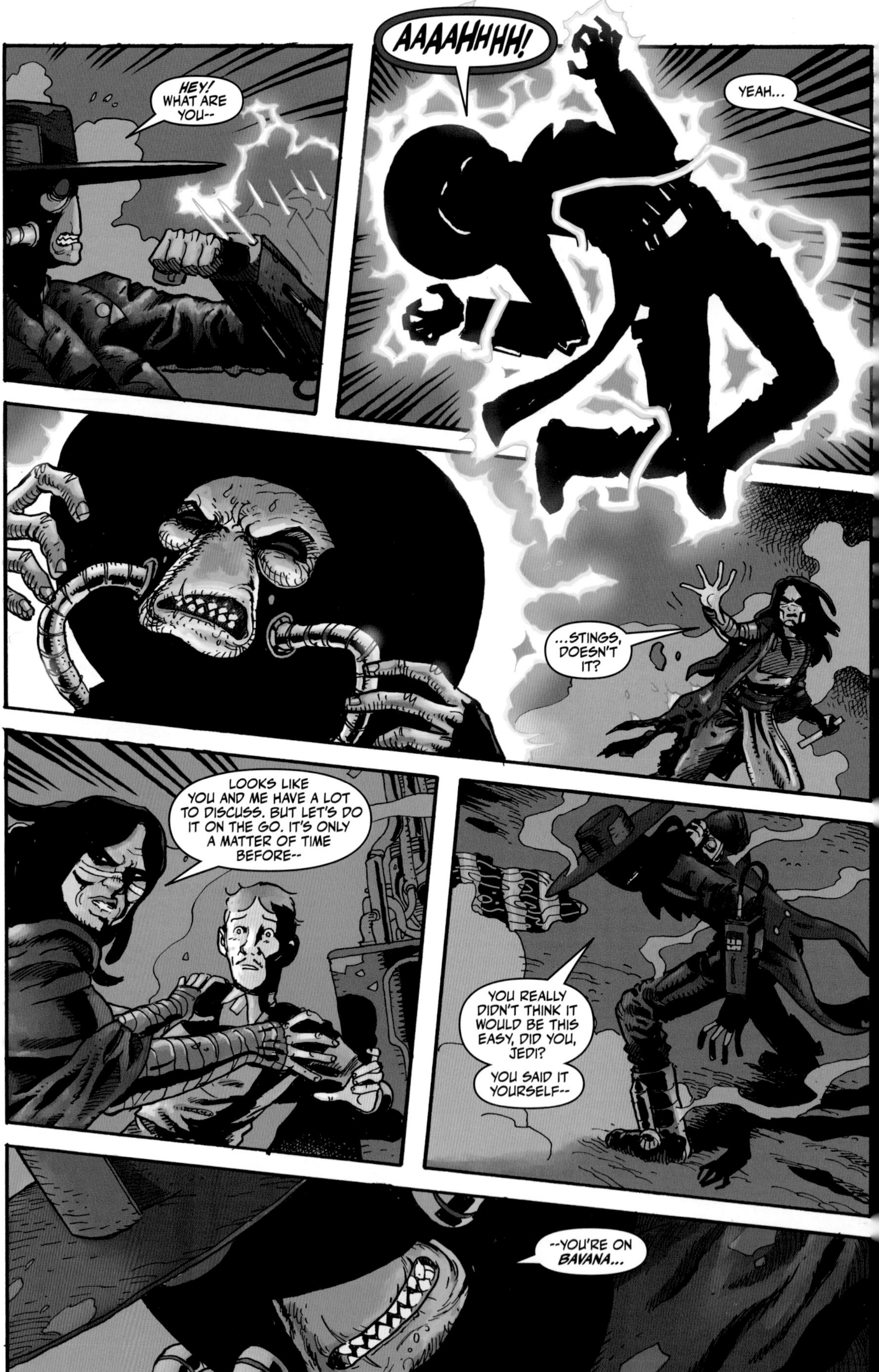
HEY! WHAT ARE YOU--
AAAAHHHH!
YEAH...
...STINGS, DOESN'T IT?
LOOKS LIKE YOU AND ME HAVE A LOT TO DISCUSS. BUT LET'S DO IT ON THE GO. IT'S ONLY A MATTER OF TIME BEFORE--
YOU REALLY DIDN'T THINK IT WOULD BE THIS EASY, DID YOU, JEDI?
YOU SAID IT YOURSELF--
--YOU'RE ON BAVANA...

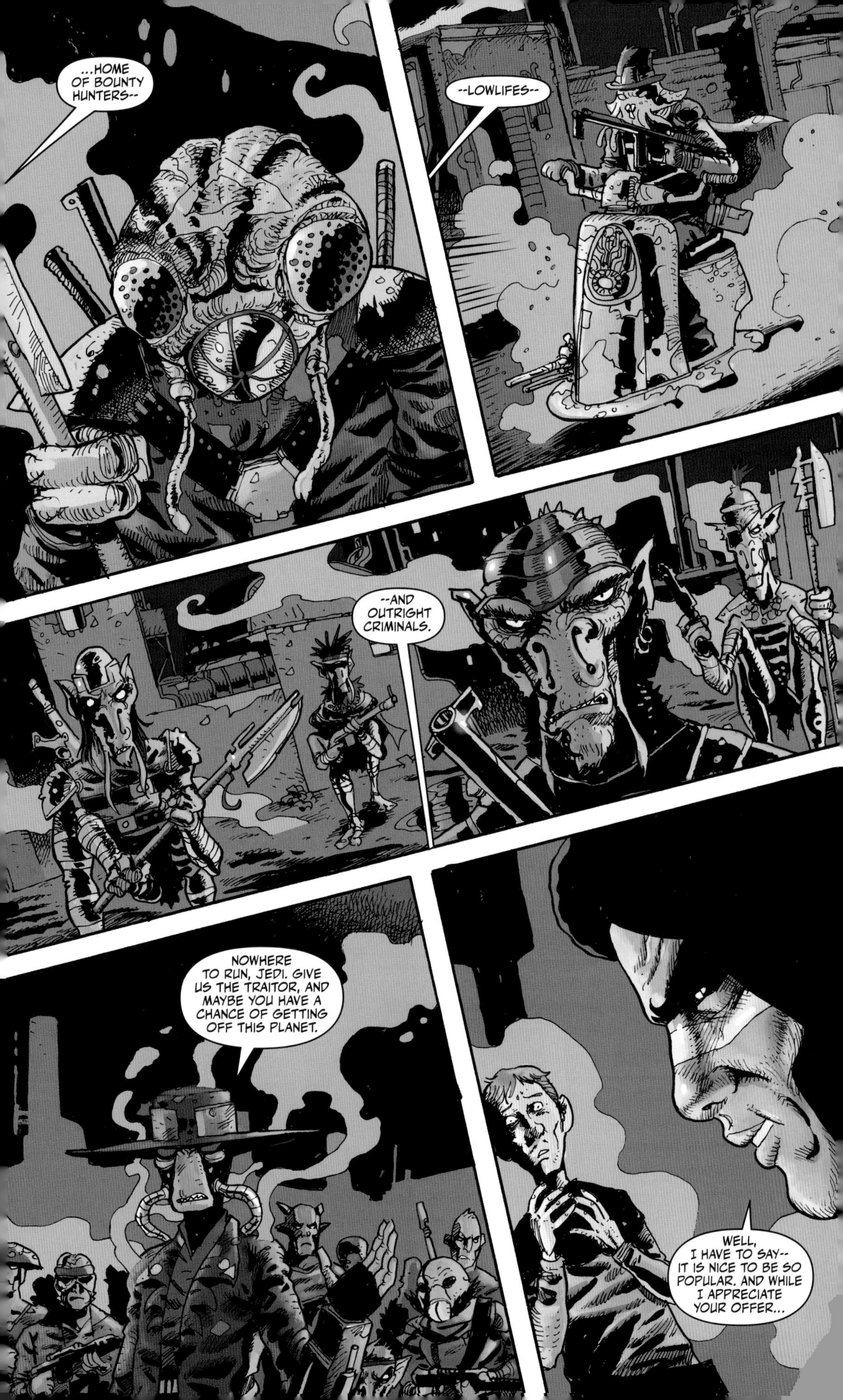
...HOME OF BOUNTY HUNTERS--
--LOWLIFES--
--AND OUTRIGHT CRIMINALS.
NOWHERE TO RUN, JEDI. GIVE US THE TRAITOR, AND MAYBE YOU HAVE A CHANCE OF GETTING OFF THIS PLANET.
WELL, I HAVE TO SAY-- IT IS NICE TO BE SO POPULAR. AND WHILE I APPRECIATE YOUR OFFER...

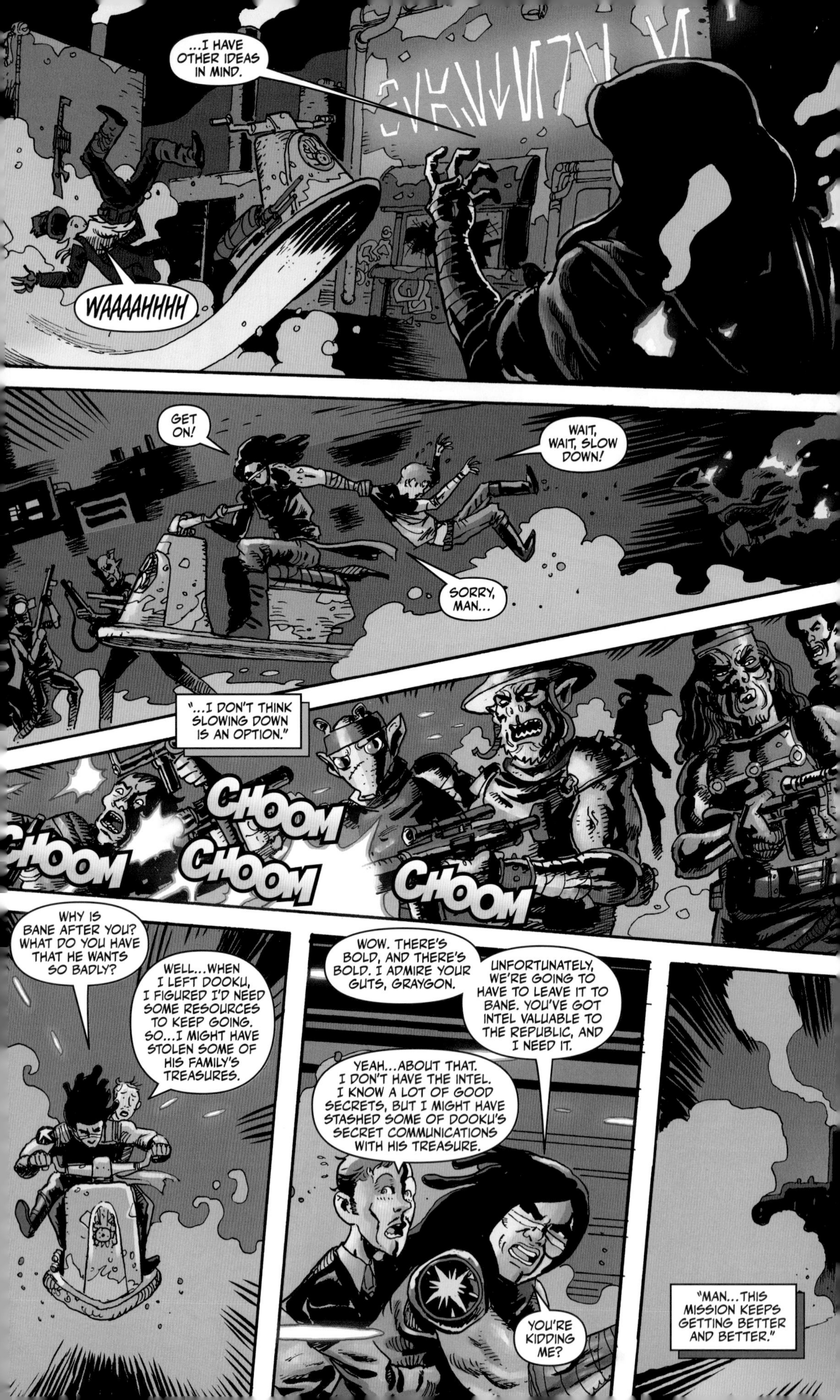
...I HAVE OTHER IDEAS IN MIND.
WAAAAHHHH
GET ON!
WAIT, WAIT, SLOW DOWN!
SORRY, MAN...
"...I DON'T THINK SLOWING DOWN IS AN OPTION."
CHOOM
CHOOM
CHOOM
CHOOM
WHY IS BANE AFTER YOU? WHAT DO YOU HAVE THAT HE WANTS SO BADLY?
WELL...WHEN I LEFT DOOKU, I FIGURED I'D NEED SOME RESOURCES TO KEEP GOING. SO...I MIGHT HAVE STOLEN SOME OF HIS FAMILY'S TREASURES.
WOW. THERE'S BOLD, AND THERE'S BOLD. I ADMIRE YOUR GUTS, GRAYGON.
UNFORTUNATELY, WE'RE GOING TO HAVE TO LEAVE IT TO BANE. YOU'VE GOT INTEL VALUABLE TO THE REPUBLIC, AND I NEED IT.
YEAH...ABOUT THAT. I DON'T HAVE THE INTEL. I KNOW A LOT OF GOOD SECRETS, BUT I MIGHT HAVE STASHED SOME OF DOOKU'S SECRET COMMUNICATIONS WITH HIS TREASURE.
YOU'RE KIDDING ME?
"MAN...THIS MISSION KEEPS GETTING BETTER AND BETTER."

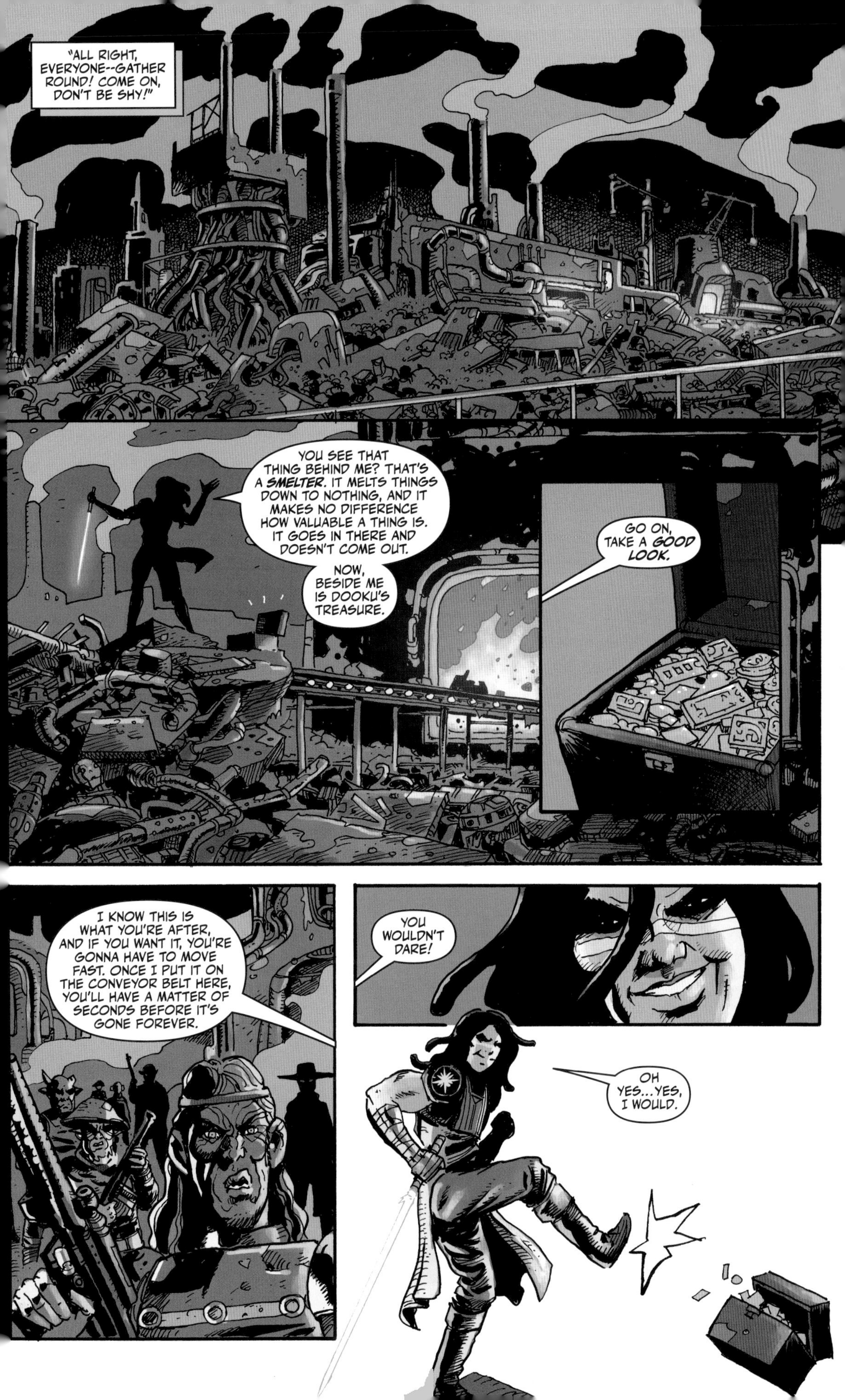
"ALL RIGHT, EVERYONE--GATHER ROUND! COME ON, DON'T BE SHY!"
YOU SEE THAT THING BEHIND ME? THAT'S A SMELTER. IT MELTS THINGS DOWN TO NOTHING, AND IT MAKES NO DIFFERENCE HOW VALUABLE A THING IS. IT GOES IN THERE AND DOESN'T COME OUT.
NOW, BESIDE ME IS DOOKU'S TREASURE.
GO ON, TAKE A GOOD LOOK.
I KNOW THIS IS WHAT YOU'RE AFTER, AND IF YOU WANT IT, YOU'RE GONNA HAVE TO MOVE FAST. ONCE I PUT IT ON THE CONVEYOR BELT HERE, YOU'LL HAVE A MATTER OF SECONDS BEFORE IT'S GONE FOREVER.
YOU WOULDN'T DARE!
OH YES...YES, I WOULD.

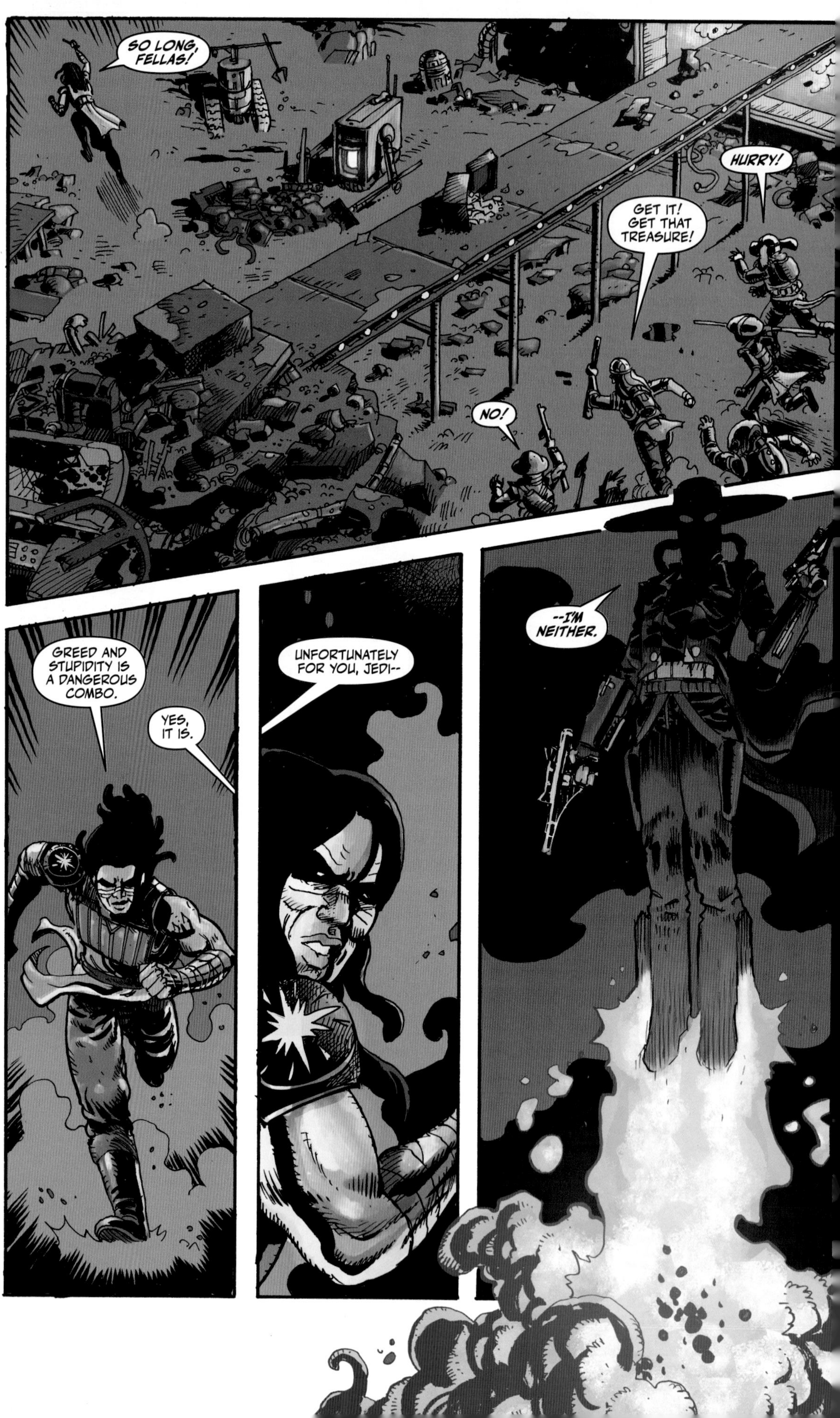
SO LONG, FELLAS!
HURRY!
GET IT! GET THAT TREASURE!
NO!
GREED AND STUPIDITY IS A DANGEROUS COMBO.
YES, IT IS.
UNFORTUNATELY FOR YOU, JEDI--
--I'M NEITHER.

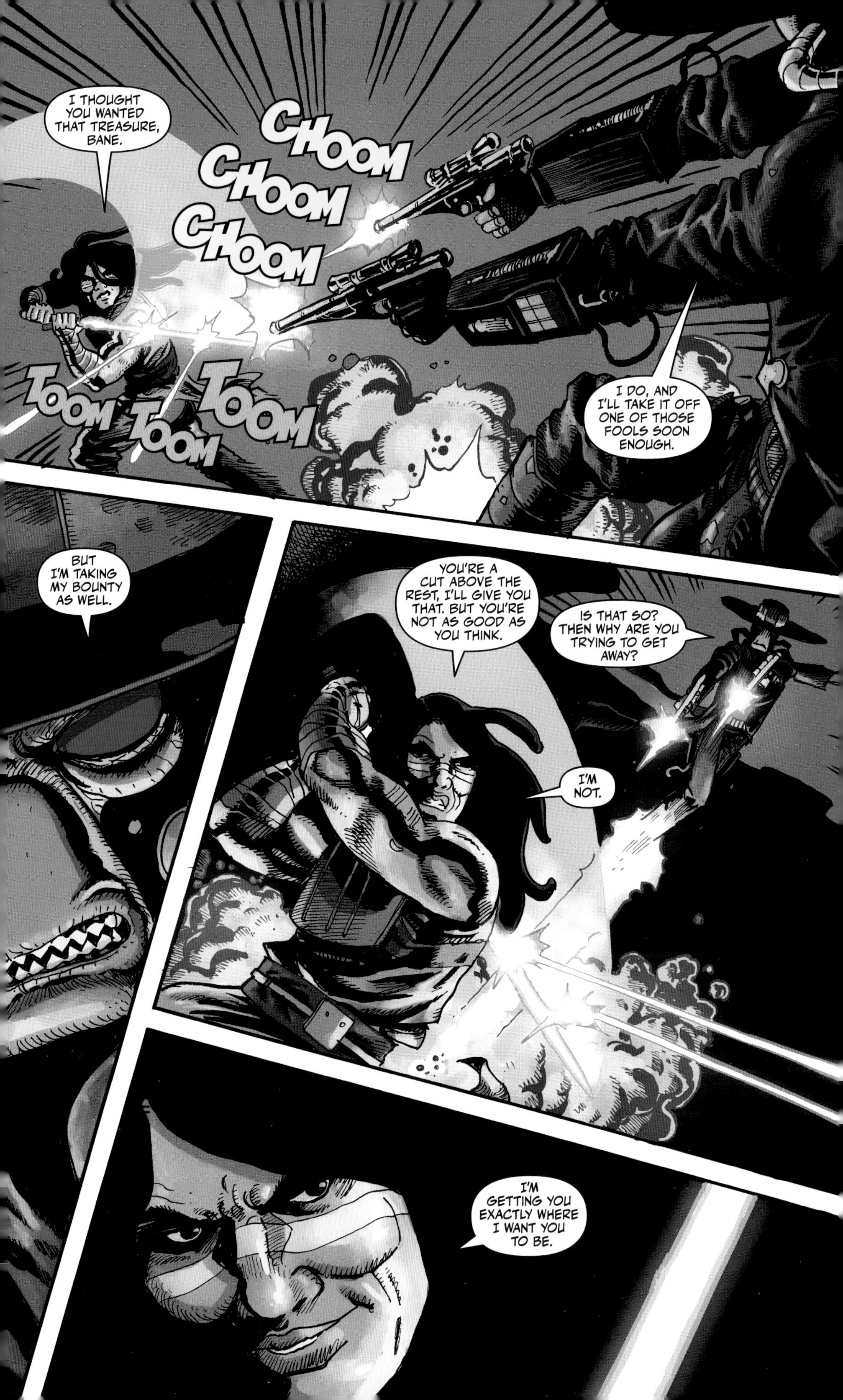
I THOUGHT YOU WANTED THAT TREASURE, BANE.
CHOOM
CHOOM
CHOOM
TOOM
TOOM
TOOM
I DO, AND I'LL TAKE IT OFF ONE OF THOSE FOOLS SOON ENOUGH.
BUT I'M TAKING MY BOUNTY AS WELL.
YOU'RE A CUT ABOVE THE REST, I'LL GIVE YOU THAT. BUT YOU'RE NOT AS GOOD AS YOU THINK.
IS THAT SO? THEN WHY ARE YOU TRYING TO GET AWAY?
I'M NOT.
I'M GETTING YOU EXACTLY WHERE I WANT YOU TO BE.

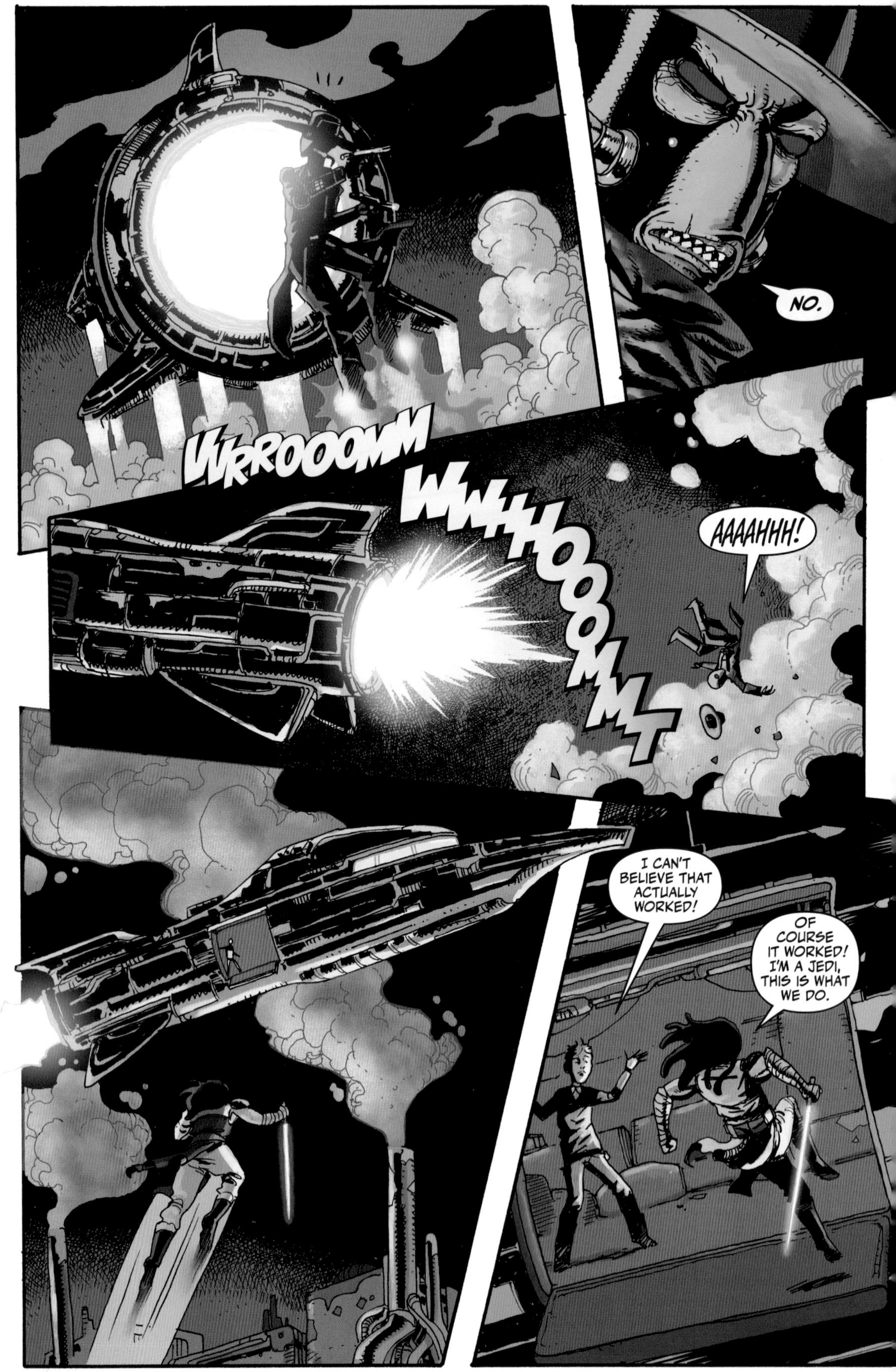

NO.
VRROOOMM
WWHOOOMMT
AAAAHHH!
I CAN'T BELIEVE THAT ACTUALLY WORKED!
OF COURSE IT WORKED! I'M A JEDI, THIS IS WHAT WE DO.

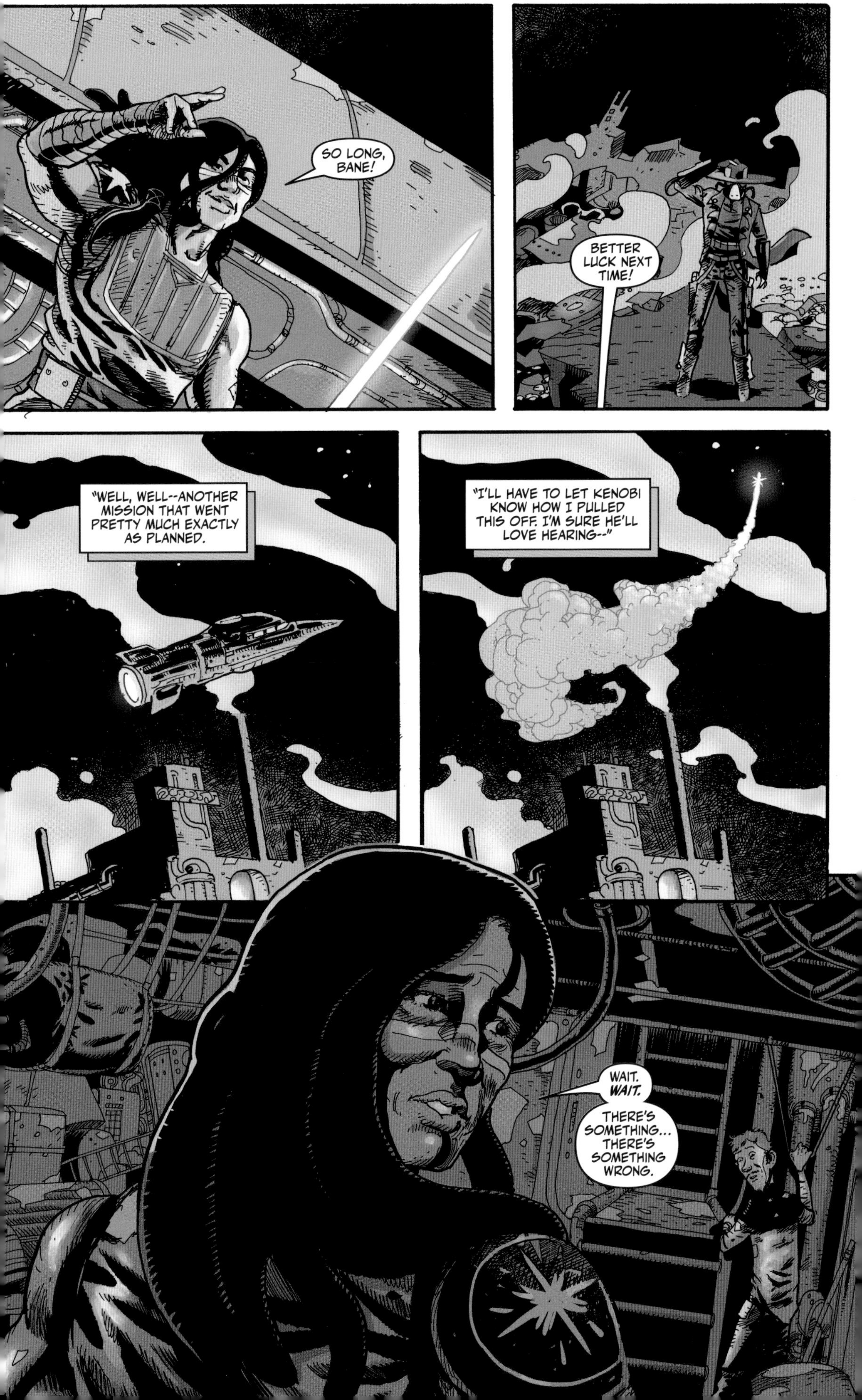
SO LONG, BANE!
BETTER LUCK NEXT TIME!
"WELL, WELL--ANOTHER MISSION THAT WENT PRETTY MUCH EXACTLY AS PLANNED.
"I'LL HAVE TO LET KENOBI KNOW HOW I PULLED THIS OFF. I'M SURE HE'LL LOVE HEARING--"
WAIT. *WAIT.*
THERE'S SOMETHING... THERE'S SOMETHING WRONG.

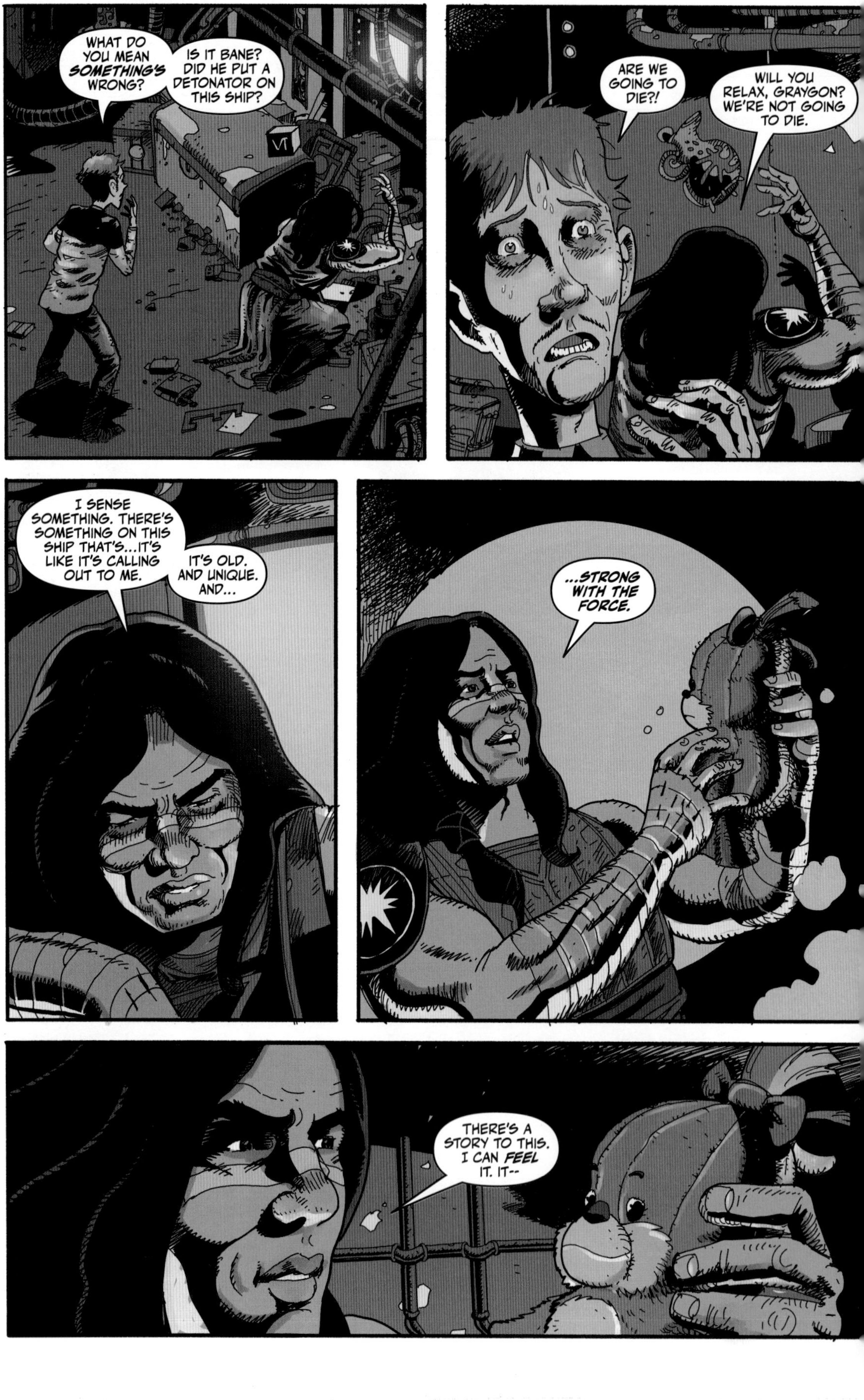
WHAT DO YOU MEAN *SOMETHING'S* WRONG?
IS IT BANE? DID HE PUT A DETONATOR ON THIS SHIP?
ARE WE GOING TO DIE?!
WILL YOU RELAX, GRAYGON? WE'RE NOT GOING TO DIE.
I SENSE SOMETHING. THERE'S SOMETHING ON THIS SHIP THAT'S...IT'S LIKE IT'S CALLING OUT TO ME.
IT'S OLD. AND UNIQUE. AND...
...STRONG WITH THE FORCE.
THERE'S A STORY TO THIS. I CAN *FEEL* IT. IT--

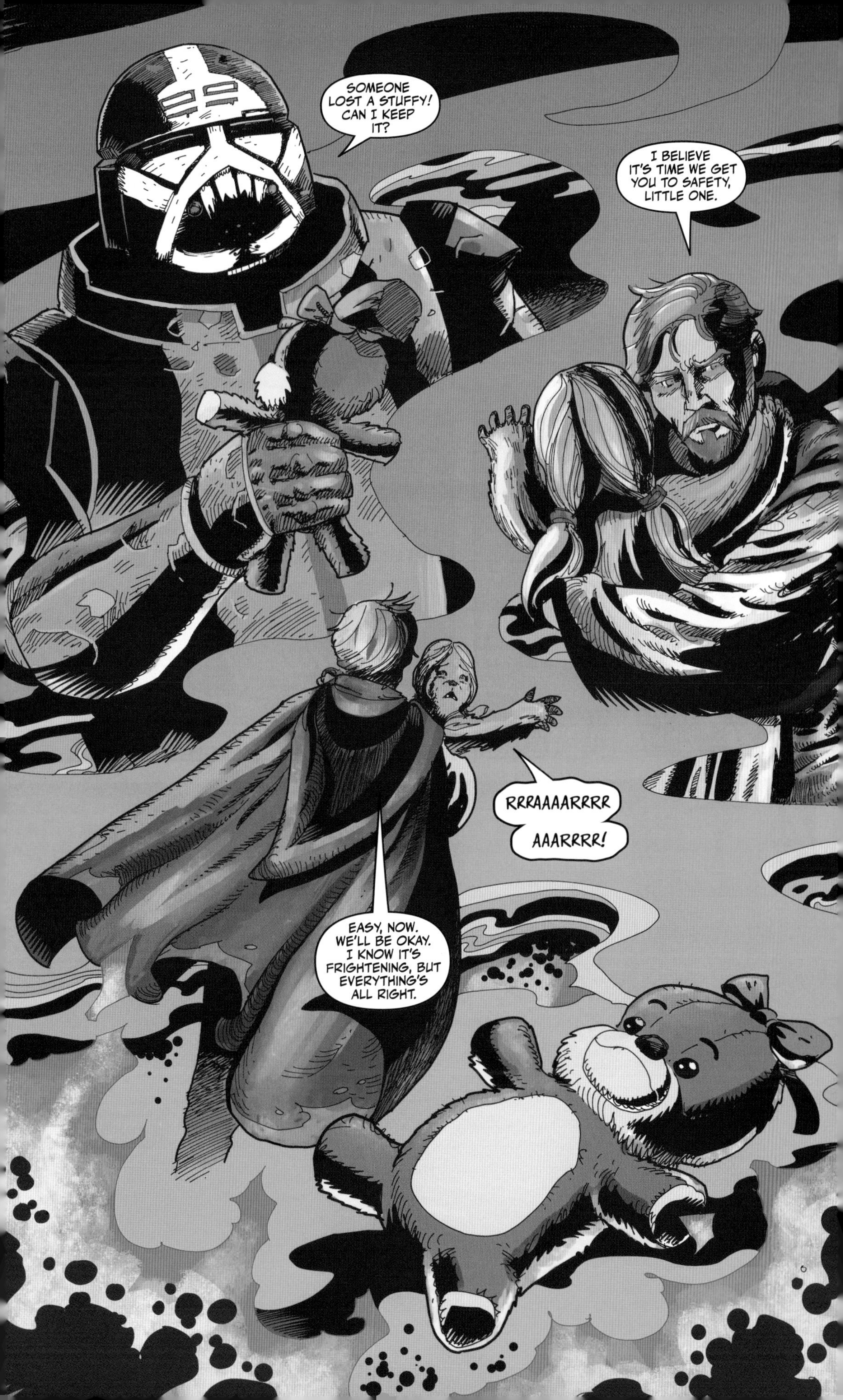
SOMEONE LOST A STUFFY! CAN I KEEP IT?
I BELIEVE IT'S TIME WE GET YOU TO SAFETY, LITTLE ONE.
RRRAAAARRRR
AAARRRR!
EASY, NOW. WE'LL BE OKAY. I KNOW IT'S FRIGHTENING, BUT EVERYTHING'S ALL RIGHT.

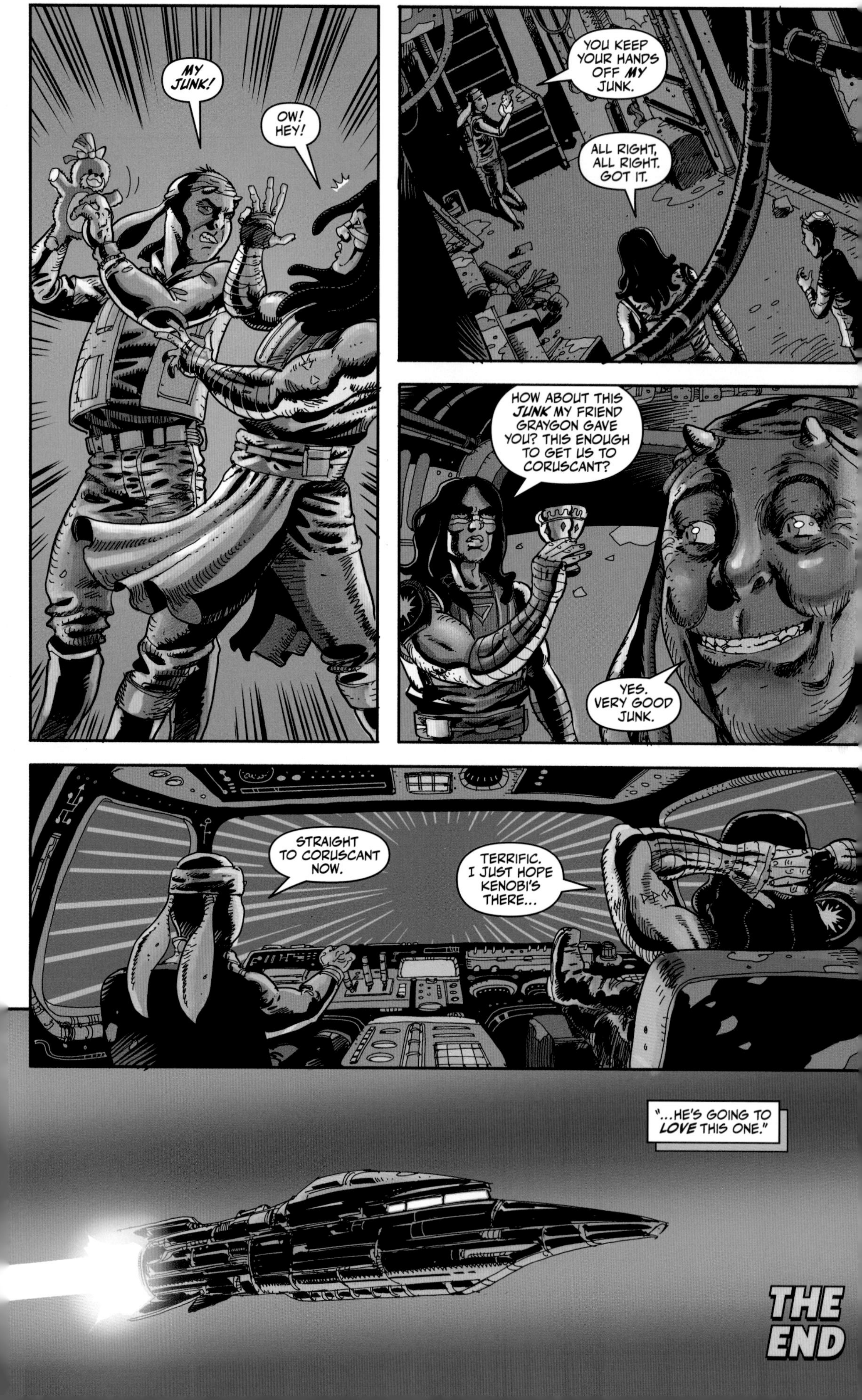
MY JUNK!
OW! HEY!
YOU KEEP YOUR HANDS OFF MY JUNK.
ALL RIGHT, ALL RIGHT. GOT IT.
HOW ABOUT THIS JUNK MY FRIEND GRAYGON GAVE YOU? THIS ENOUGH TO GET US TO CORUSCANT?
YES. VERY GOOD JUNK.
STRAIGHT TO CORUSCANT NOW.
TERRIFIC. I JUST HOPE KENOBI'S THERE...
"...HE'S GOING TO LOVE THIS ONE."
THE END

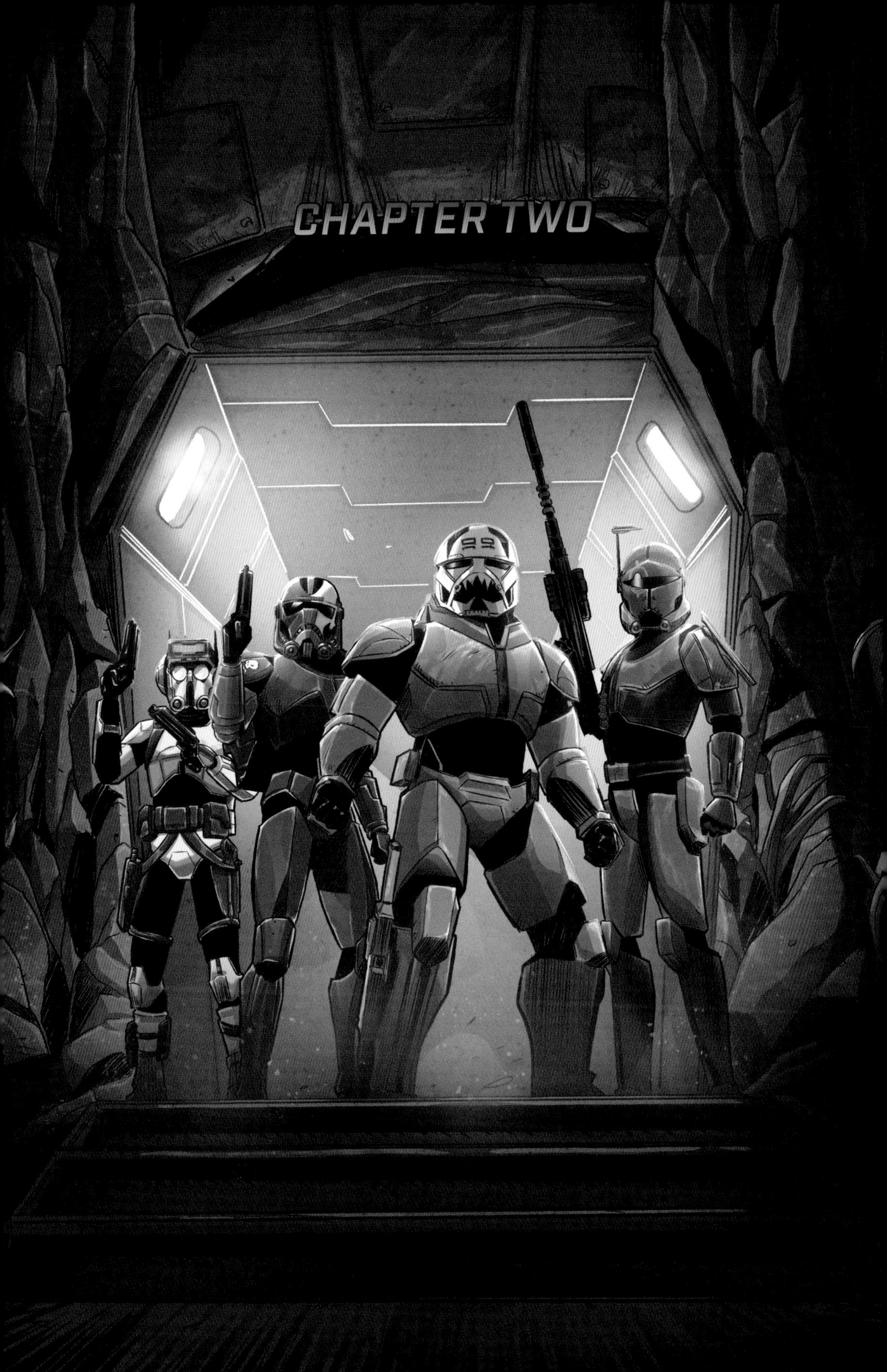
CHAPTER TWO

Art by Riccardo Faccini with Nicola Righi

Art by Lucas Marang

CHAPTER TWO:
BAD BATCH, RIGHT STUFF

written by
MICHAEL MORECI

art by
RICCARDO FACCINI

colors by
NICOLA RIGHI

letters by
COMICRAFT'S TYLER SMITH and
JIMMY BETANCOURT

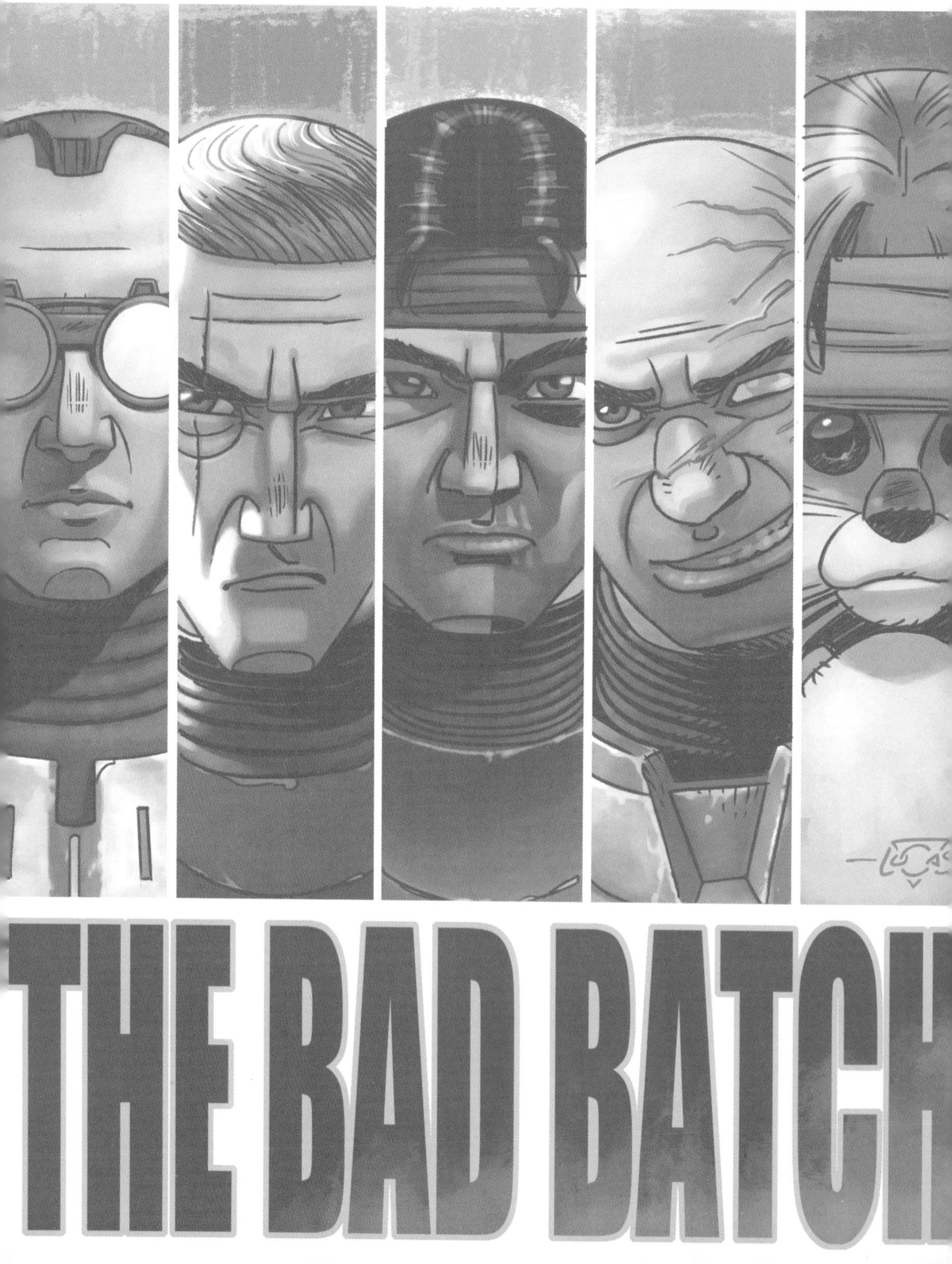
THE BAD BATCH

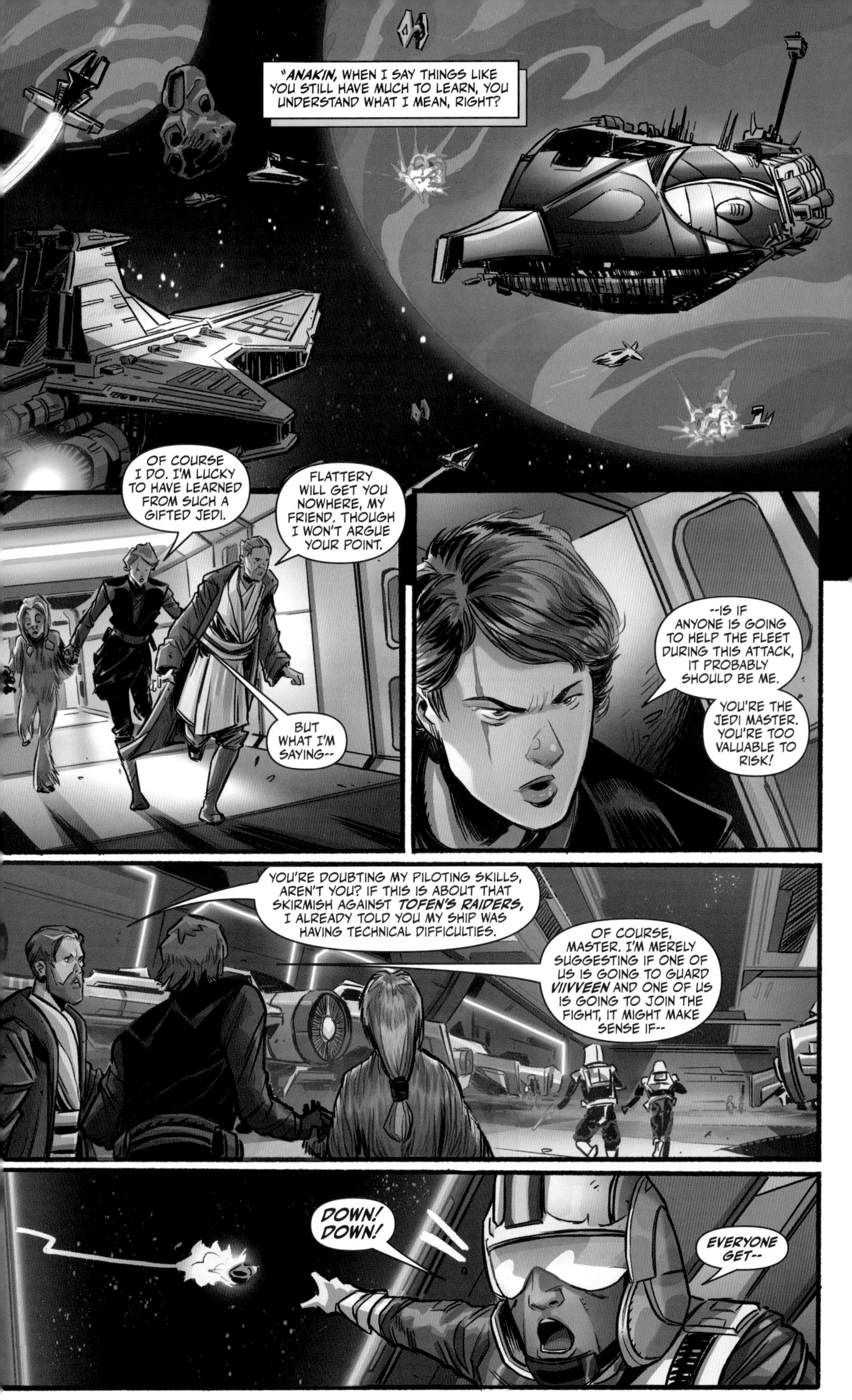
"ANAKIN, WHEN I SAY THINGS LIKE YOU STILL HAVE MUCH TO LEARN, YOU UNDERSTAND WHAT I MEAN, RIGHT?
OF COURSE I DO. I'M LUCKY TO HAVE LEARNED FROM SUCH A GIFTED JEDI.
FLATTERY WILL GET YOU NOWHERE, MY FRIEND. THOUGH I WON'T ARGUE YOUR POINT.
BUT WHAT I'M SAYING--
--IS IF ANYONE IS GOING TO HELP THE FLEET DURING THIS ATTACK, IT PROBABLY SHOULD BE ME.
YOU'RE THE JEDI MASTER. YOU'RE TOO VALUABLE TO RISK!
YOU'RE DOUBTING MY PILOTING SKILLS, AREN'T YOU? IF THIS IS ABOUT THAT SKIRMISH AGAINST TOFEN'S RAIDERS, I ALREADY TOLD YOU MY SHIP WAS HAVING TECHNICAL DIFFICULTIES.
OF COURSE, MASTER. I'M MERELY SUGGESTING IF ONE OF US IS GOING TO GUARD VIIVVEEN AND ONE OF US IS GOING TO JOIN THE FIGHT, IT MIGHT MAKE SENSE IF--
DOWN! DOWN!
EVERYONE GET--

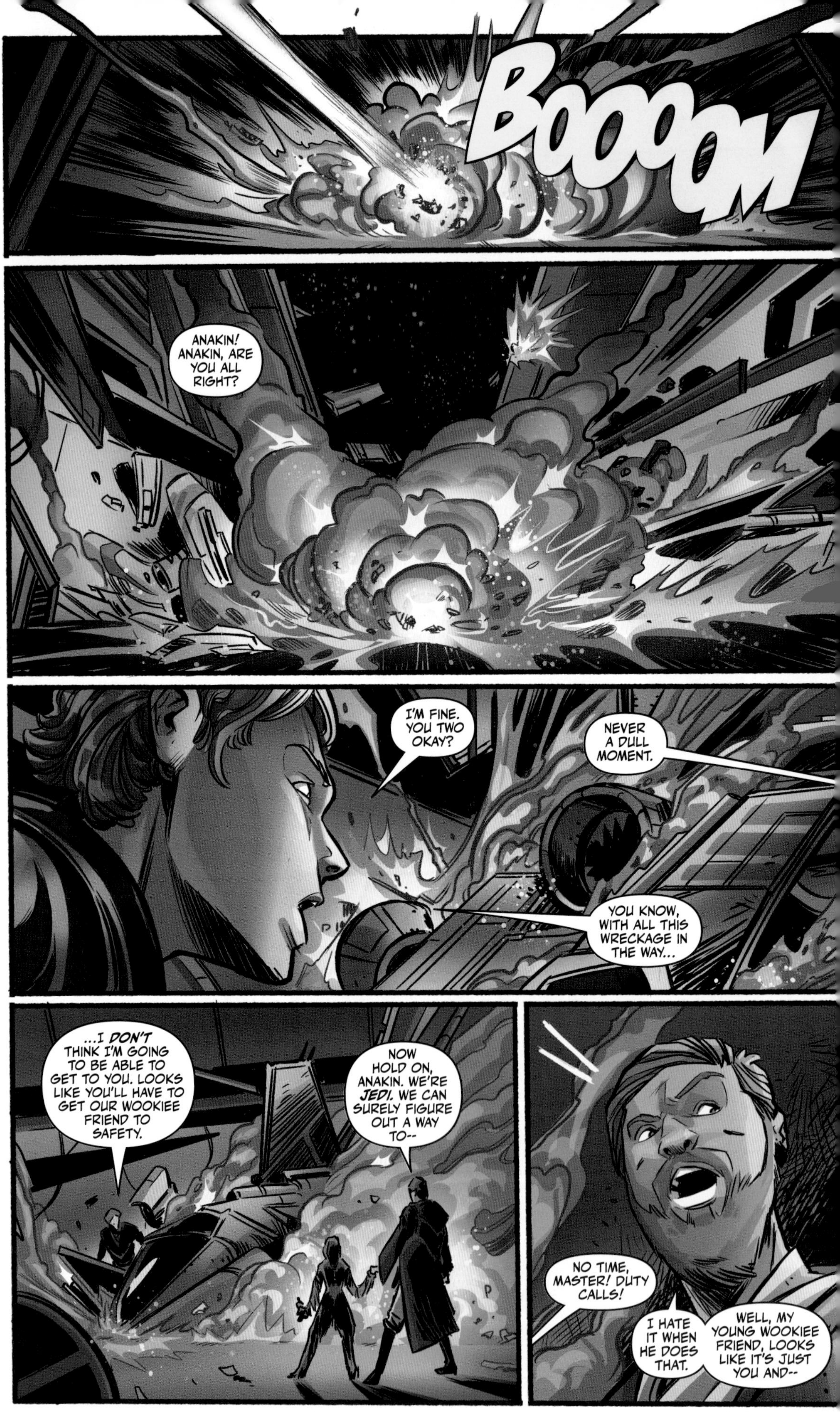
BOOOOM
ANAKIN! ANAKIN, ARE YOU ALL RIGHT?
I'M FINE. YOU TWO OKAY?
NEVER A DULL MOMENT.
YOU KNOW, WITH ALL THIS WRECKAGE IN THE WAY...
...I DON'T THINK I'M GOING TO BE ABLE TO GET TO YOU. LOOKS LIKE YOU'LL HAVE TO GET OUR WOOKIEE FRIEND TO SAFETY.
NOW HOLD ON, ANAKIN. WE'RE JEDI. WE CAN SURELY FIGURE OUT A WAY TO--
NO TIME, MASTER! DUTY CALLS!
I HATE IT WHEN HE DOES THAT.
WELL, MY YOUNG WOOKIEE FRIEND, LOOKS LIKE IT'S JUST YOU AND--

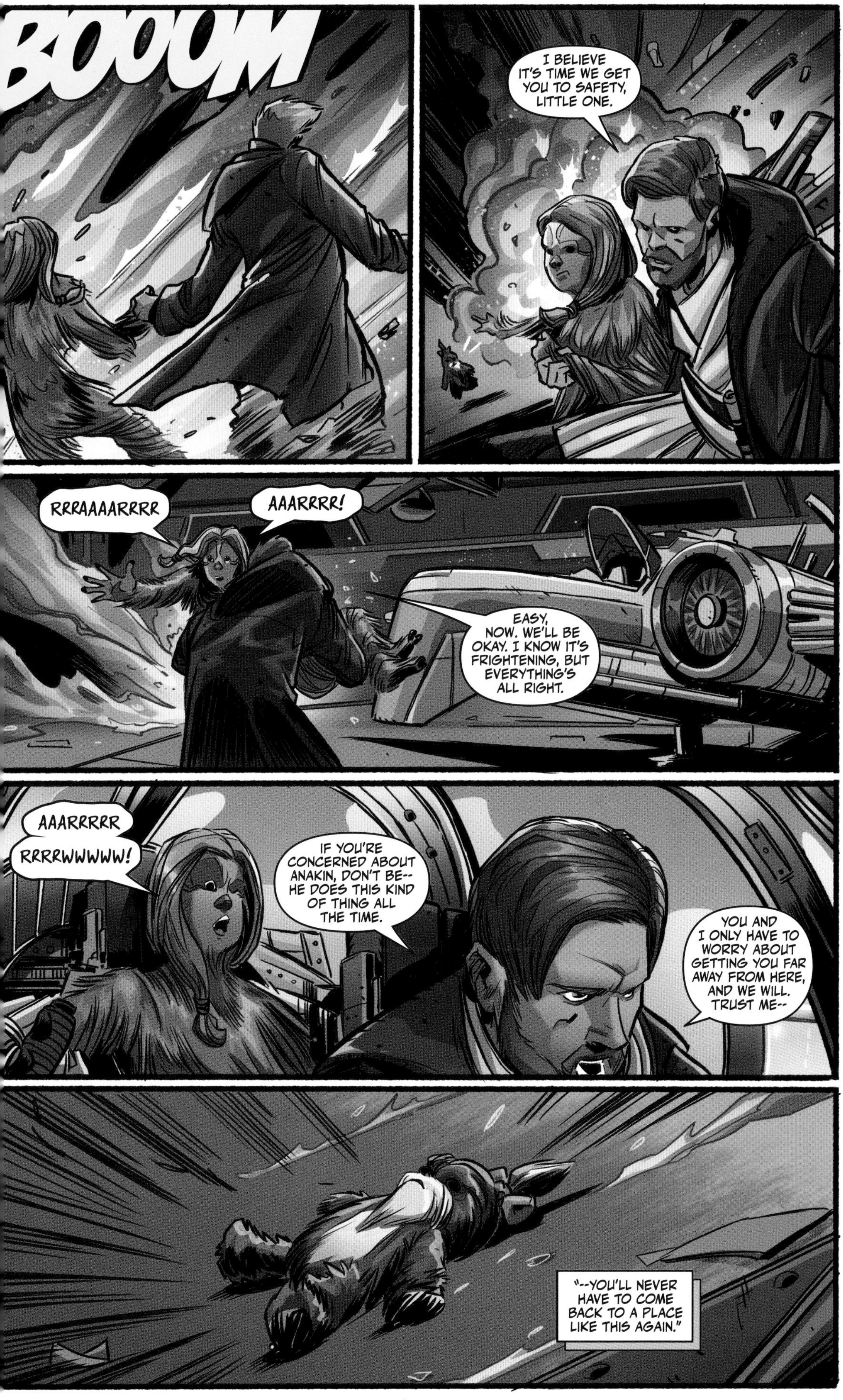
BOOOM
I BELIEVE IT'S TIME WE GET YOU TO SAFETY, LITTLE ONE.
RRRAAAARRRR
AAARRRR!
EASY, NOW. WE'LL BE OKAY. I KNOW IT'S FRIGHTENING, BUT EVERYTHING'S ALL RIGHT.
AAARRRRR
RRRRWWWWW!
IF YOU'RE CONCERNED ABOUT ANAKIN, DON'T BE-- HE DOES THIS KIND OF THING ALL THE TIME.
YOU AND I ONLY HAVE TO WORRY ABOUT GETTING YOU FAR AWAY FROM HERE, AND WE WILL. TRUST ME--
"--YOU'LL NEVER HAVE TO COME BACK TO A PLACE LIKE THIS AGAIN."

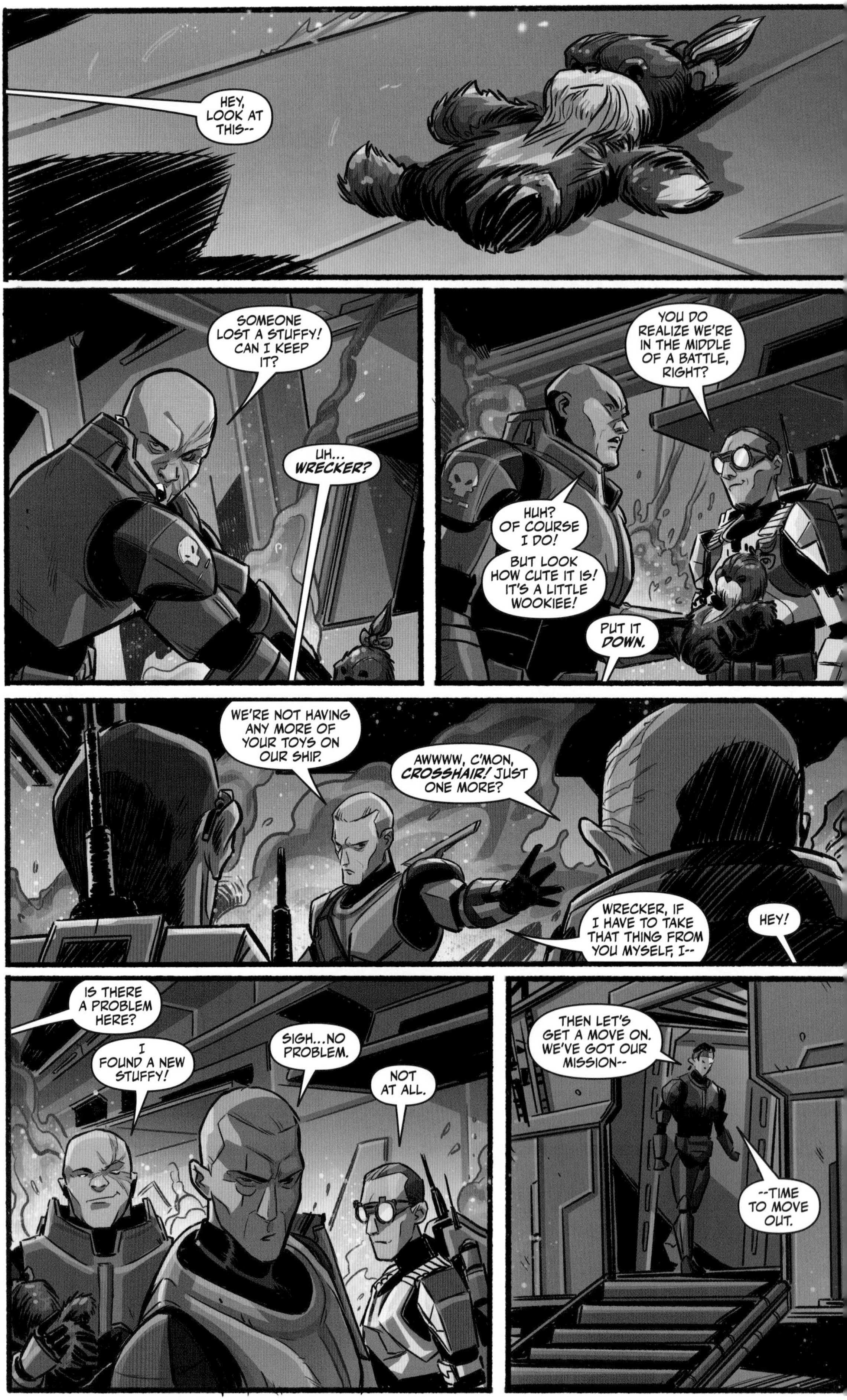
HEY, LOOK AT THIS--
SOMEONE LOST A STUFFY! CAN I KEEP IT?
UH... WRECKER?
YOU DO REALIZE WE'RE IN THE MIDDLE OF A BATTLE, RIGHT?
HUH? OF COURSE I DO!
BUT LOOK HOW CUTE IT IS! IT'S A LITTLE WOOKIEE!
PUT IT DOWN.
WE'RE NOT HAVING ANY MORE OF YOUR TOYS ON OUR SHIP.
AWWWW, C'MON, CROSSHAIR! JUST ONE MORE?
WRECKER, IF I HAVE TO TAKE THAT THING FROM YOU MYSELF, I--
HEY!
IS THERE A PROBLEM HERE?
I FOUND A NEW STUFFY!
SIGH...NO PROBLEM.
NOT AT ALL.
THEN LET'S GET A MOVE ON. WE'VE GOT OUR MISSION--
--TIME TO MOVE OUT.

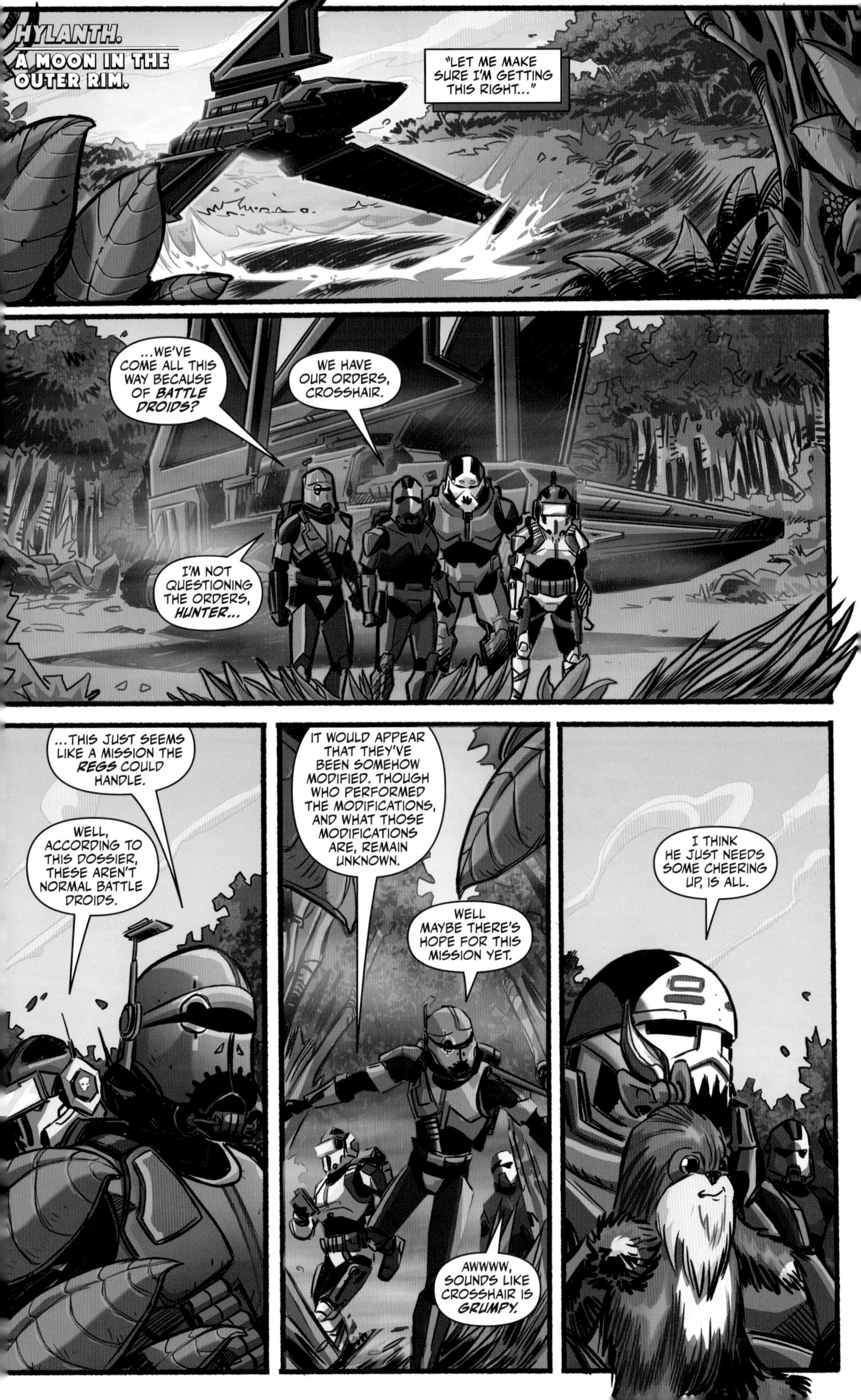
HYLANTH.
A MOON IN THE OUTER RIM.
"LET ME MAKE SURE I'M GETTING THIS RIGHT..."
...WE'VE COME ALL THIS WAY BECAUSE OF BATTLE DROIDS?
WE HAVE OUR ORDERS, CROSSHAIR.
I'M NOT QUESTIONING THE ORDERS, HUNTER...
...THIS JUST SEEMS LIKE A MISSION THE REGS COULD HANDLE.
WELL, ACCORDING TO THIS DOSSIER, THESE AREN'T NORMAL BATTLE DROIDS.
IT WOULD APPEAR THAT THEY'VE BEEN SOMEHOW MODIFIED. THOUGH WHO PERFORMED THE MODIFICATIONS, AND WHAT THOSE MODIFICATIONS ARE, REMAIN UNKNOWN.
WELL MAYBE THERE'S HOPE FOR THIS MISSION YET.
AWWWW, SOUNDS LIKE CROSSHAIR IS GRUMPY.
I THINK HE JUST NEEDS SOME CHEERING UP, IS ALL.

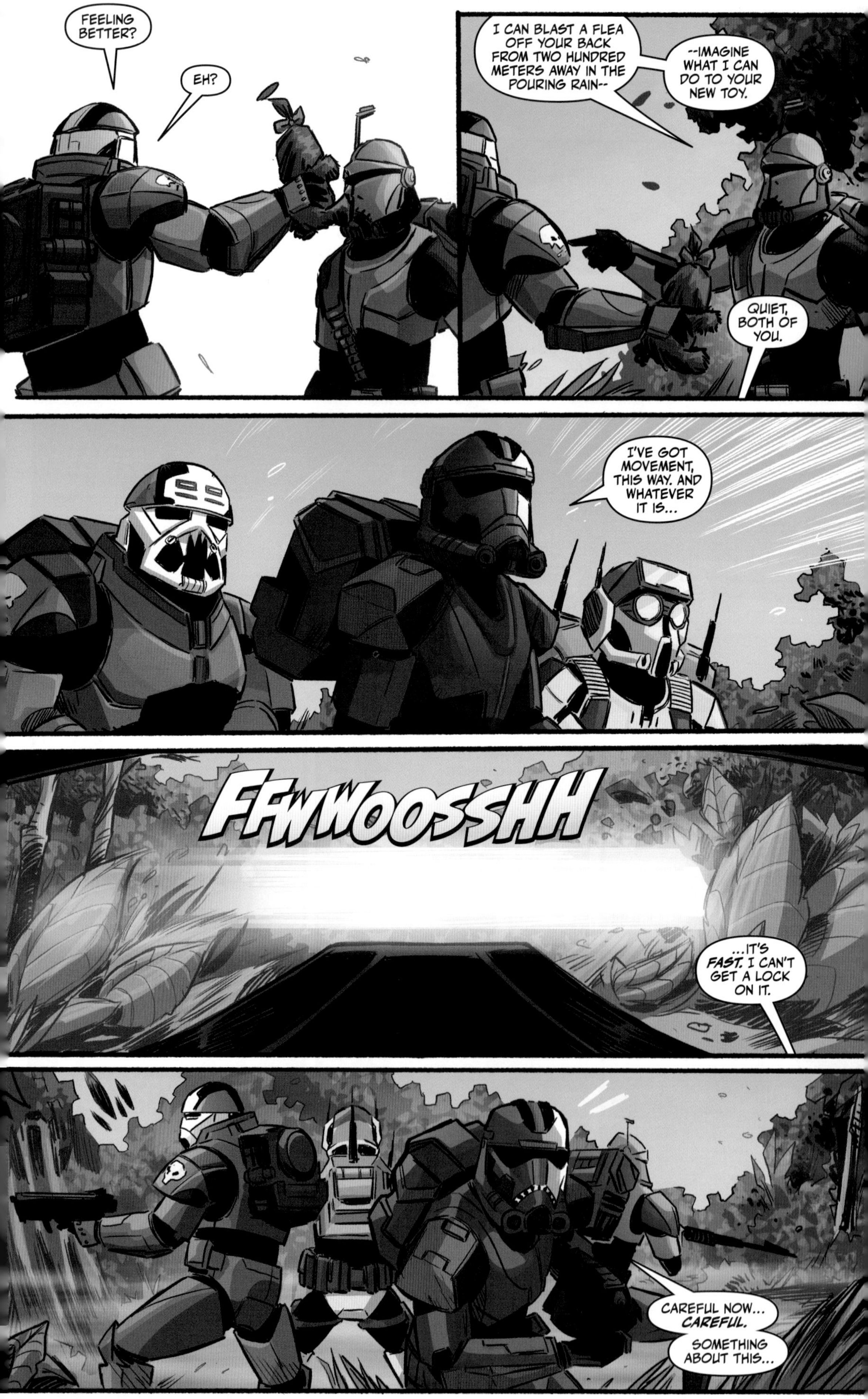
FEELING BETTER?
EH?
I CAN BLAST A FLEA OFF YOUR BACK FROM TWO HUNDRED METERS AWAY IN THE POURING RAIN--
--IMAGINE WHAT I CAN DO TO YOUR NEW TOY.
QUIET, BOTH OF YOU.
I'VE GOT MOVEMENT, THIS WAY. AND WHATEVER IT IS...
FFWWOOSSHH
...IT'S *FAST.* I CAN'T GET A LOCK ON IT.
CAREFUL NOW... *CAREFUL.*
SOMETHING ABOUT THIS...

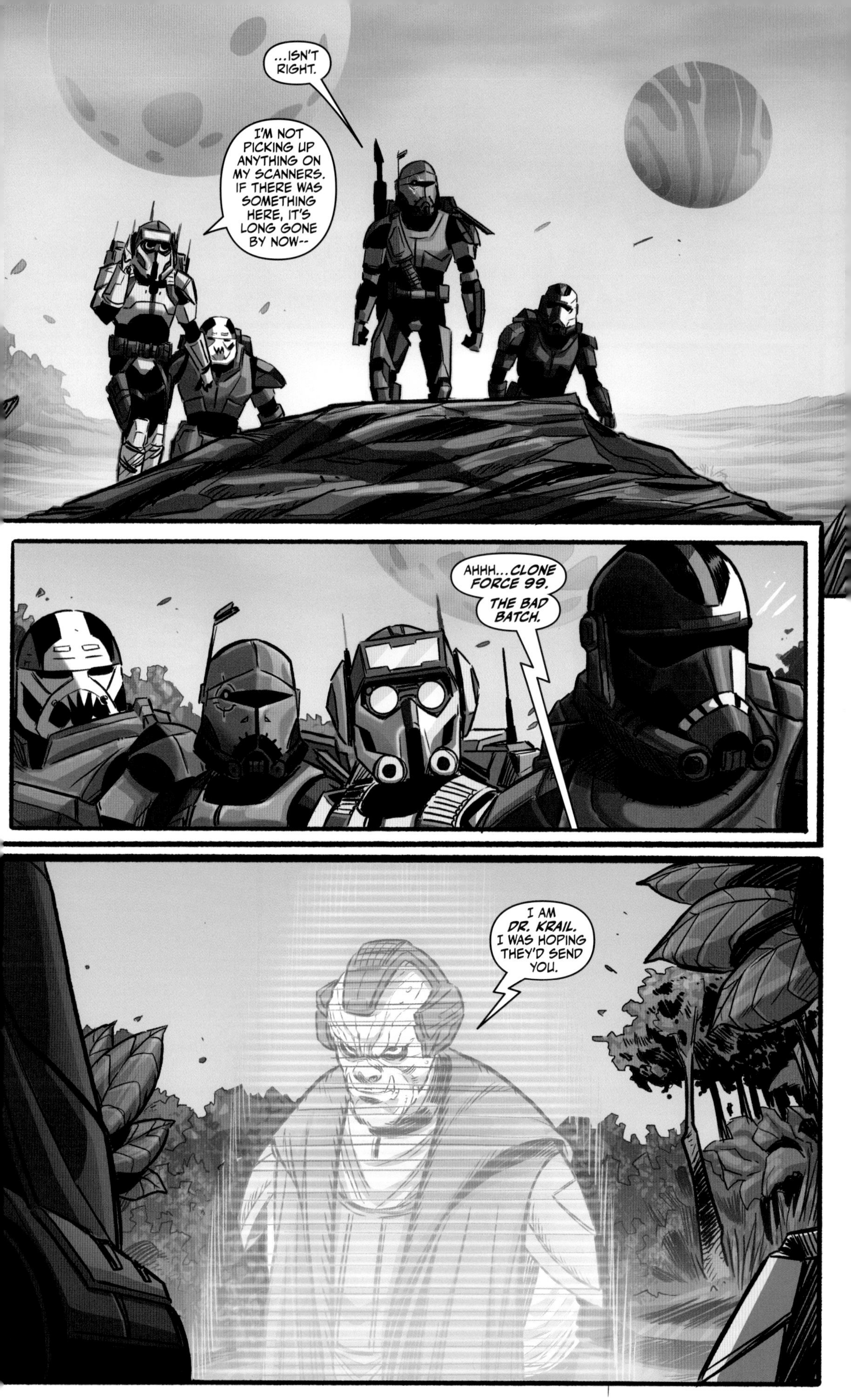
...ISN'T RIGHT.
I'M NOT PICKING UP ANYTHING ON MY SCANNERS. IF THERE WAS SOMETHING HERE, IT'S LONG GONE BY NOW--
AHHH... CLONE FORCE 99.
THE BAD BATCH.
I AM DR. KRAIL. I WAS HOPING THEY'D SEND YOU.

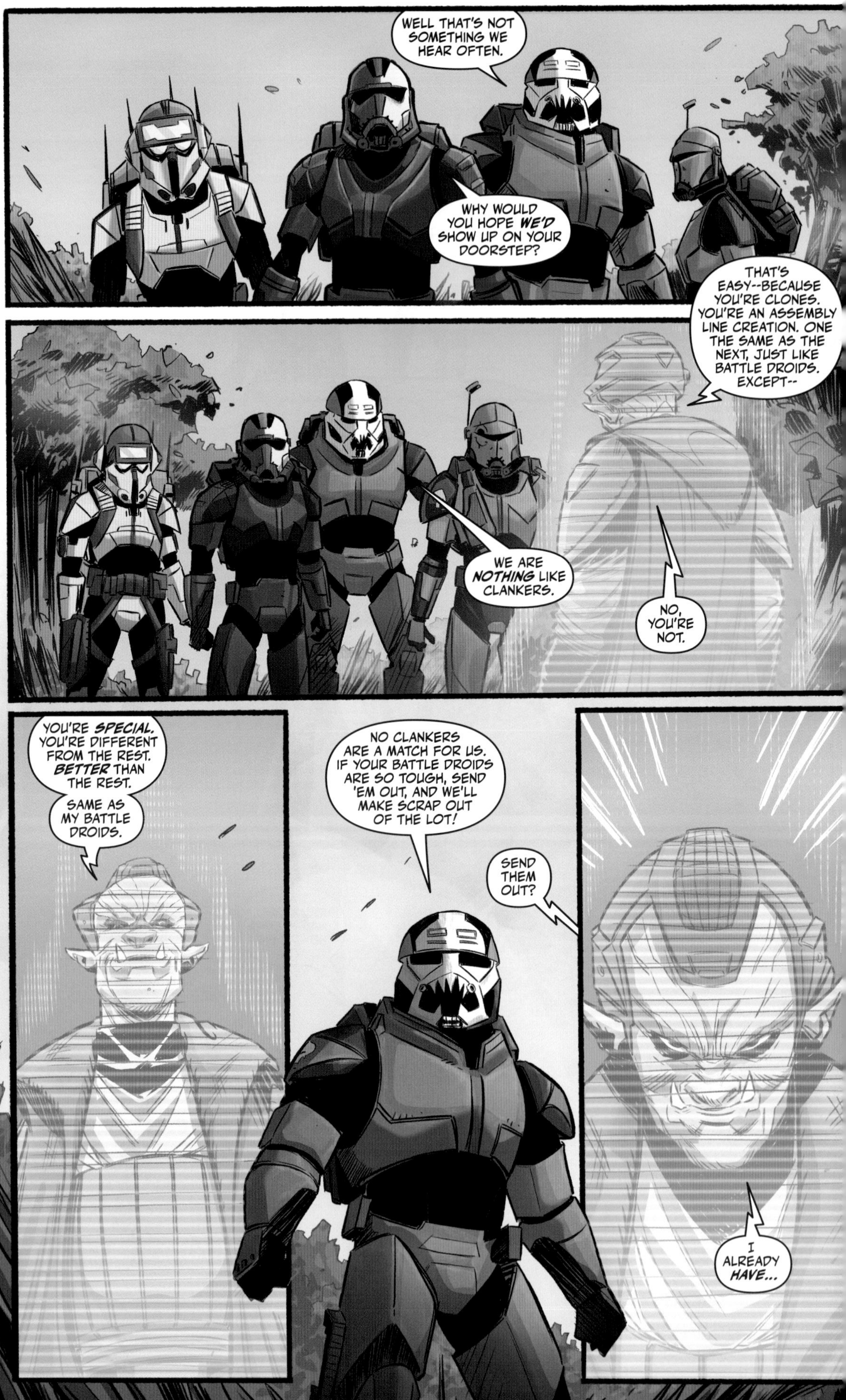
WELL THAT'S NOT SOMETHING WE HEAR OFTEN.
WHY WOULD YOU HOPE *WE'D* SHOW UP ON YOUR DOORSTEP?
THAT'S EASY--BECAUSE YOU'RE CLONES. YOU'RE AN ASSEMBLY LINE CREATION. ONE THE SAME AS THE NEXT, JUST LIKE BATTLE DROIDS. EXCEPT--
WE ARE *NOTHING* LIKE CLANKERS.
NO, YOU'RE NOT.
YOU'RE *SPECIAL.* YOU'RE DIFFERENT FROM THE REST. *BETTER* THAN THE REST.
SAME AS MY BATTLE DROIDS.
NO CLANKERS ARE A MATCH FOR US. IF YOUR BATTLE DROIDS ARE SO TOUGH, SEND 'EM OUT, AND WE'LL MAKE SCRAP OUT OF THE LOT!
SEND THEM OUT?
I ALREADY *HAVE*...

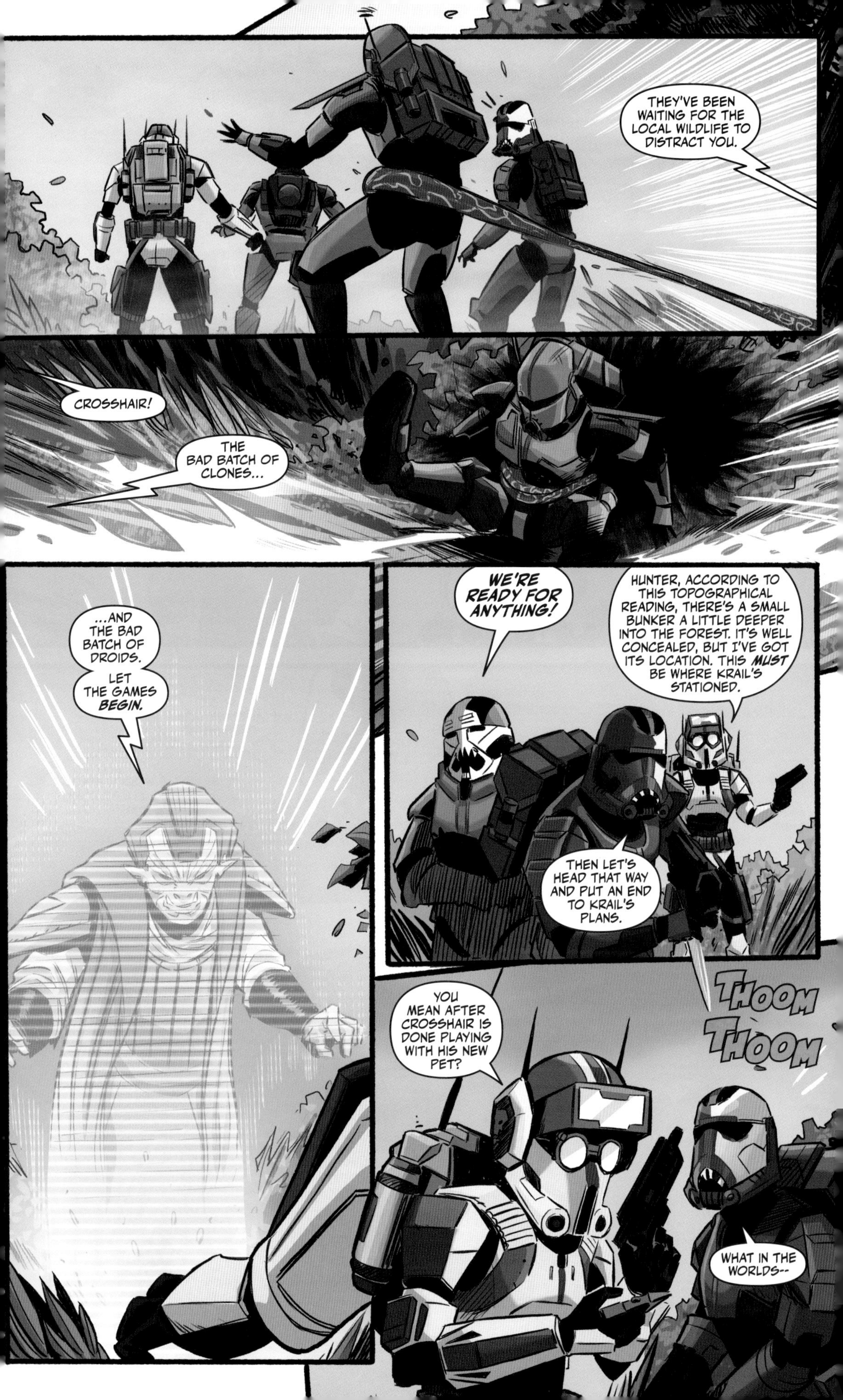
THEY'VE BEEN WAITING FOR THE LOCAL WILDLIFE TO DISTRACT YOU.
CROSSHAIR!
THE BAD BATCH OF CLONES...
...AND THE BAD BATCH OF DROIDS.
LET THE GAMES *BEGIN.*
WE'RE READY FOR ANYTHING!
HUNTER, ACCORDING TO THIS TOPOGRAPHICAL READING, THERE'S A SMALL BUNKER A LITTLE DEEPER INTO THE FOREST. IT'S WELL CONCEALED, BUT I'VE GOT ITS LOCATION. THIS *MUST* BE WHERE KRAIL'S STATIONED.
THEN LET'S HEAD THAT WAY AND PUT AN END TO KRAIL'S PLANS.
YOU MEAN AFTER CROSSHAIR IS DONE PLAYING WITH HIS NEW PET?
THOOM
THOOM
WHAT IN THE WORLDS--

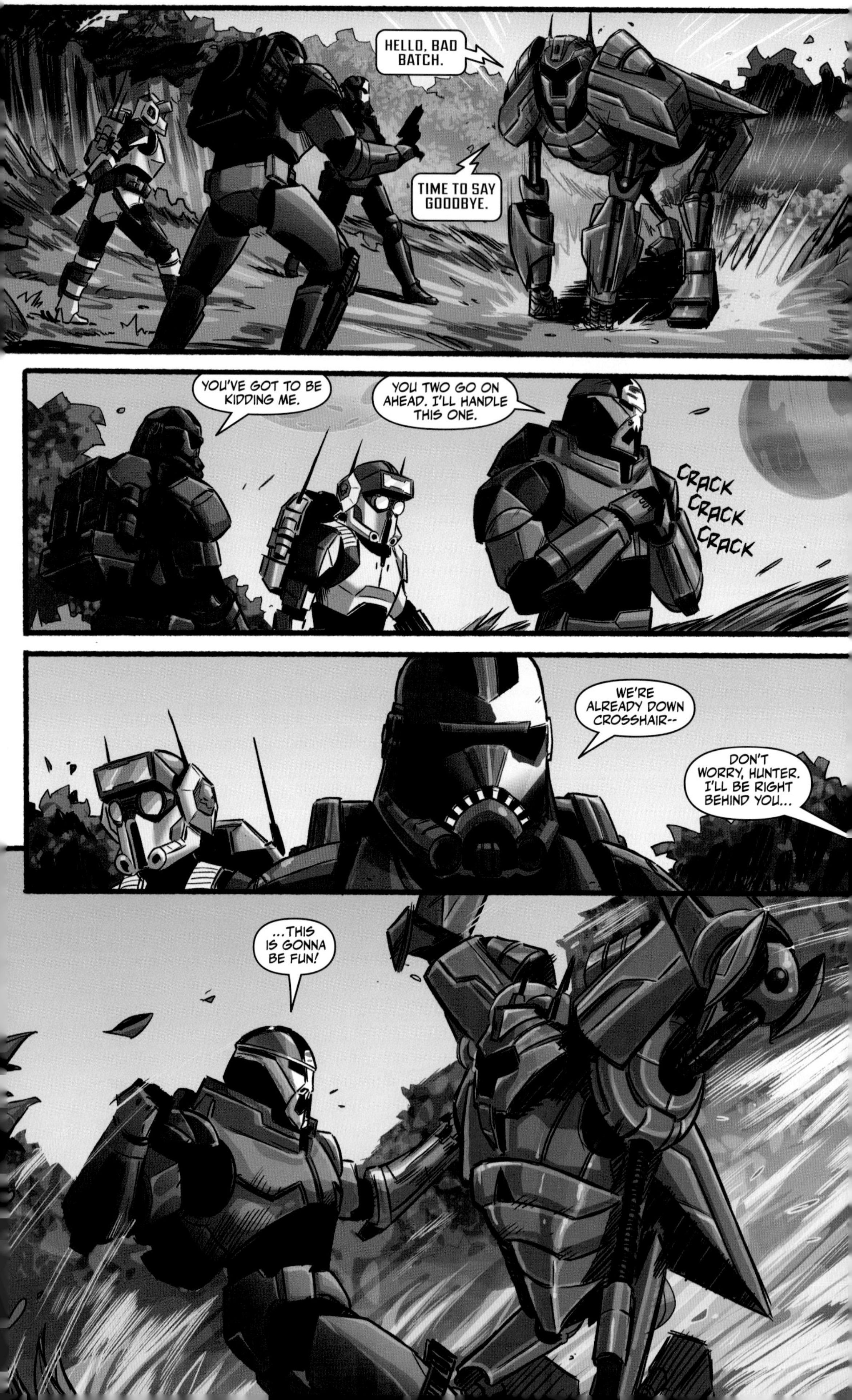
HELLO, BAD BATCH.
TIME TO SAY GOODBYE.
YOU'VE GOT TO BE KIDDING ME.
YOU TWO GO ON AHEAD. I'LL HANDLE THIS ONE.
CRACK CRACK CRACK
WE'RE ALREADY DOWN CROSSHAIR--
DON'T WORRY, HUNTER. I'LL BE RIGHT BEHIND YOU...
...THIS IS GONNA BE FUN!

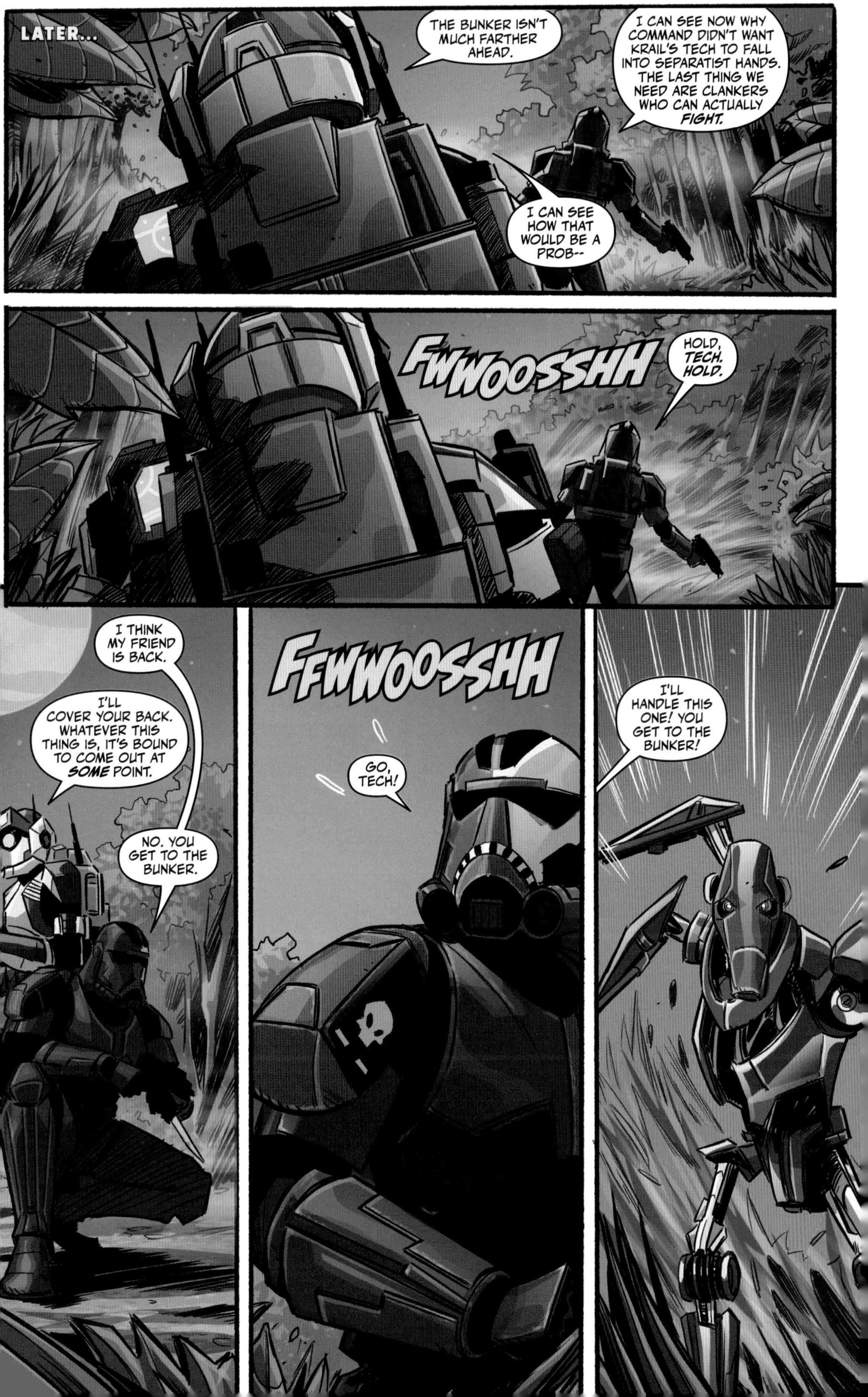
LATER...
THE BUNKER ISN'T MUCH FARTHER AHEAD.
I CAN SEE NOW WHY COMMAND DIDN'T WANT KRAIL'S TECH TO FALL INTO SEPARATIST HANDS. THE LAST THING WE NEED ARE CLANKERS WHO CAN ACTUALLY *FIGHT.*
I CAN SEE HOW THAT WOULD BE A PROB--
FWWOOSSHH
HOLD, *TECH.* *HOLD.*
I THINK MY FRIEND IS BACK.
I'LL COVER YOUR BACK. WHATEVER THIS THING IS, IT'S BOUND TO COME OUT AT ***SOME*** POINT.
NO. YOU GET TO THE BUNKER.
FFWWOOSSHH
GO, TECH!
I'LL HANDLE THIS ONE! YOU GET TO THE BUNKER!

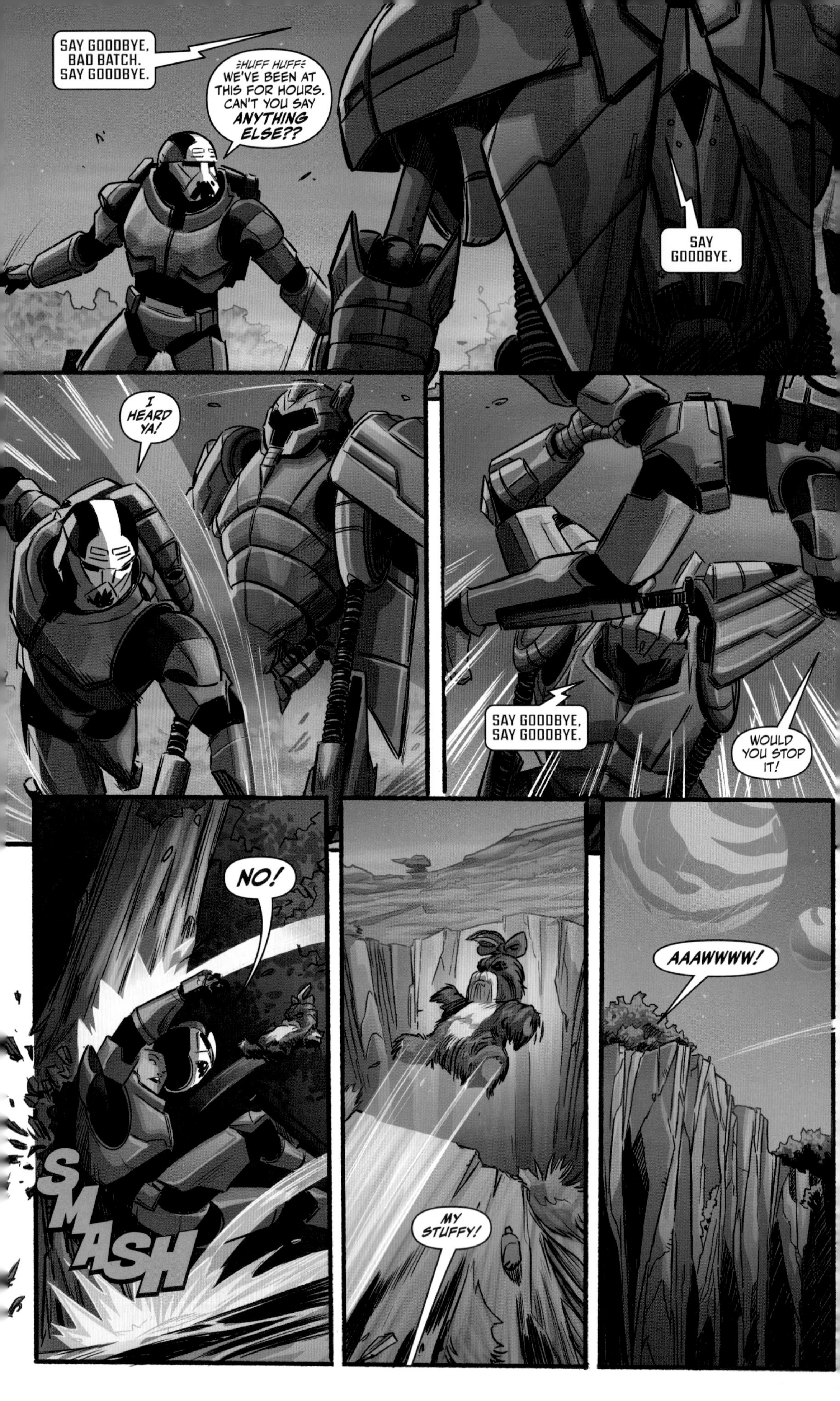
SAY GOODBYE, BAD BATCH. SAY GOODBYE.
HUFF HUFF WE'VE BEEN AT THIS FOR HOURS. CAN'T YOU SAY ANYTHING ELSE??
SAY GOODBYE.
I HEARD YA!
SAY GOODBYE, SAY GOODBYE.
WOULD YOU STOP IT!
NO!
SMASH
MY STUFFY!
AAAWWWW!

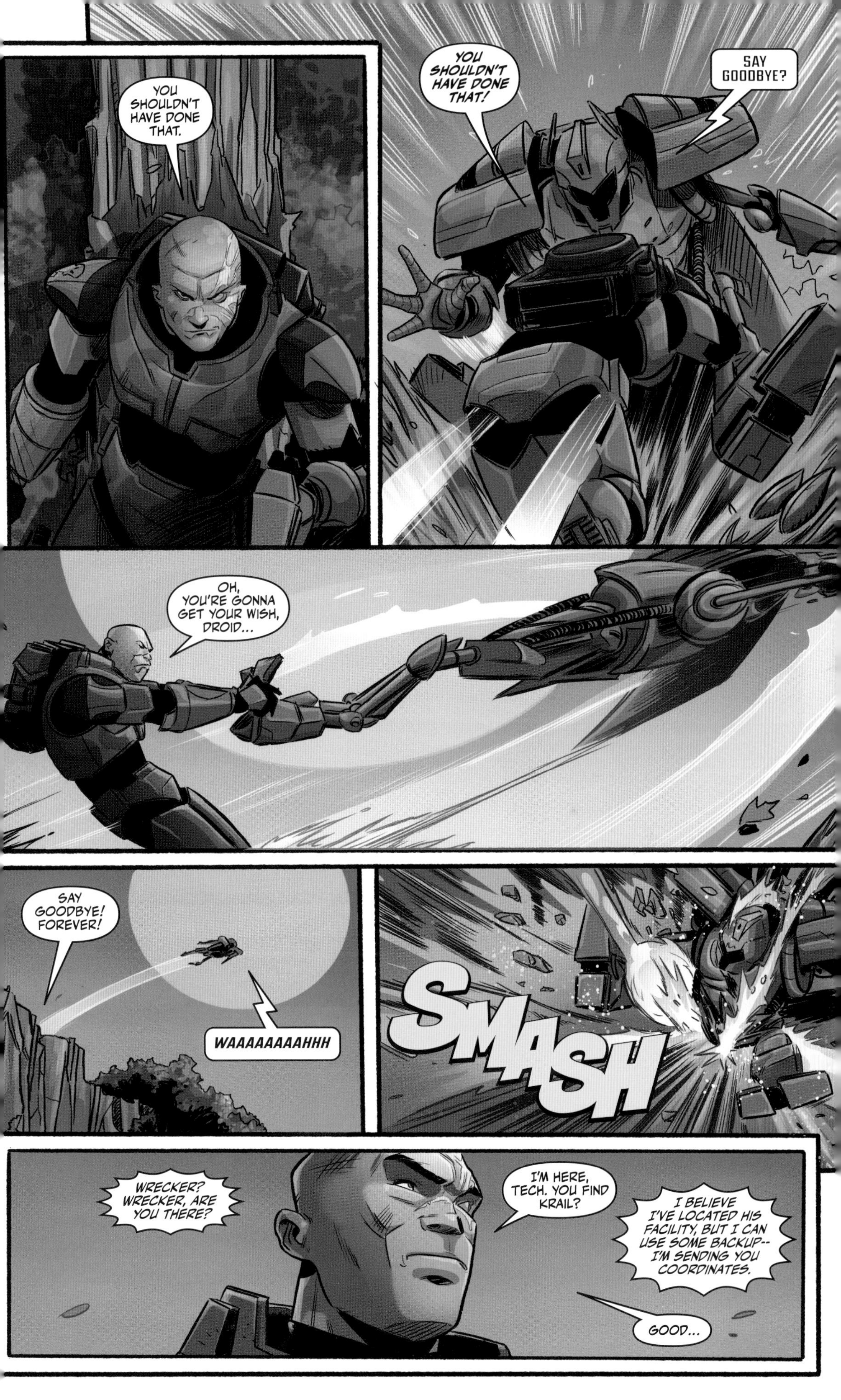
YOU SHOULDN'T HAVE DONE THAT.
YOU SHOULDN'T HAVE DONE THAT!
SAY GOODBYE?
OH, YOU'RE GONNA GET YOUR WISH, DROID...
SAY GOODBYE! FOREVER!
WAAAAAAAAAHHH
SMASH
WRECKER? WRECKER, ARE YOU THERE?
I'M HERE, TECH. YOU FIND KRAIL?
I BELIEVE I'VE LOCATED HIS FACILITY, BUT I CAN USE SOME BACKUP-- I'M SENDING YOU COORDINATES.
GOOD...

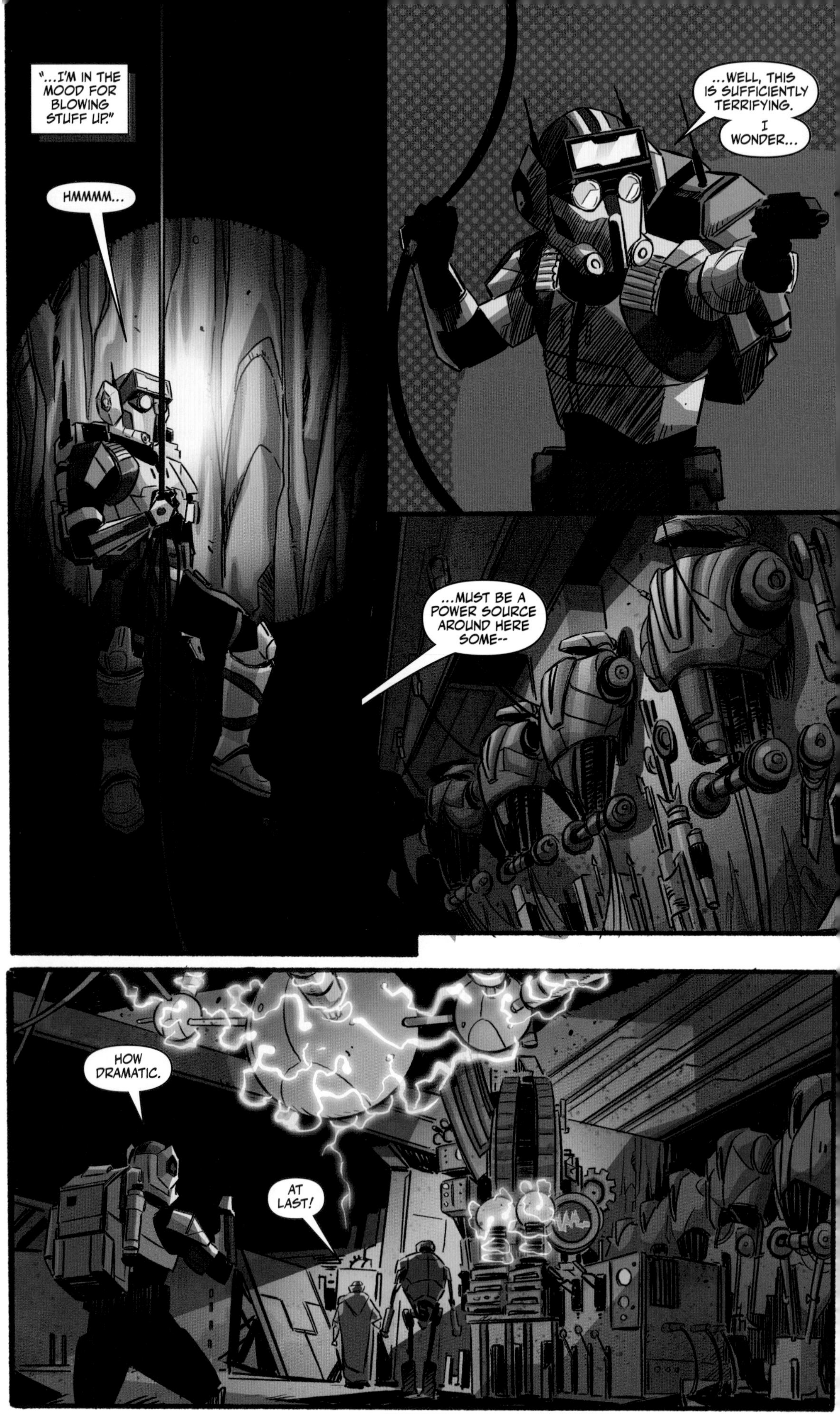
"...I'M IN THE MOOD FOR BLOWING STUFF UP."
HMMMM...
...WELL, THIS IS SUFFICIENTLY TERRIFYING.
I WONDER...
...MUST BE A POWER SOURCE AROUND HERE SOME--
HOW DRAMATIC.
AT LAST!

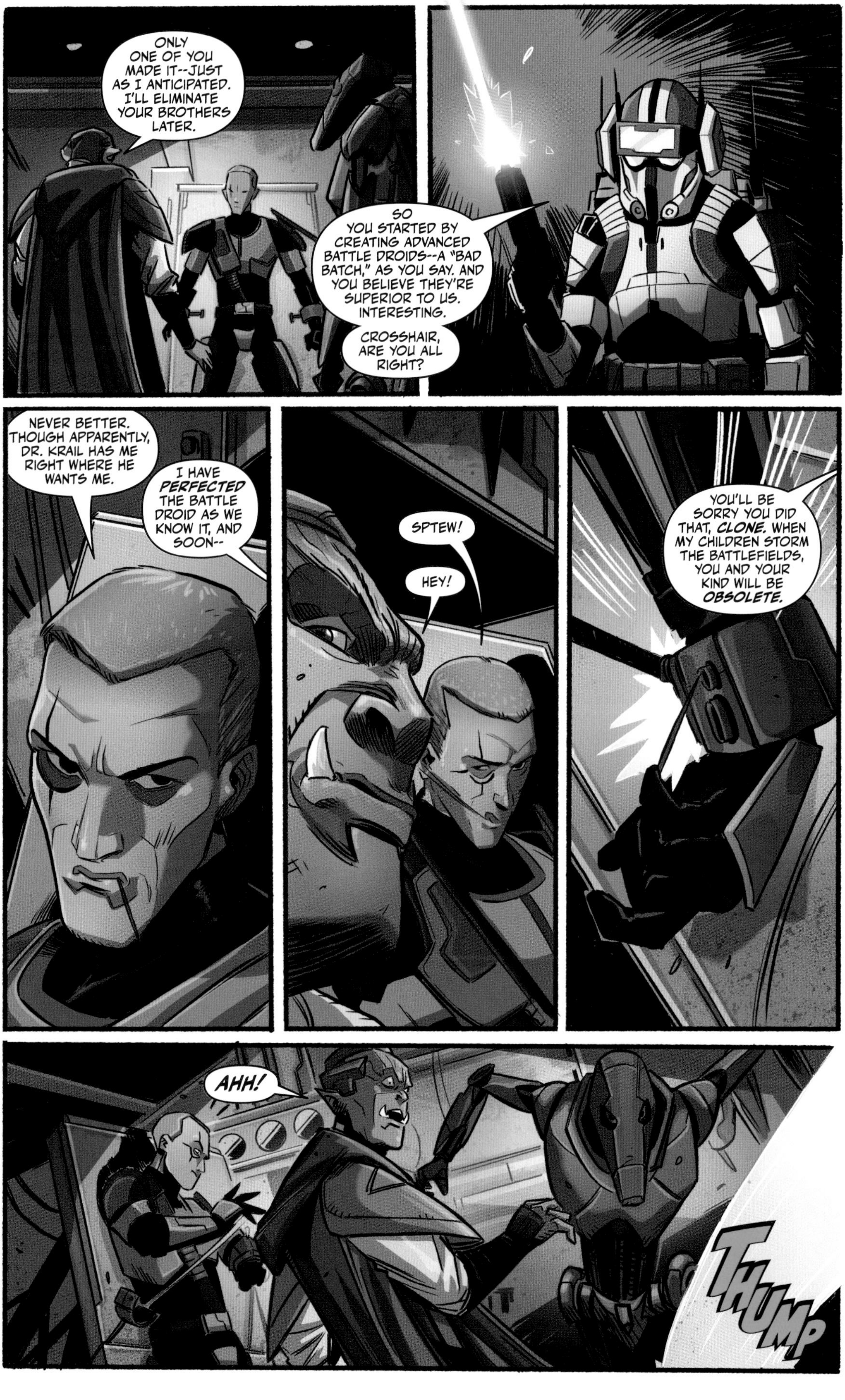
ONLY ONE OF YOU MADE IT--JUST AS I ANTICIPATED. I'LL ELIMINATE YOUR BROTHERS LATER.
SO YOU STARTED BY CREATING ADVANCED BATTLE DROIDS--A "BAD BATCH," AS YOU SAY. AND YOU BELIEVE THEY'RE SUPERIOR TO US. INTERESTING.
CROSSHAIR, ARE YOU ALL RIGHT?
NEVER BETTER. THOUGH APPARENTLY, DR. KRAIL HAS ME RIGHT WHERE HE WANTS ME.
I HAVE PERFECTED THE BATTLE DROID AS WE KNOW IT, AND SOON--
SPTEW!
HEY!
YOU'LL BE SORRY YOU DID THAT, CLONE. WHEN MY CHILDREN STORM THE BATTLEFIELDS, YOU AND YOUR KIND WILL BE OBSOLETE.
AHH!
THUMP

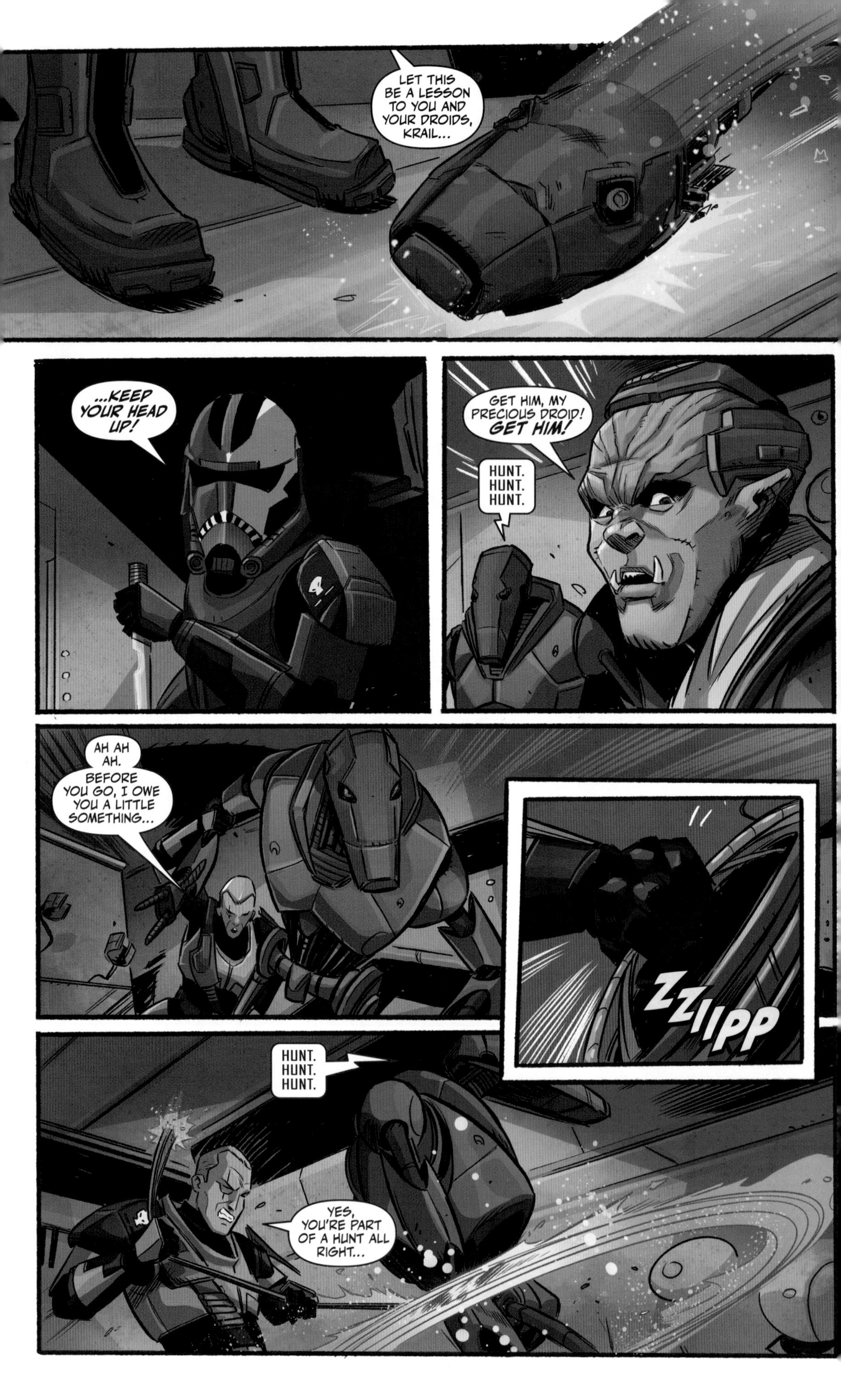
LET THIS BE A LESSON TO YOU AND YOUR DROIDS, KRAIL...
...KEEP YOUR HEAD UP!
GET HIM, MY PRECIOUS DROID! GET HIM!
HUNT. HUNT. HUNT.
AH AH AH. BEFORE YOU GO, I OWE YOU A LITTLE SOMETHING...
ZZIIPP
HUNT. HUNT. HUNT.
YES, YOU'RE PART OF A HUNT ALL RIGHT...

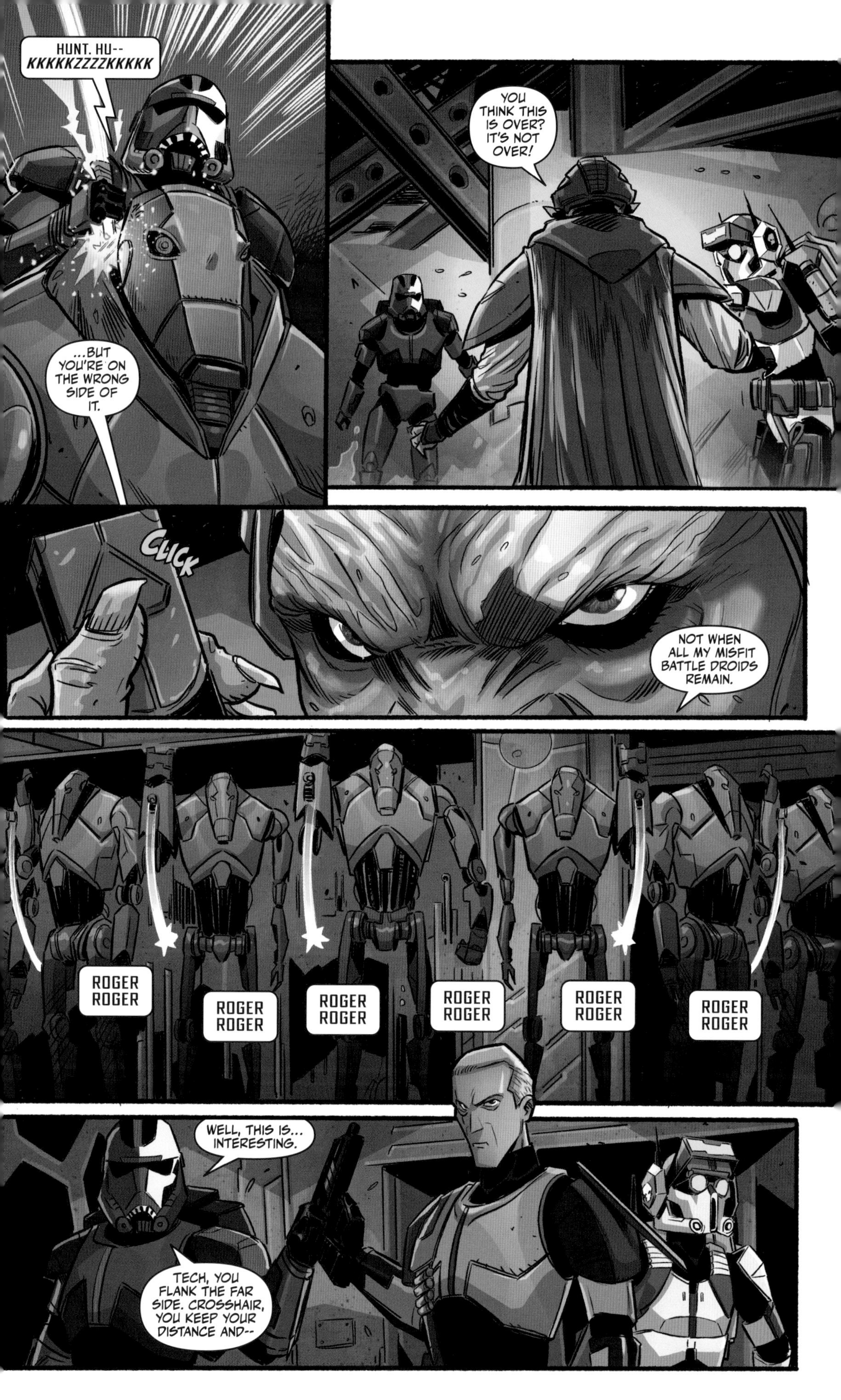
HUNT. HU-- KKKKKZZZZKKKKK
...BUT YOU'RE ON THE WRONG SIDE OF IT.
YOU THINK THIS IS OVER? IT'S NOT OVER!
CLICK
NOT WHEN ALL MY MISFIT BATTLE DROIDS REMAIN.
ROGER ROGER
ROGER ROGER
ROGER ROGER
ROGER ROGER
ROGER ROGER
ROGER ROGER
WELL, THIS IS... INTERESTING.
TECH, YOU FLANK THE FAR SIDE. CROSSHAIR, YOU KEEP YOUR DISTANCE AND--

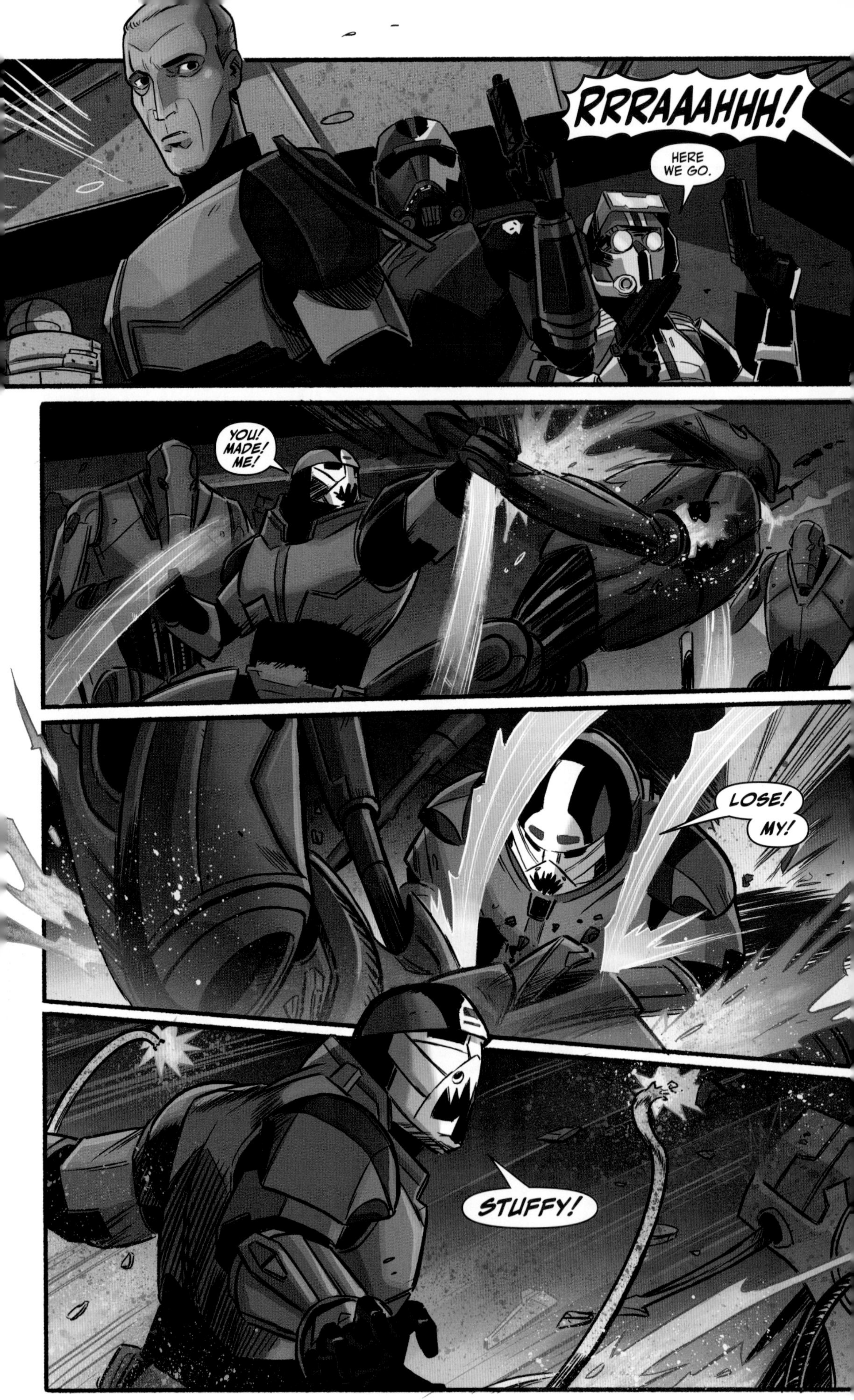
RRRAAAHHH!
HERE WE GO.
YOU! MADE! ME!
LOSE! MY!
STUFFY!

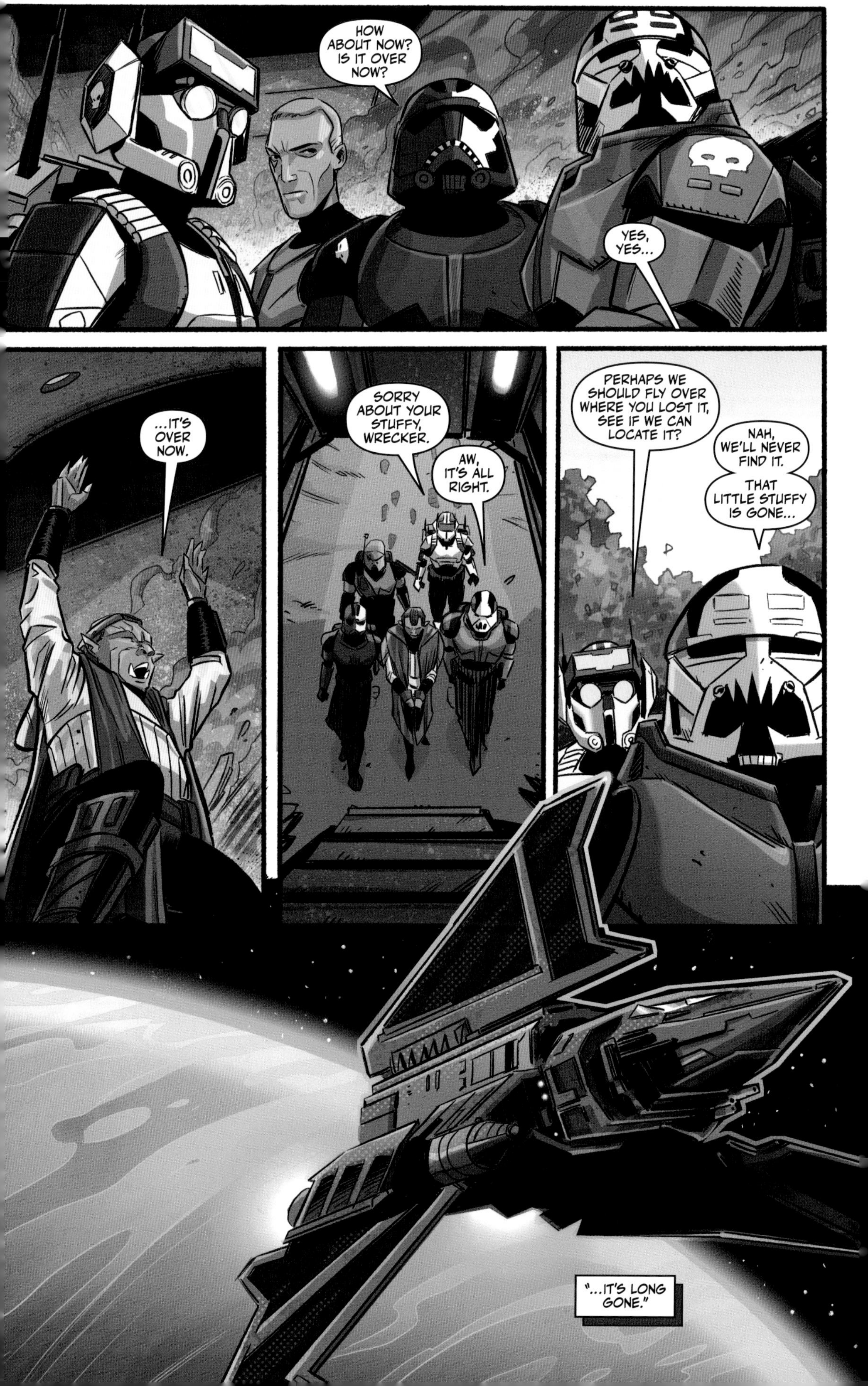
HOW ABOUT NOW? IS IT OVER NOW?
YES, YES...
...IT'S OVER NOW.
SORRY ABOUT YOUR STUFFY, WRECKER.
AW, IT'S ALL RIGHT.
PERHAPS WE SHOULD FLY OVER WHERE YOU LOST IT, SEE IF WE CAN LOCATE IT?
NAH, WE'LL NEVER FIND IT.
THAT LITTLE STUFFY IS GONE...
"...IT'S LONG GONE."

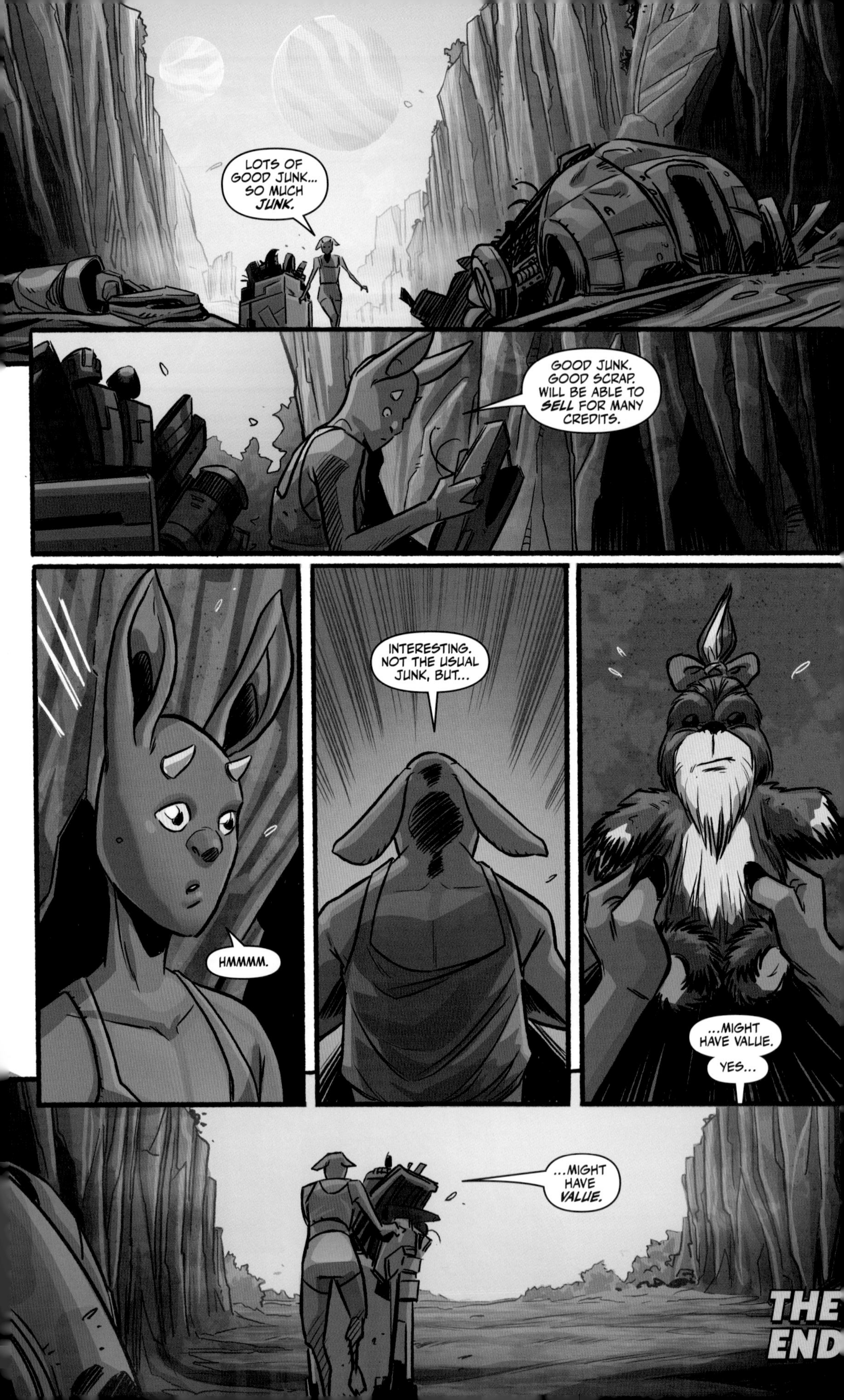
LOTS OF GOOD JUNK... SO MUCH JUNK.
GOOD JUNK. GOOD SCRAP. WILL BE ABLE TO SELL FOR MANY CREDITS.
HMMMM.
INTERESTING. NOT THE USUAL JUNK, BUT...
...MIGHT HAVE VALUE.
YES...
...MIGHT HAVE VALUE.
THE END

Art by Tom Fowler with Bill Crabtree

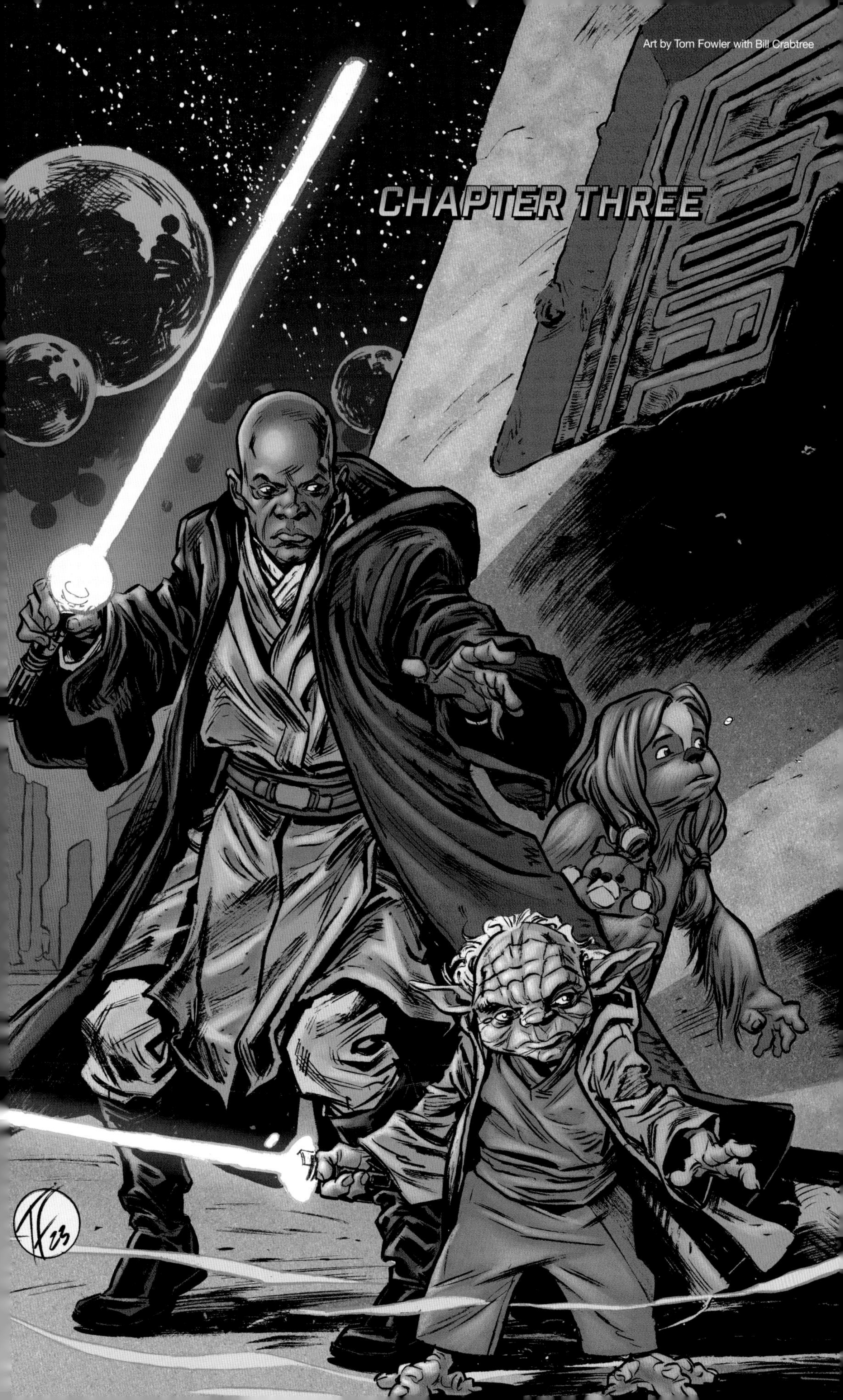
CHAPTER THREE

Art by Cary Nor

CHAPTER THREE:
A FORCE UNITED

written by
AMANDA DEIBERT

art and colors by
MEGAN HUANG

letters by
COMICRAFT'S TYLER SMITH and
JIMMY BETANCOURT

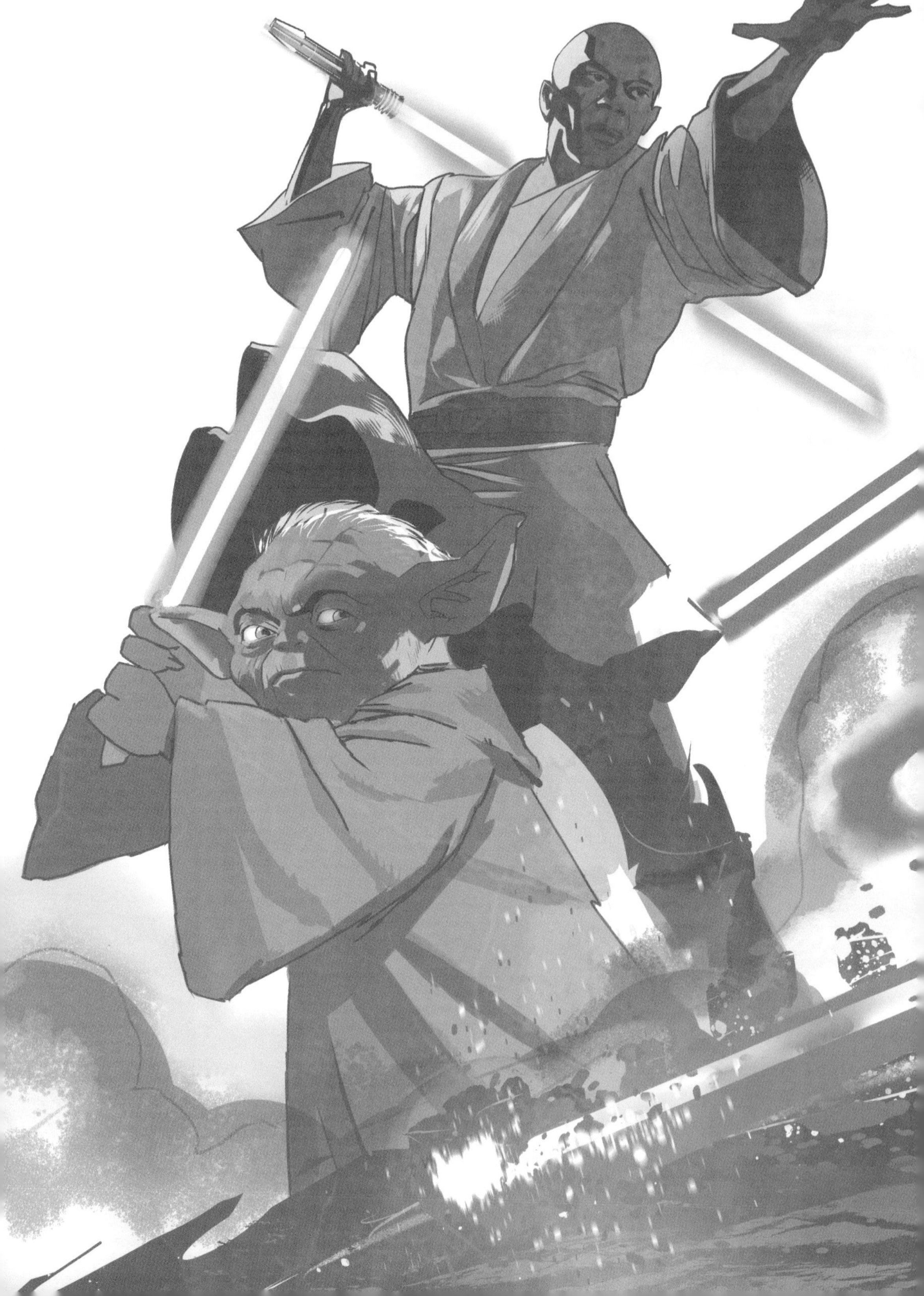

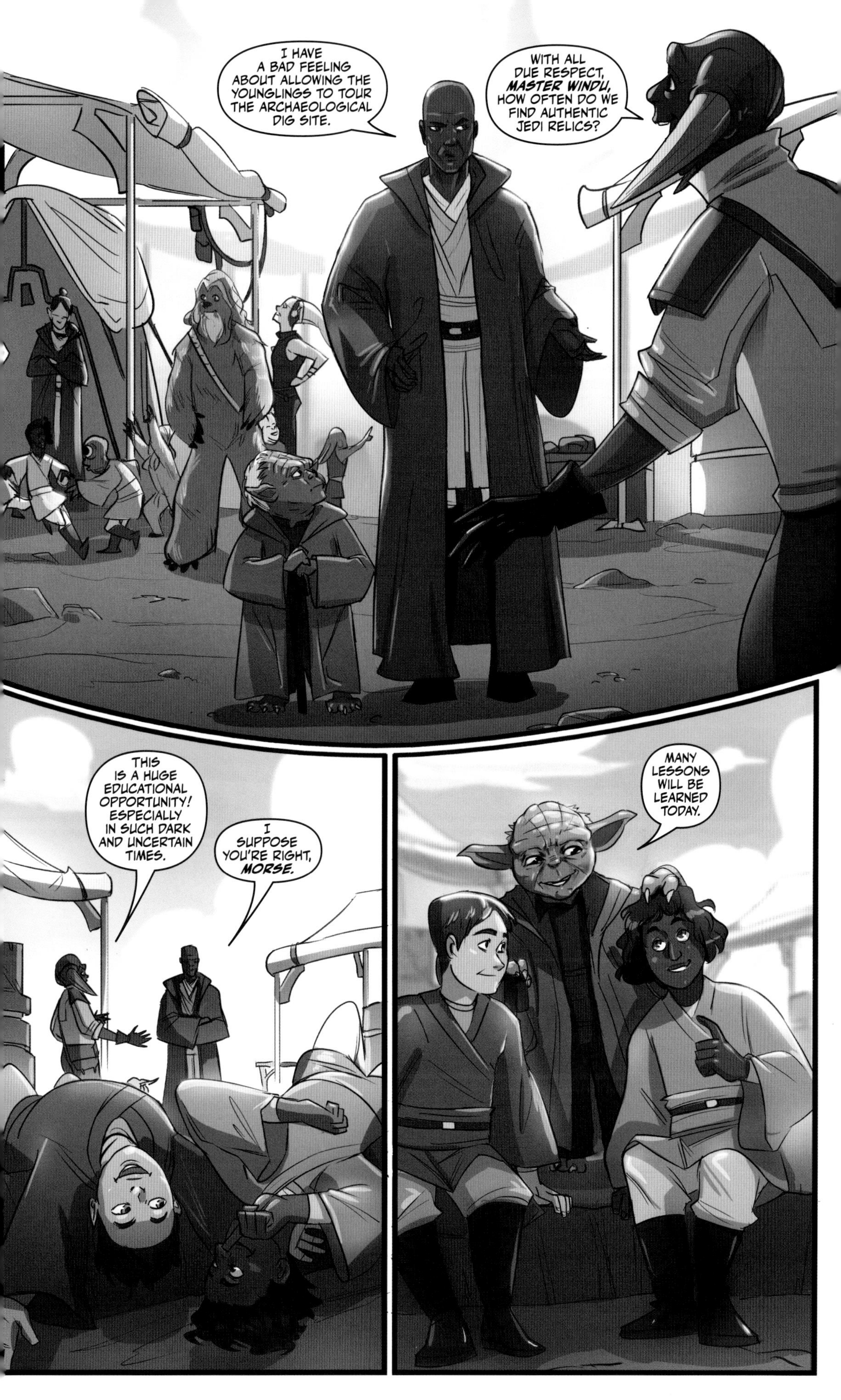
I HAVE A BAD FEELING ABOUT ALLOWING THE YOUNGLINGS TO TOUR THE ARCHAEOLOGICAL DIG SITE.
WITH ALL DUE RESPECT, MASTER WINDU, HOW OFTEN DO WE FIND AUTHENTIC JEDI RELICS?
THIS IS A HUGE EDUCATIONAL OPPORTUNITY! ESPECIALLY IN SUCH DARK AND UNCERTAIN TIMES.
I SUPPOSE YOU'RE RIGHT, MORSE.
MANY LESSONS WILL BE LEARNED TODAY.

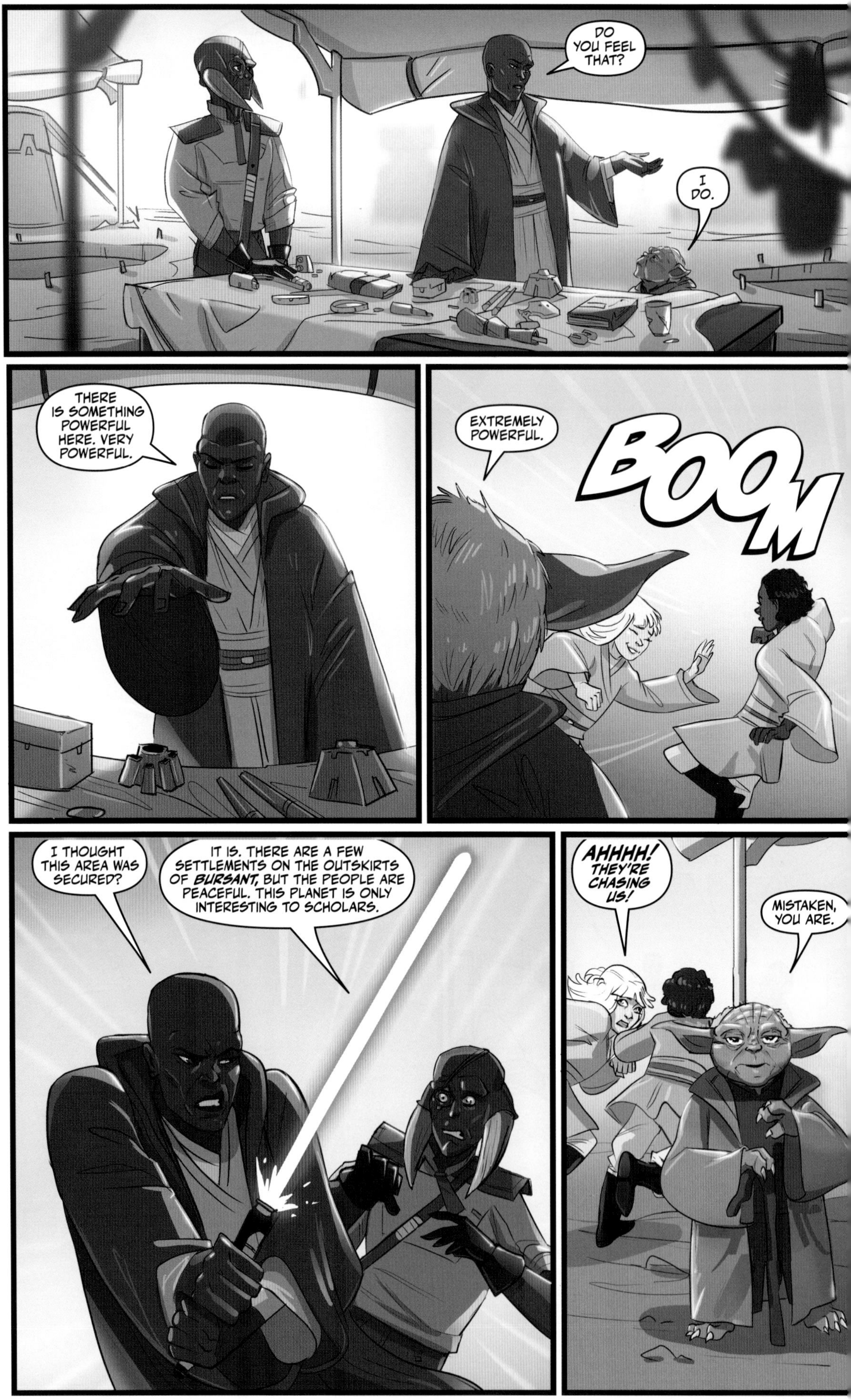
DO YOU FEEL THAT?
I DO.
THERE IS SOMETHING POWERFUL HERE. VERY POWERFUL.
EXTREMELY POWERFUL.
BOOM
I THOUGHT THIS AREA WAS SECURED?
IT IS. THERE ARE A FEW SETTLEMENTS ON THE OUTSKIRTS OF BURSANT, BUT THE PEOPLE ARE PEACEFUL. THIS PLANET IS ONLY INTERESTING TO SCHOLARS.
AHHHH! THEY'RE CHASING US!
MISTAKEN, YOU ARE.

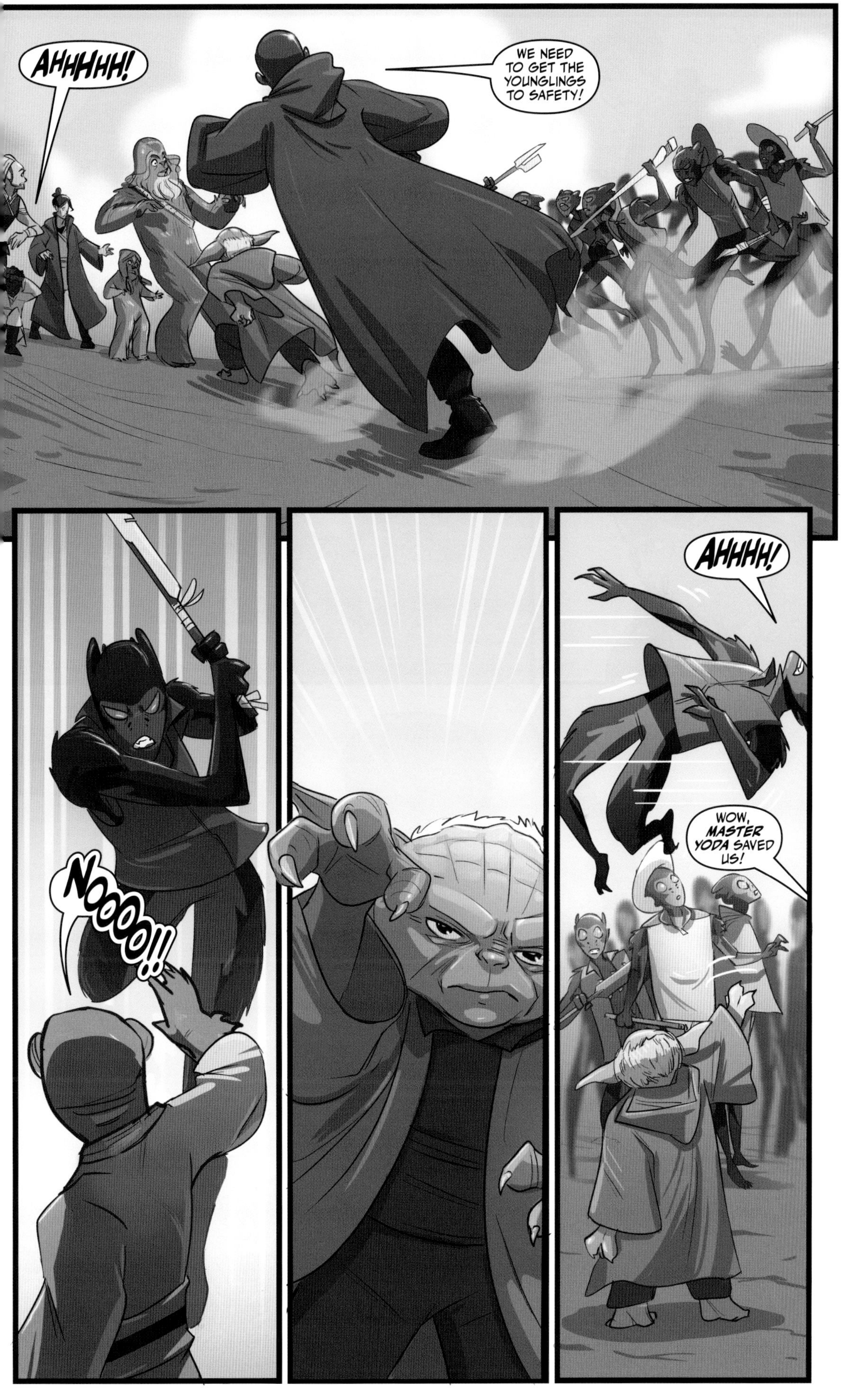
AHHHHH!
WE NEED TO GET THE YOUNGLINGS TO SAFETY!
NOOOO!!
AHHHH!
WOW, MASTER YODA SAVED US!

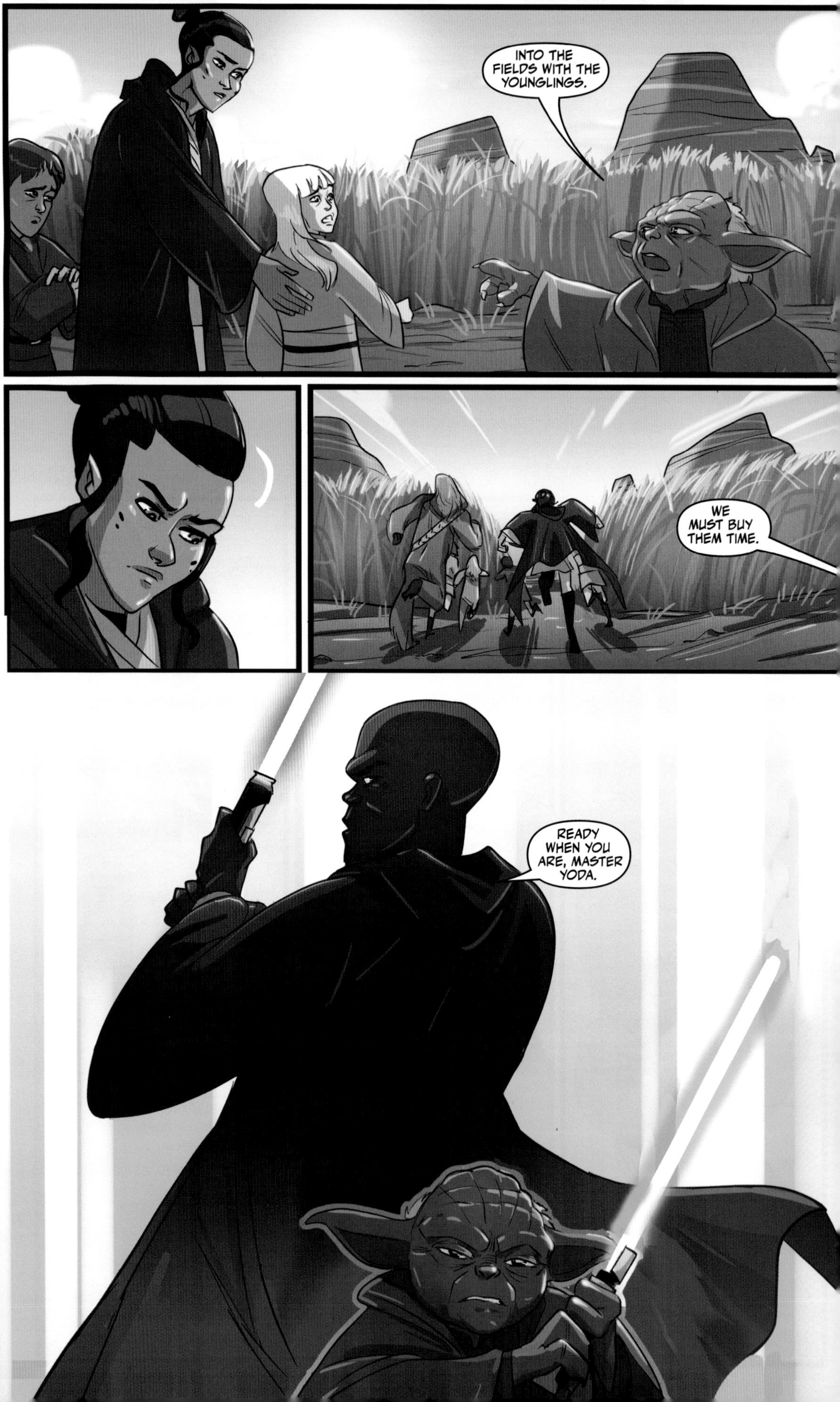
INTO THE FIELDS WITH THE YOUNGLINGS.
WE MUST BUY THEM TIME.
READY WHEN YOU ARE, MASTER YODA.

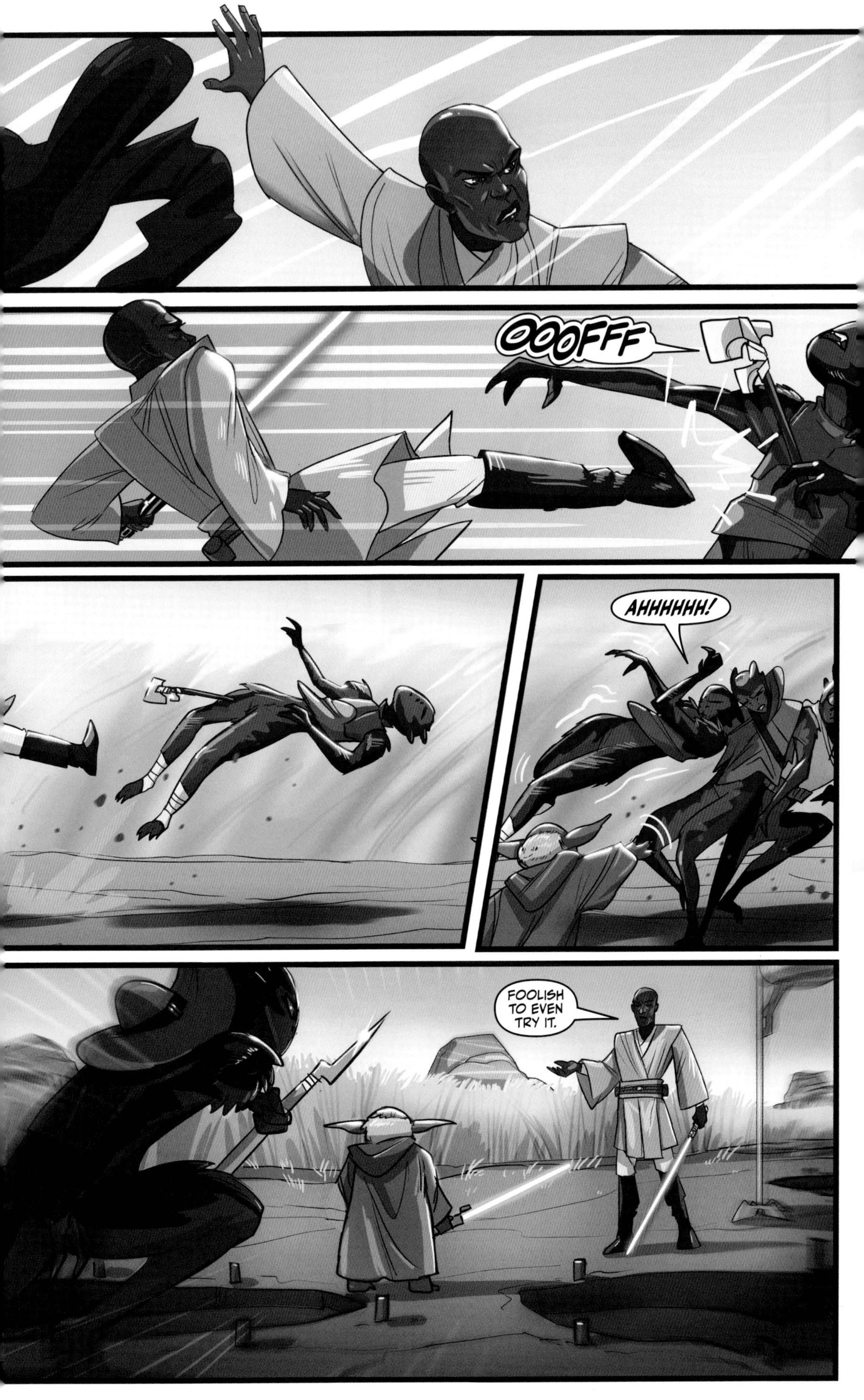
OOOFFF
AHHHHHH!
FOOLISH TO EVEN TRY IT.

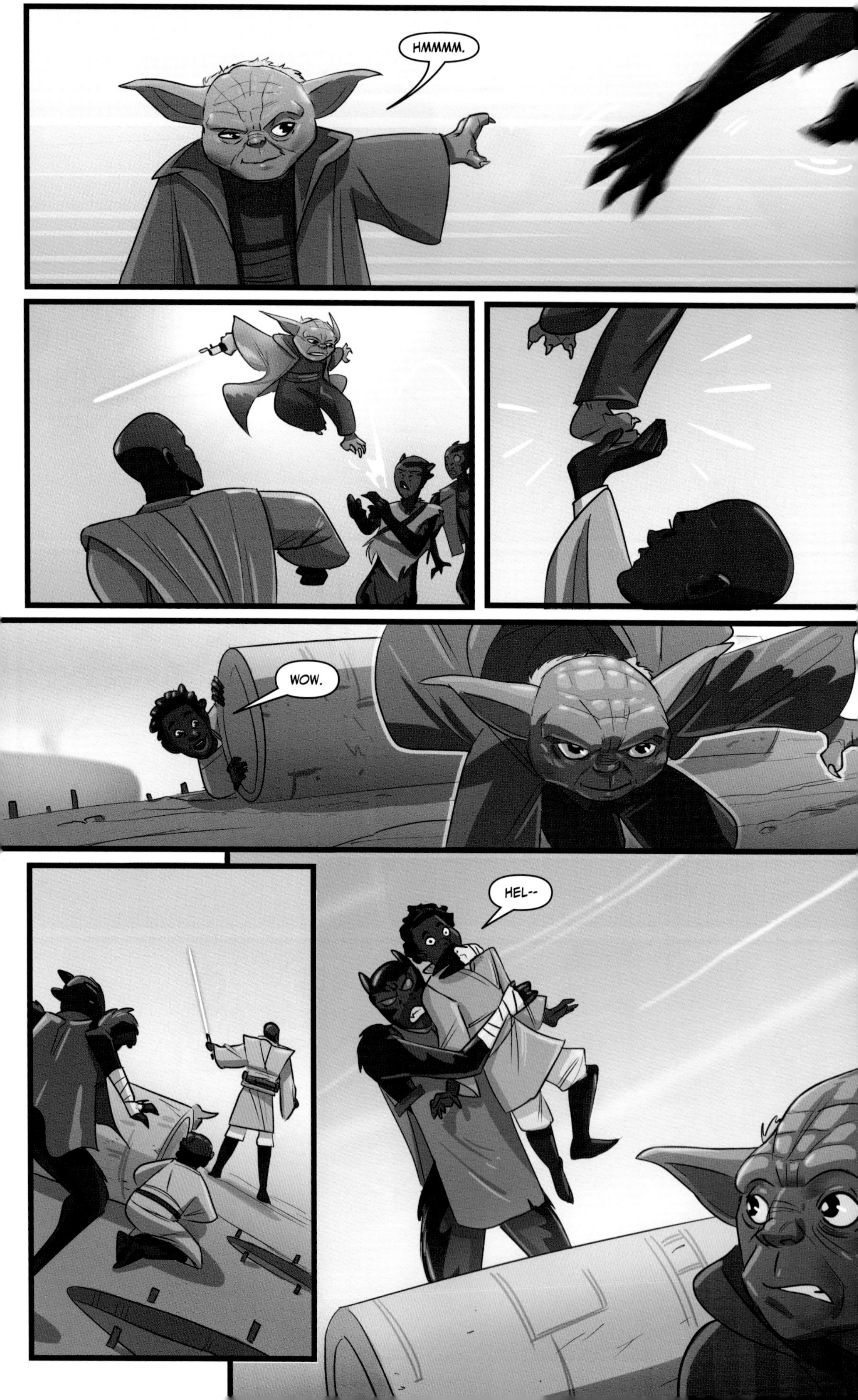
HMMMM.
WOW.
HEL--

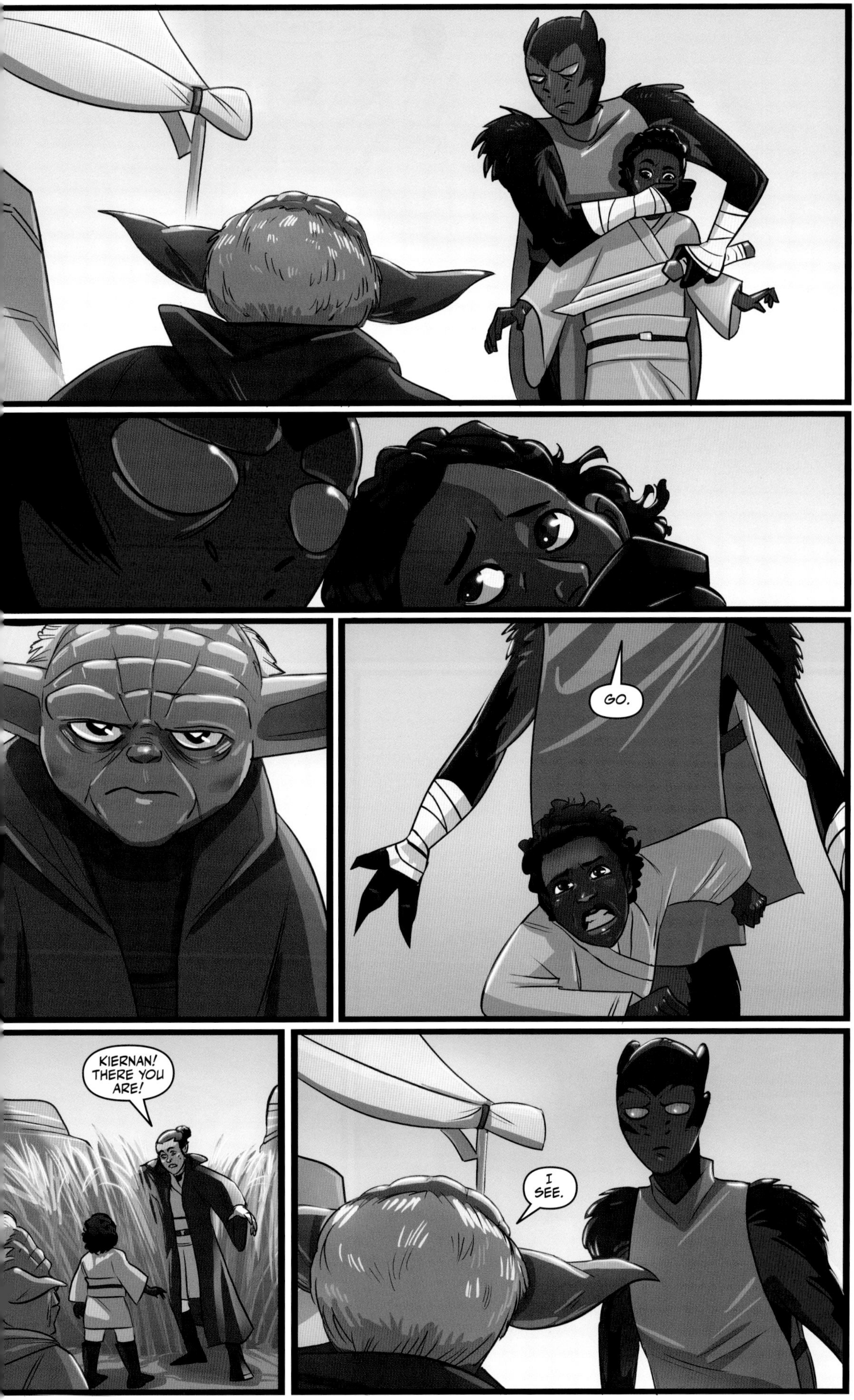
GO.
KIERNAN! THERE YOU ARE!
I SEE.

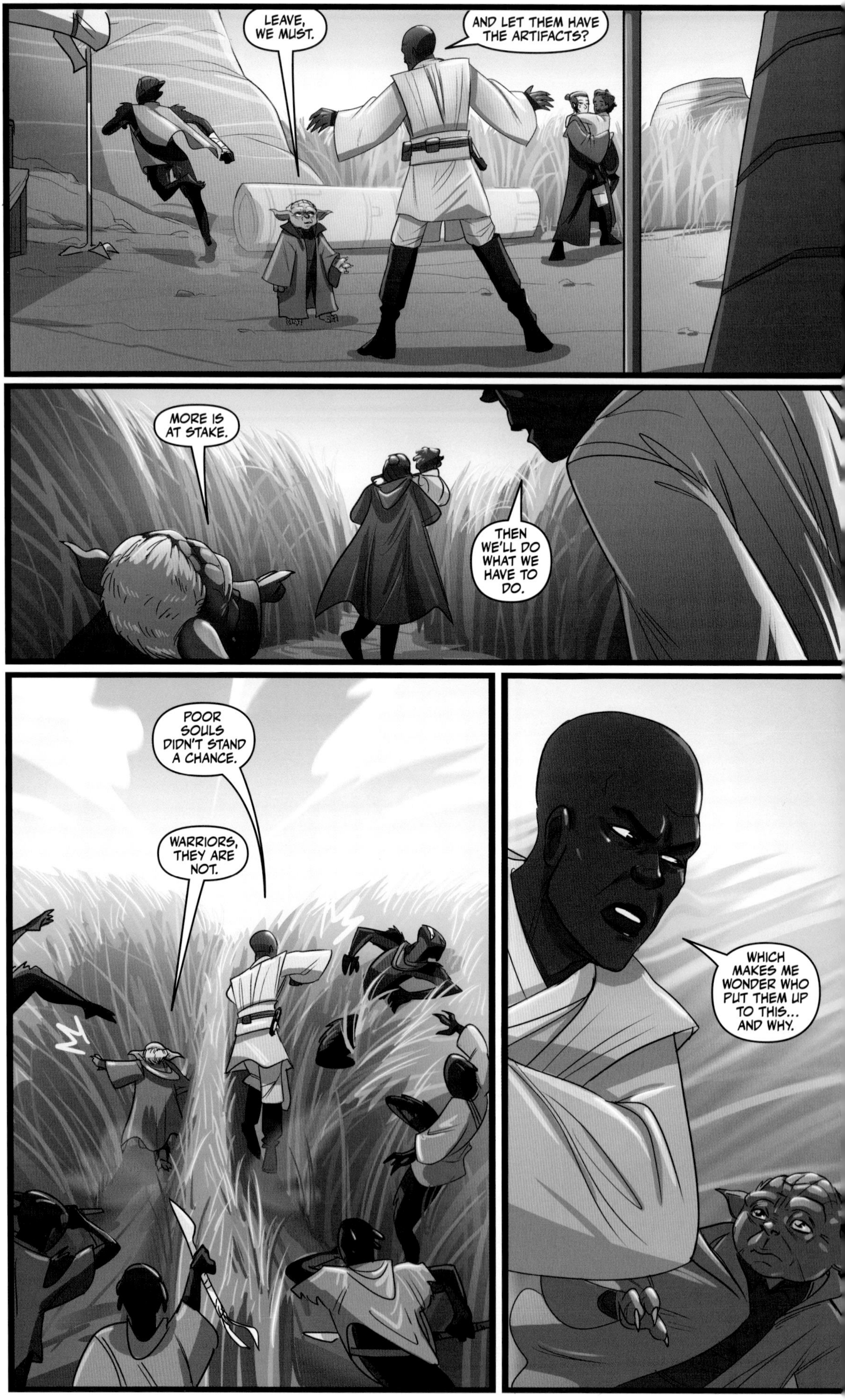

LEAVE, WE MUST.
AND LET THEM HAVE THE ARTIFACTS?
MORE IS AT STAKE.
THEN WE'LL DO WHAT WE HAVE TO DO.
POOR SOULS DIDN'T STAND A CHANCE.
WARRIORS, THEY ARE NOT.
WHICH MAKES ME WONDER WHO PUT THEM UP TO THIS... AND WHY.

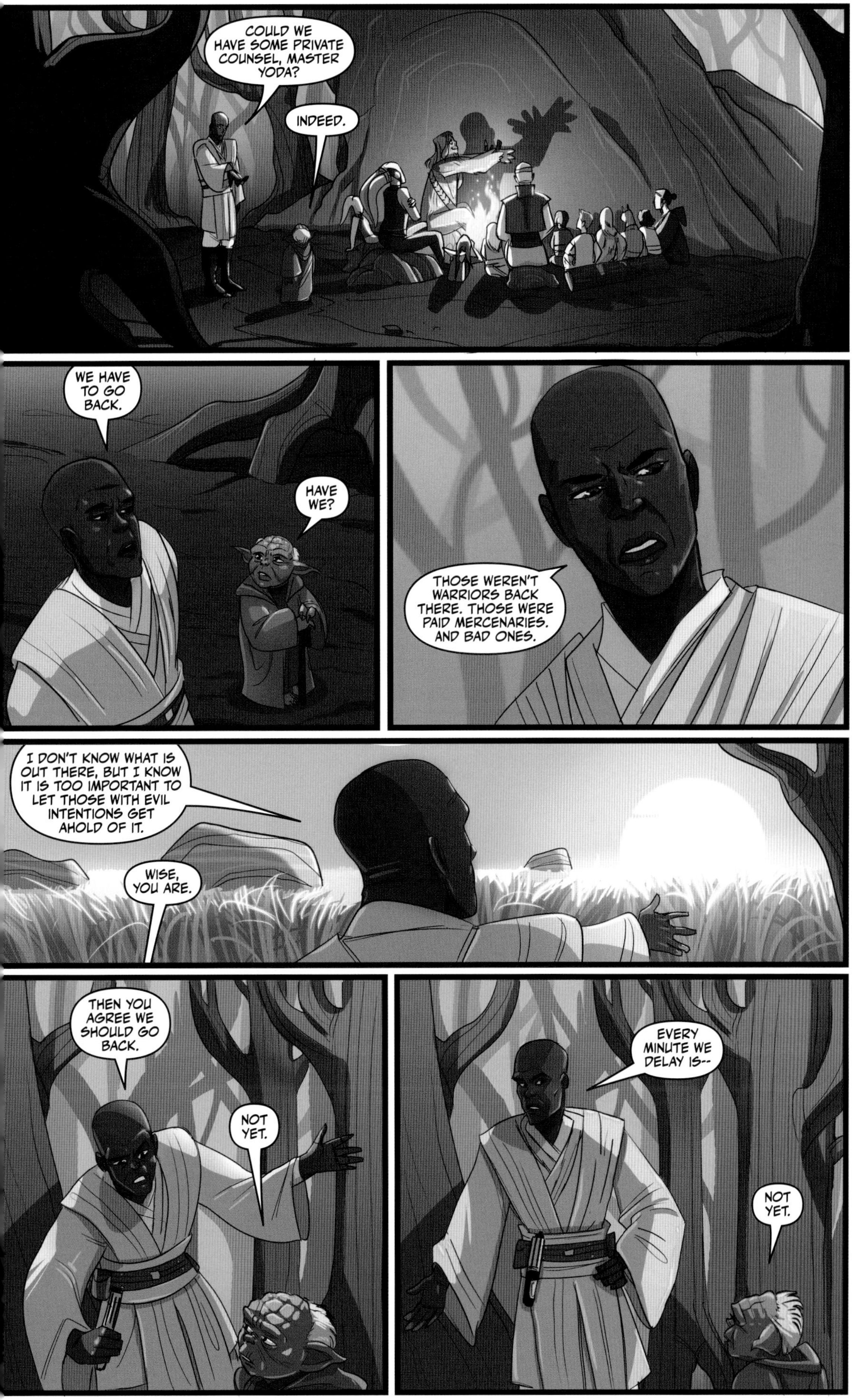
COULD WE HAVE SOME PRIVATE COUNSEL, MASTER YODA?
INDEED.
WE HAVE TO GO BACK.
HAVE WE?
THOSE WEREN'T WARRIORS BACK THERE. THOSE WERE PAID MERCENARIES. AND BAD ONES.
I DON'T KNOW WHAT IS OUT THERE, BUT I KNOW IT IS TOO IMPORTANT TO LET THOSE WITH EVIL INTENTIONS GET AHOLD OF IT.
WISE, YOU ARE.
THEN YOU AGREE WE SHOULD GO BACK.
NOT YET.
EVERY MINUTE WE DELAY IS--
NOT YET.

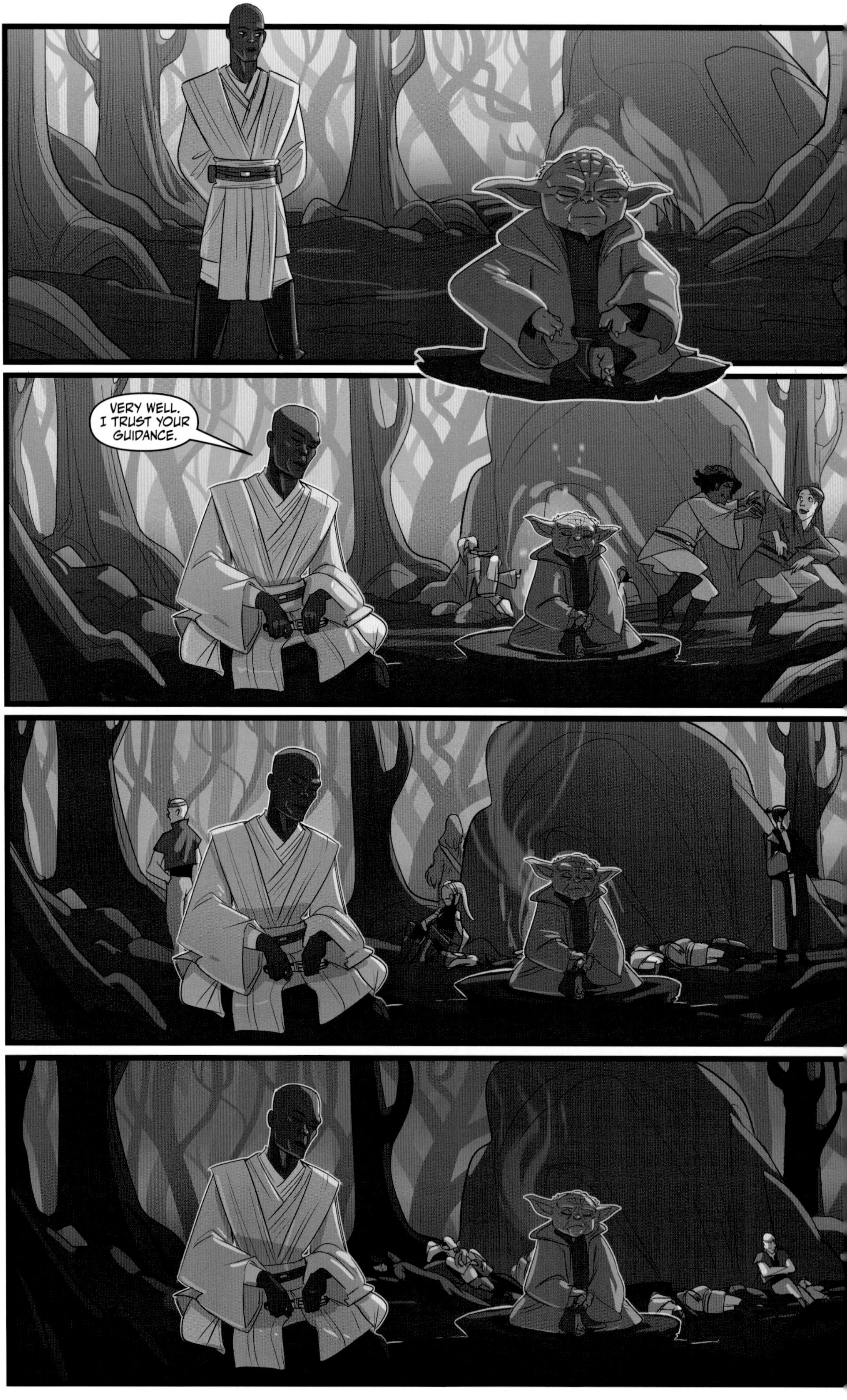
VERY WELL. I TRUST YOUR GUIDANCE.

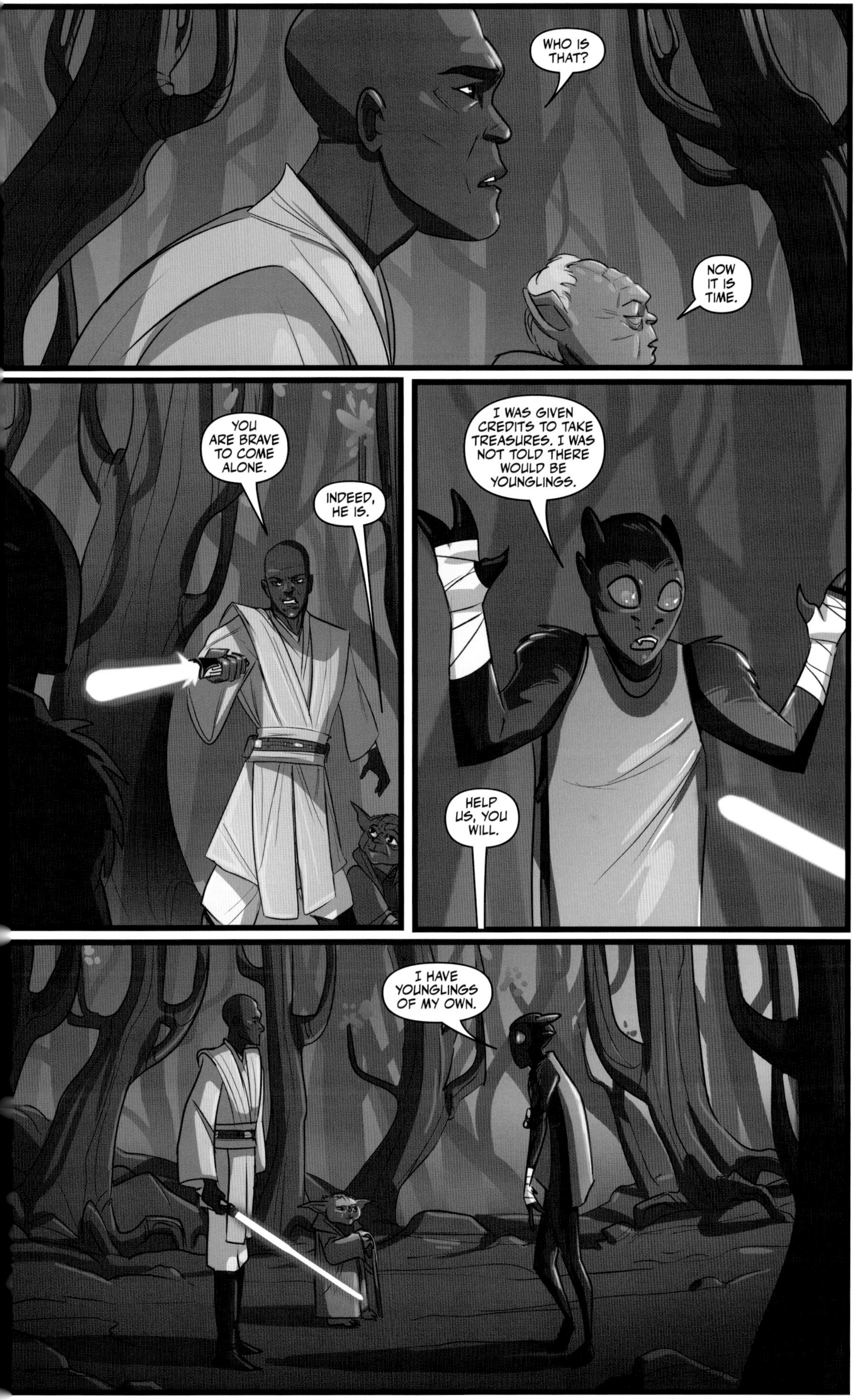
WHO IS THAT?
NOW IT IS TIME.
YOU ARE BRAVE TO COME ALONE.
INDEED, HE IS.
I WAS GIVEN CREDITS TO TAKE TREASURES. I WAS NOT TOLD THERE WOULD BE YOUNGLINGS.
HELP US, YOU WILL.
I HAVE YOUNGLINGS OF MY OWN.

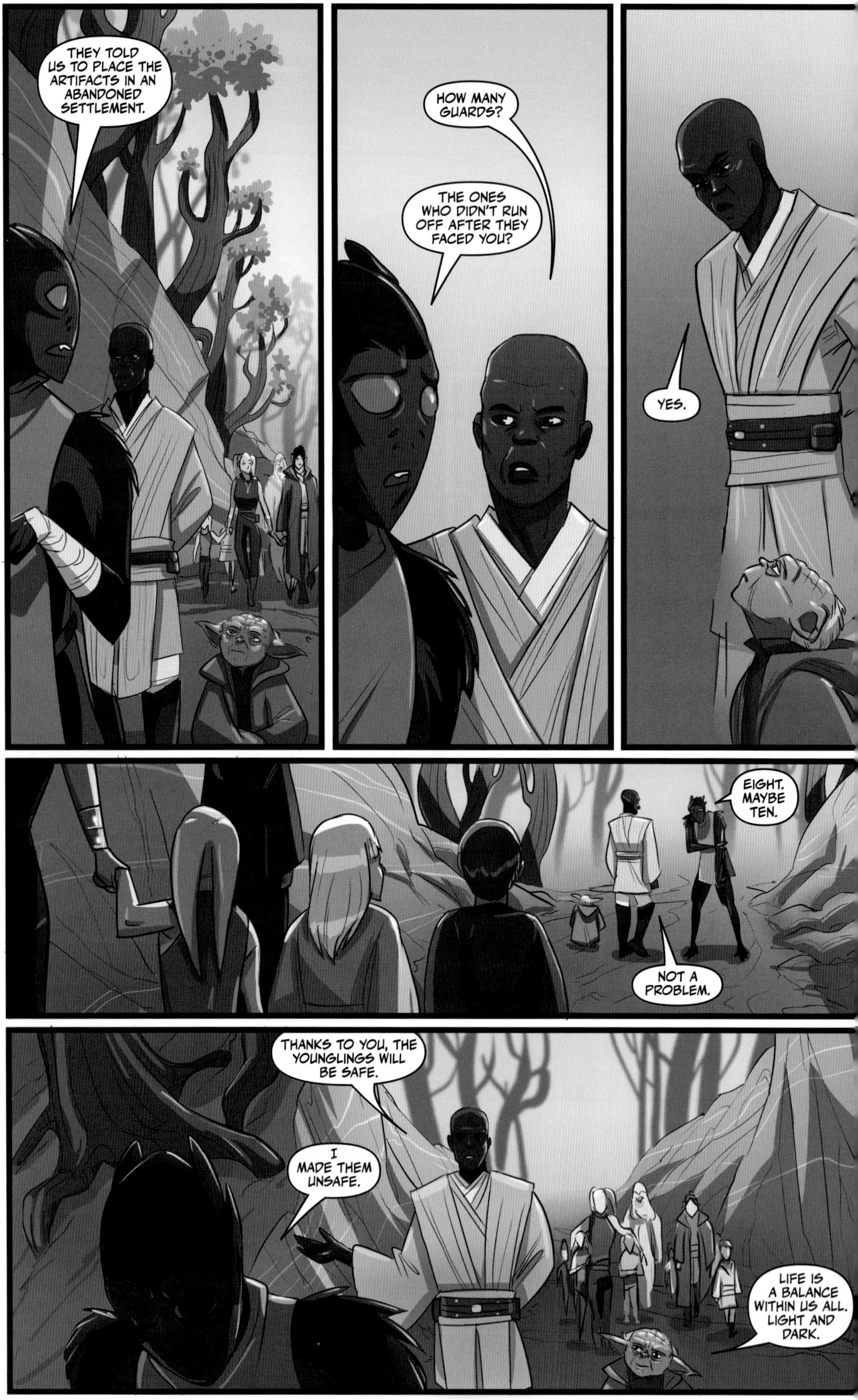
THEY TOLD US TO PLACE THE ARTIFACTS IN AN ABANDONED SETTLEMENT.
HOW MANY GUARDS?
THE ONES WHO DIDN'T RUN OFF AFTER THEY FACED YOU?
YES.
EIGHT. MAYBE TEN.
NOT A PROBLEM.
THANKS TO YOU, THE YOUNGLINGS WILL BE SAFE.
I MADE THEM UNSAFE.
LIFE IS A BALANCE WITHIN US ALL. LIGHT AND DARK.

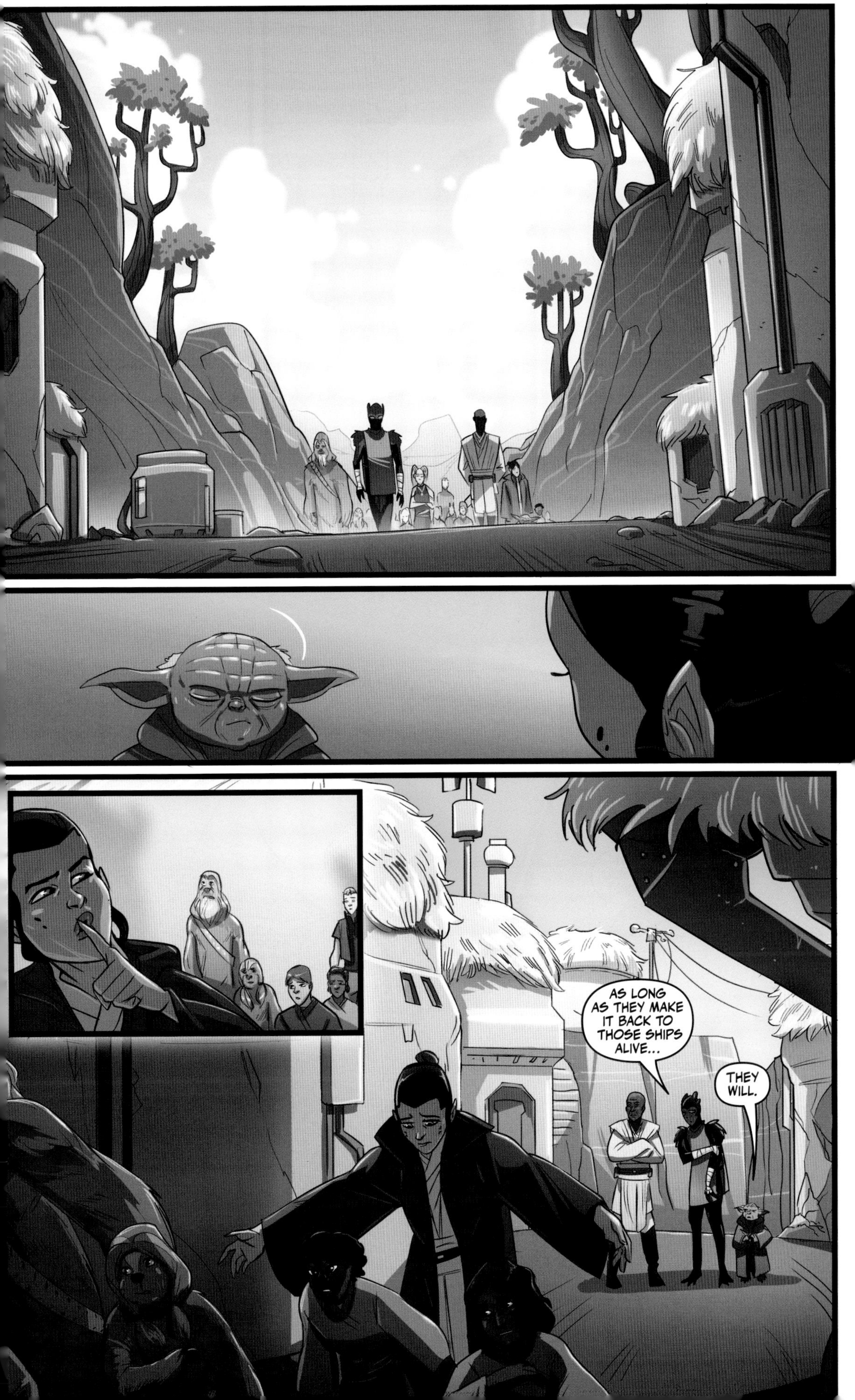
AS LONG AS THEY MAKE IT BACK TO THOSE SHIPS ALIVE...
THEY WILL.

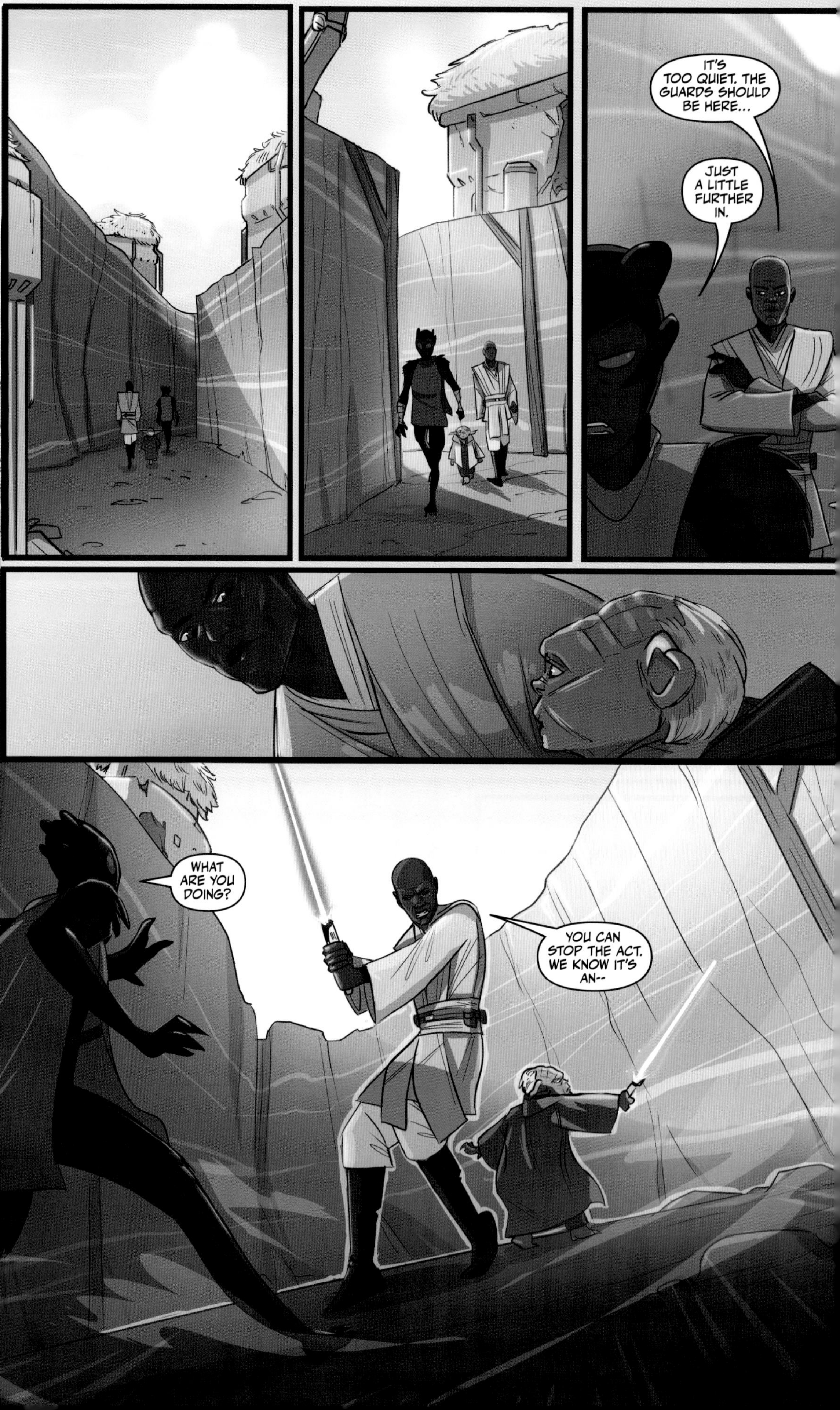
IT'S TOO QUIET. THE GUARDS SHOULD BE HERE...
JUST A LITTLE FURTHER IN.
WHAT ARE YOU DOING?
YOU CAN STOP THE ACT. WE KNOW IT'S AN--

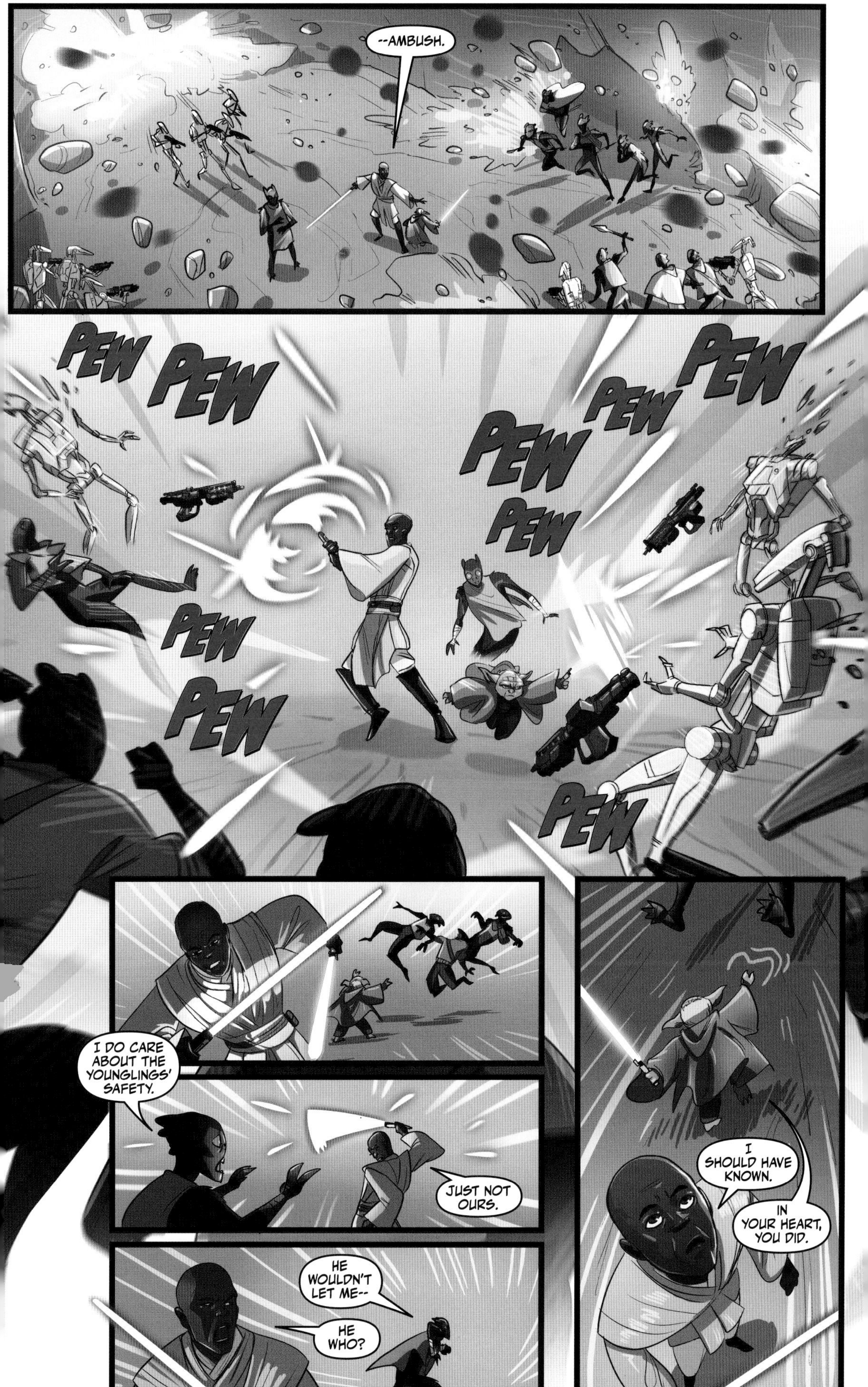
--AMBUSH.
PEW PEW
PEW PEW
PEW
PEW
PEW
PEW
PEW
I DO CARE ABOUT THE YOUNGLINGS' SAFETY.
JUST NOT OURS.
HE WOULDN'T LET ME--
HE WHO?
I SHOULD HAVE KNOWN.
IN YOUR HEART, YOU DID.

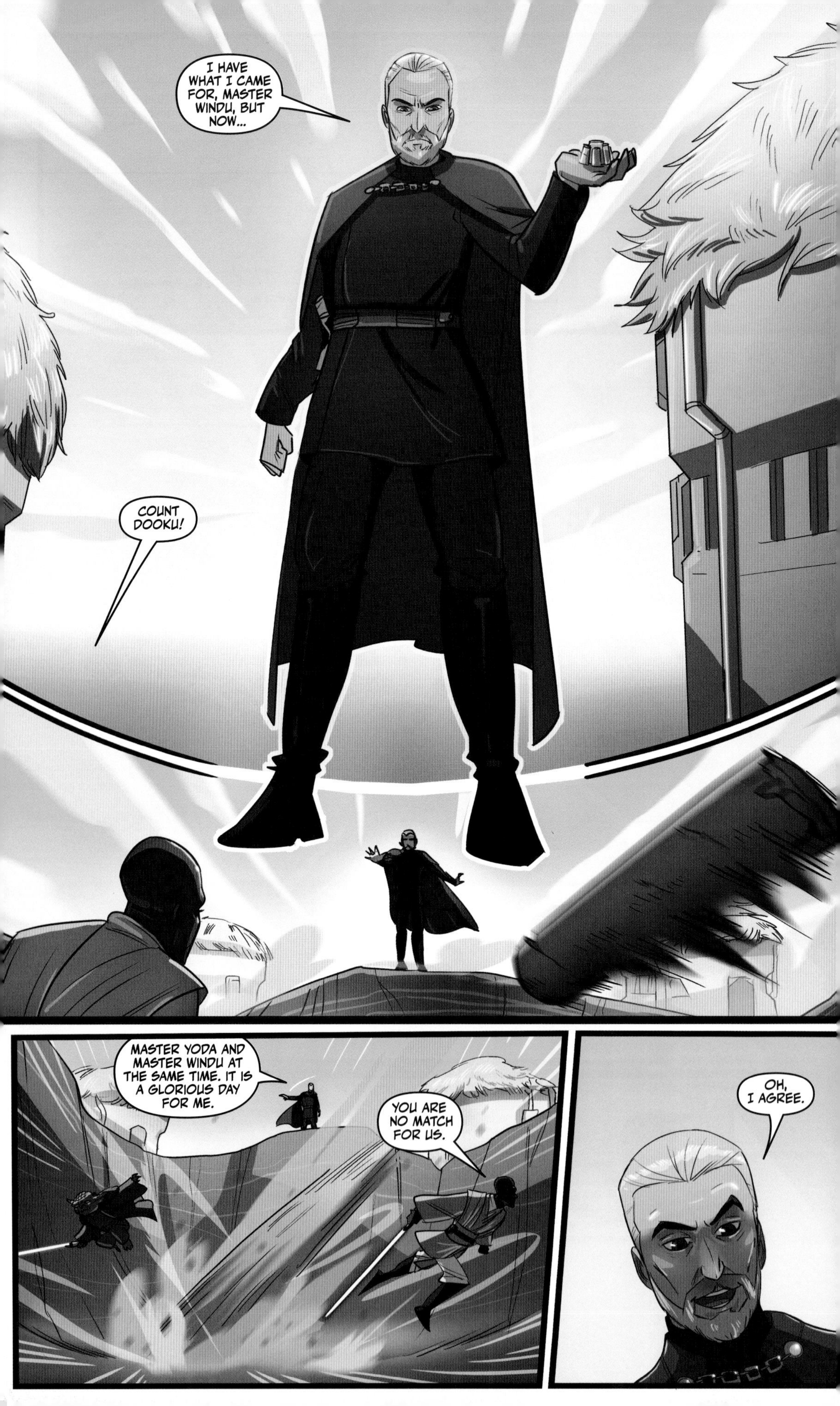
I HAVE WHAT I CAME FOR, MASTER WINDU, BUT NOW...
COUNT DOOKU!
MASTER YODA AND MASTER WINDU AT THE SAME TIME. IT IS A GLORIOUS DAY FOR ME.
YOU ARE NO MATCH FOR US.
OH, I AGREE.

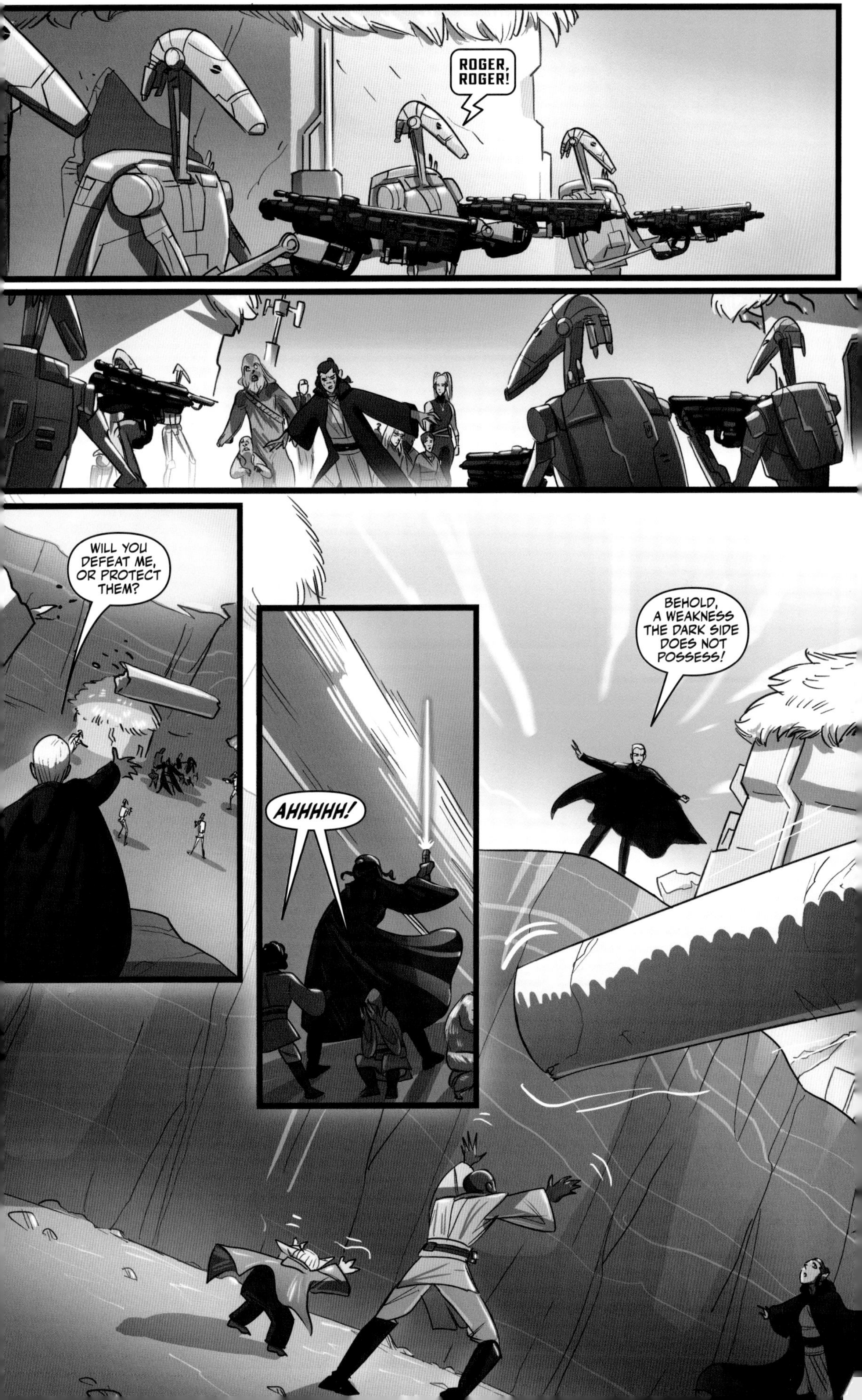
ROGER, ROGER!
WILL YOU DEFEAT ME, OR PROTECT THEM?
AHHHHH!
BEHOLD, A WEAKNESS THE DARK SIDE DOES NOT POSSESS!

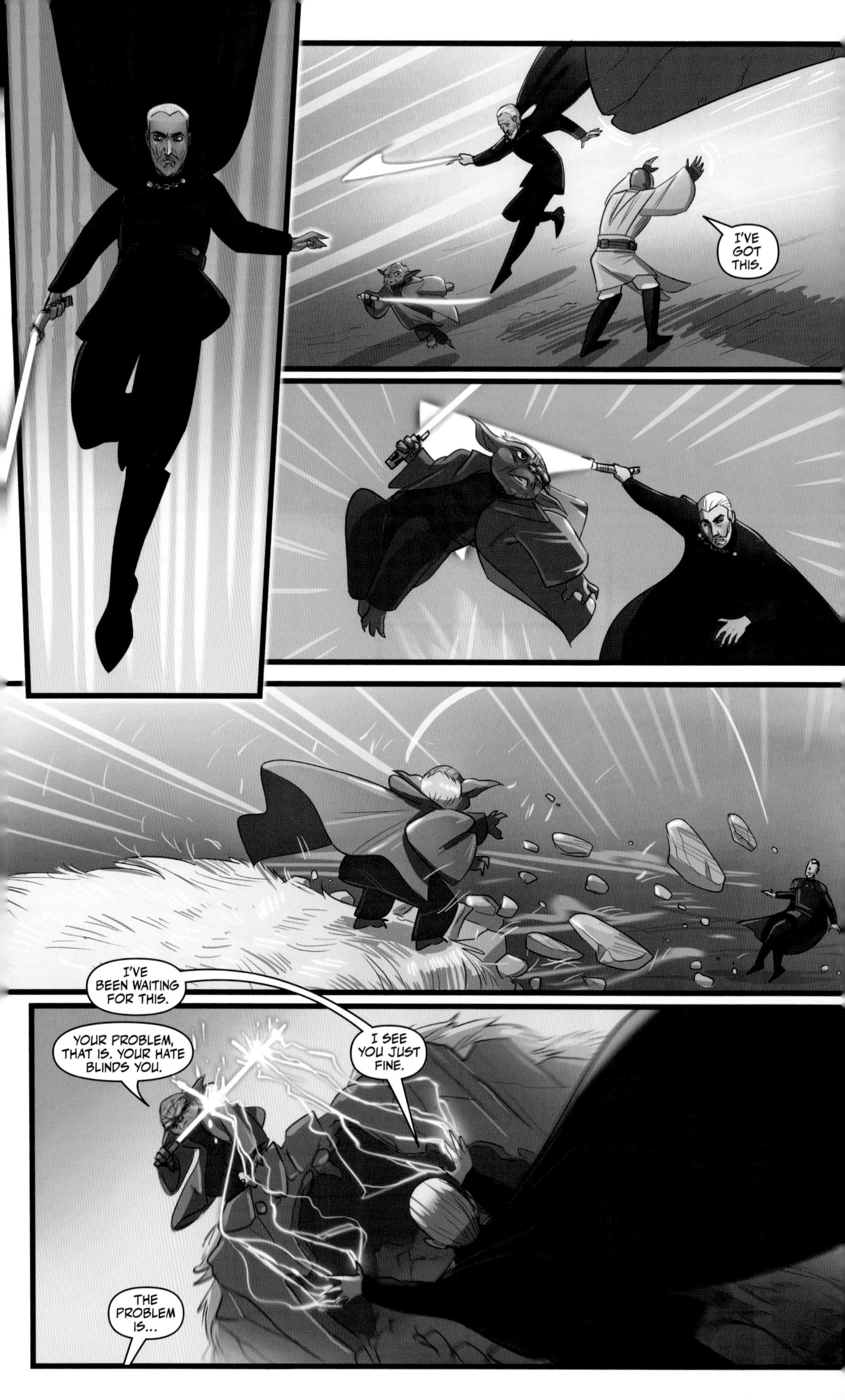
I'VE GOT THIS.
I'VE BEEN WAITING FOR THIS.
YOUR PROBLEM, THAT IS. YOUR HATE BLINDS YOU.
I SEE YOU JUST FINE.
THE PROBLEM IS...

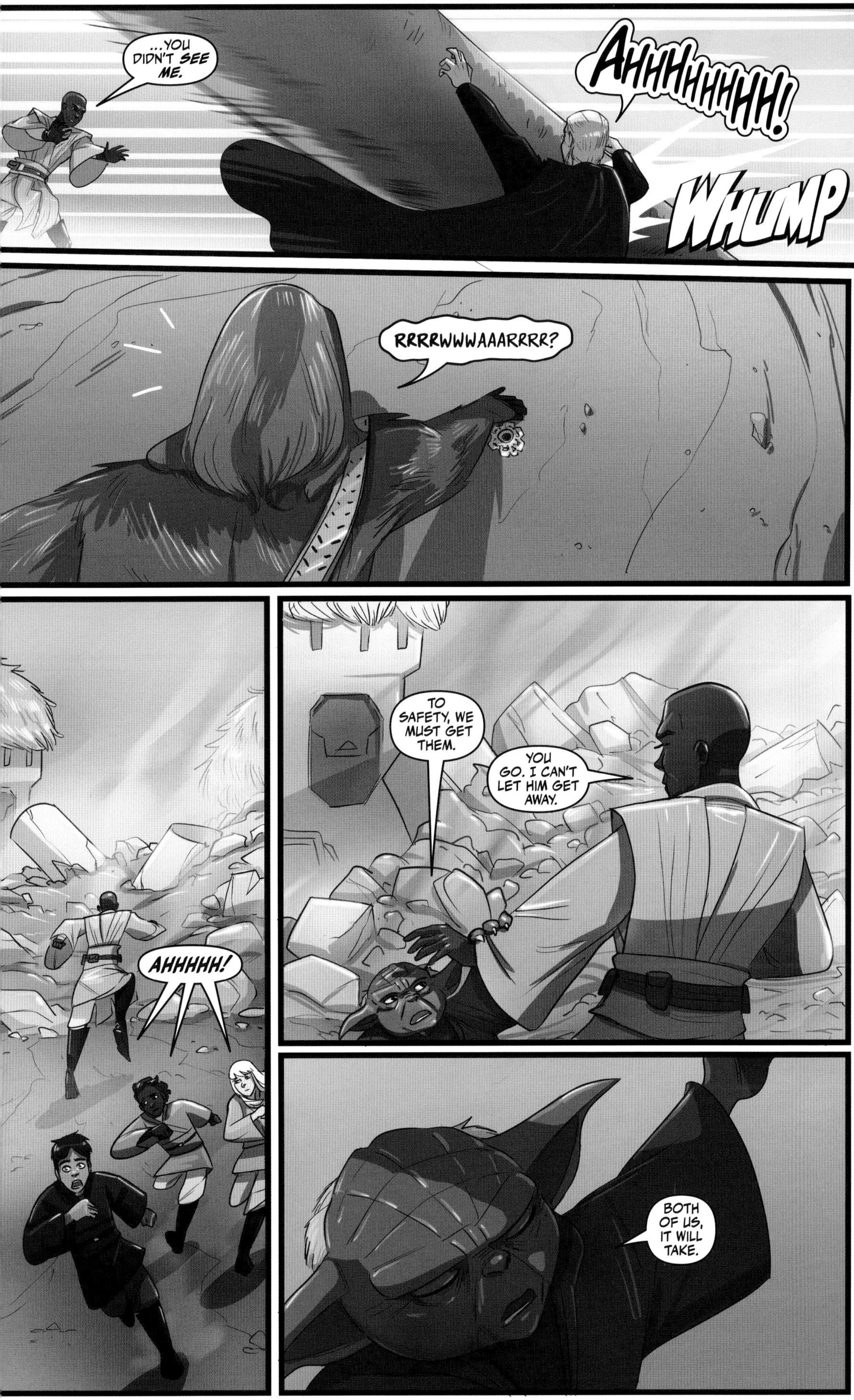
...YOU DIDN'T SEE ME.
AHHHHHHHH!
WHUMP
RRRRWWWAAARRRR?
AHHHHH!
TO SAFETY, WE MUST GET THEM.
YOU GO. I CAN'T LET HIM GET AWAY.
BOTH OF US, IT WILL TAKE.

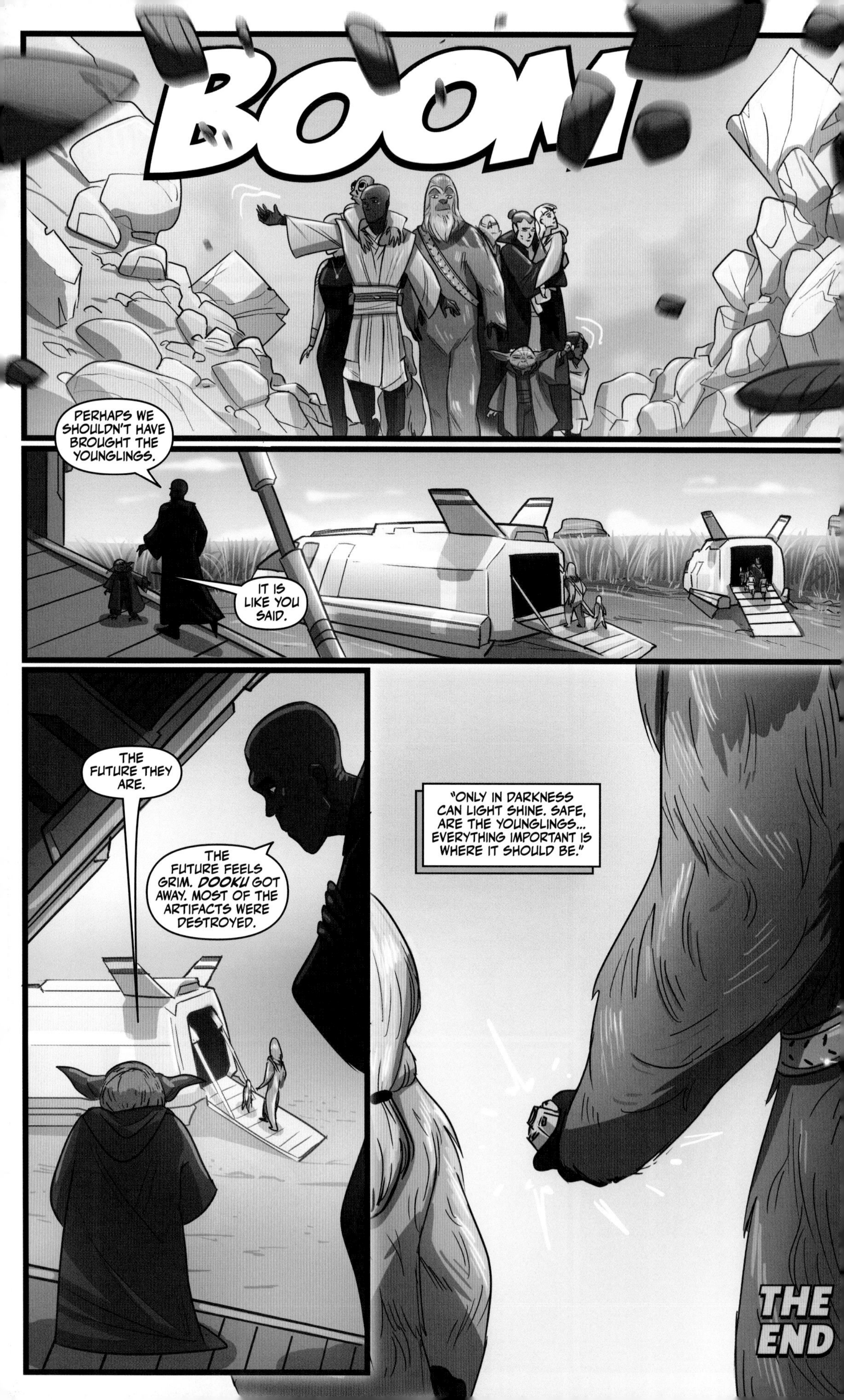
BOOM!
PERHAPS WE SHOULDN'T HAVE BROUGHT THE YOUNGLINGS.
IT IS LIKE YOU SAID.
THE FUTURE FEELS GRIM. DOOKU GOT AWAY. MOST OF THE ARTIFACTS WERE DESTROYED.
THE FUTURE THEY ARE.
"ONLY IN DARKNESS CAN LIGHT SHINE. SAFE, ARE THE YOUNGLINGS... EVERYTHING IMPORTANT IS WHERE IT SHOULD BE."
THE END

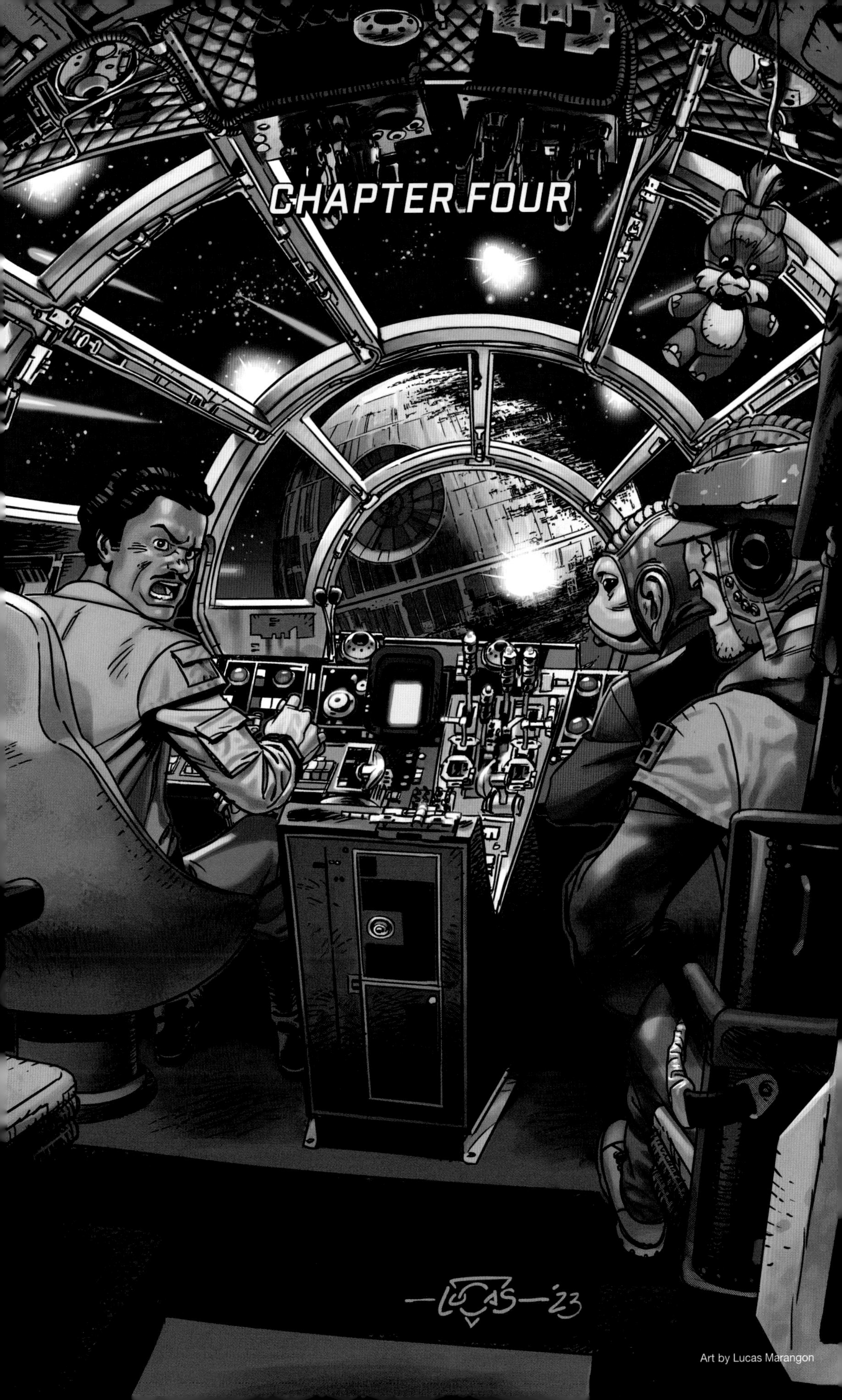
CHAPTER FOUR
LUCAS '23

Art by Lucas Marangon

Art by Cary No

CHAPTER FOUR: THE LITTLE THINGS

written by
CECIL CASTELLUCCI

art by
LUCAS MARANGON

colors by
MICHAEL ATIYEH

letters by
COMICRAFT'S TYLER SMITH and JIMMY BETANCOURT

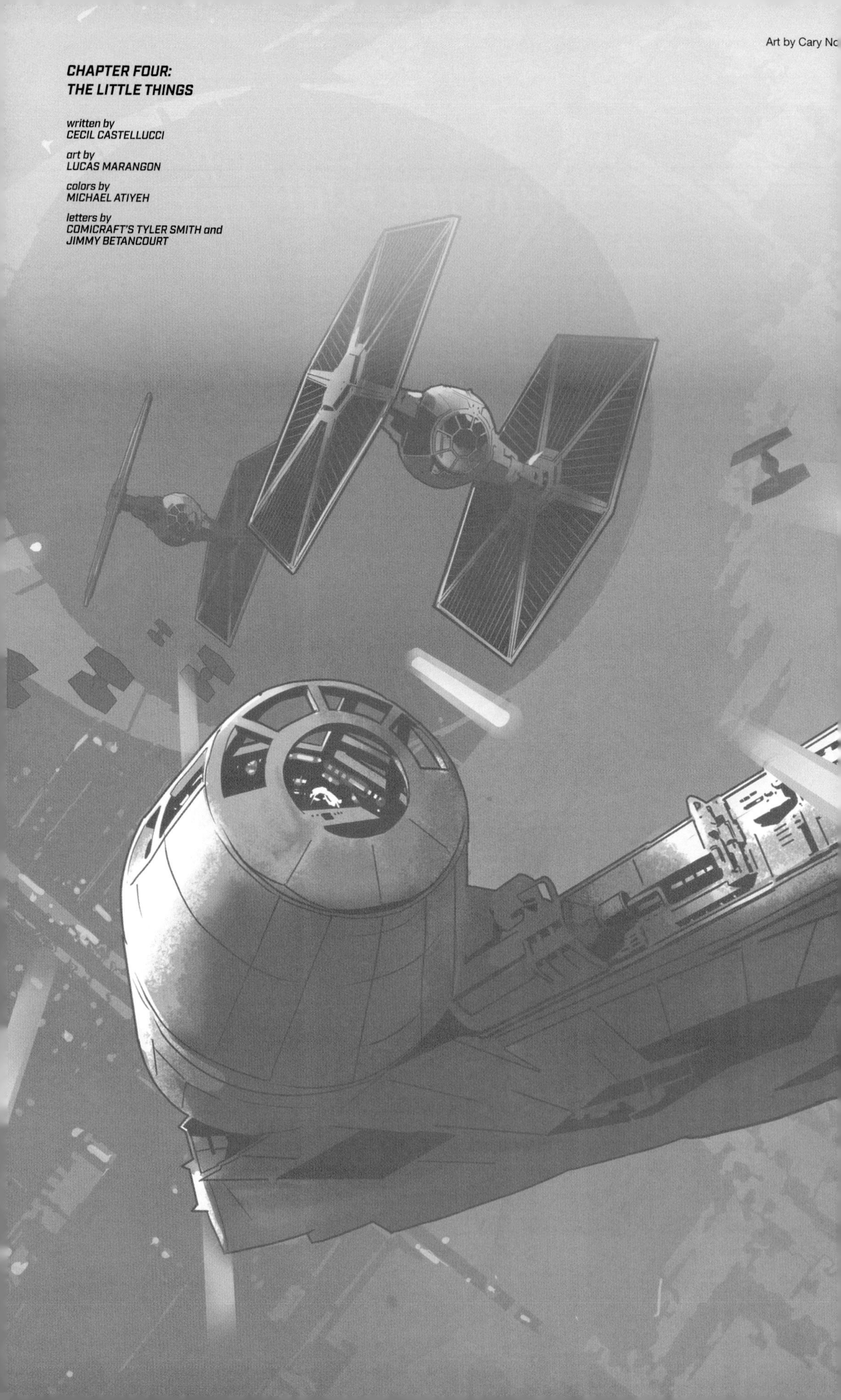

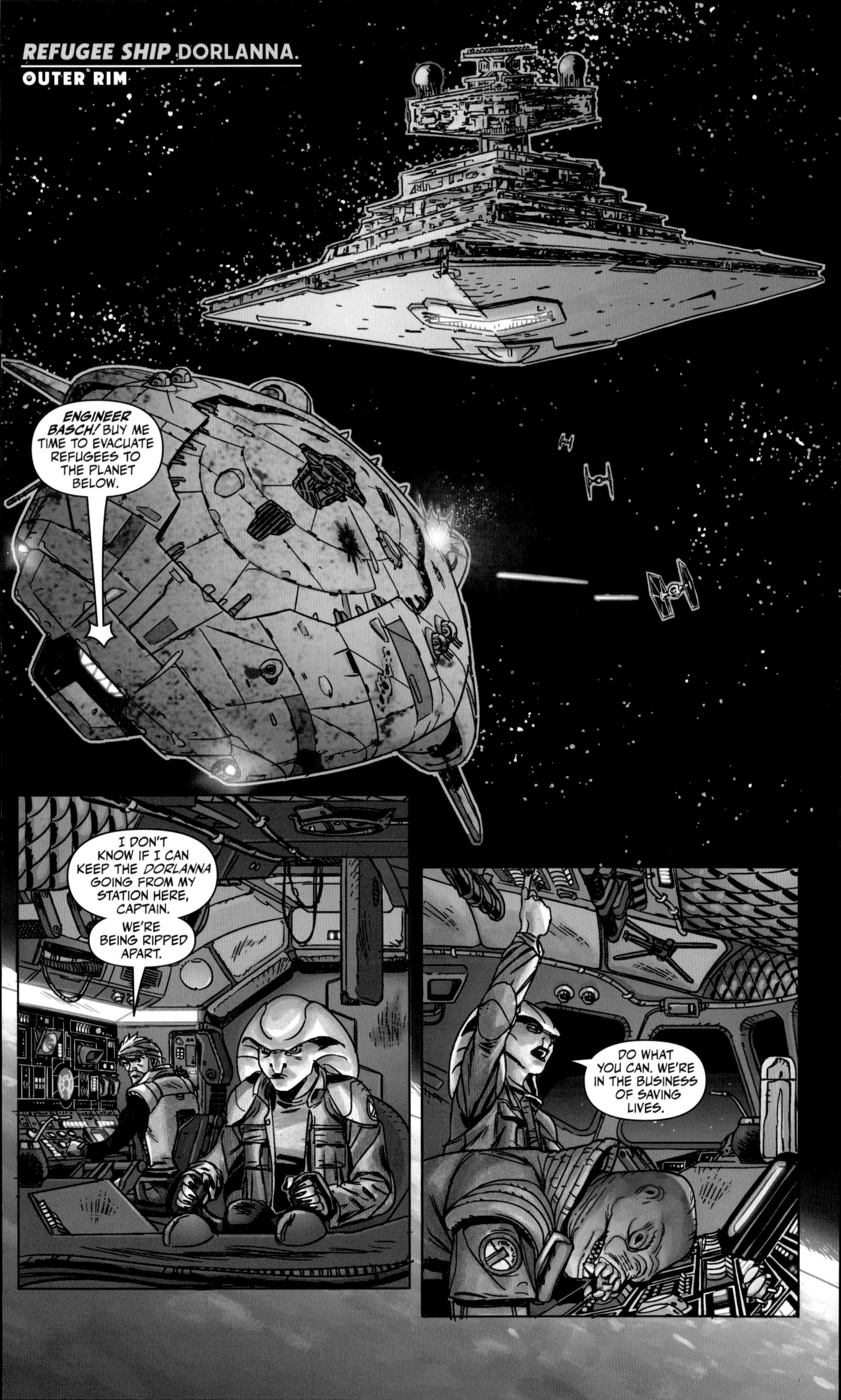
REFUGEE SHIP DORLANNA.
OUTER RIM
ENGINEER BASCH! BUY ME TIME TO EVACUATE REFUGEES TO THE PLANET BELOW.
I DON'T KNOW IF I CAN KEEP THE DORLANNA GOING FROM MY STATION HERE, CAPTAIN.
WE'RE BEING RIPPED APART.
DO WHAT YOU CAN. WE'RE IN THE BUSINESS OF SAVING LIVES.

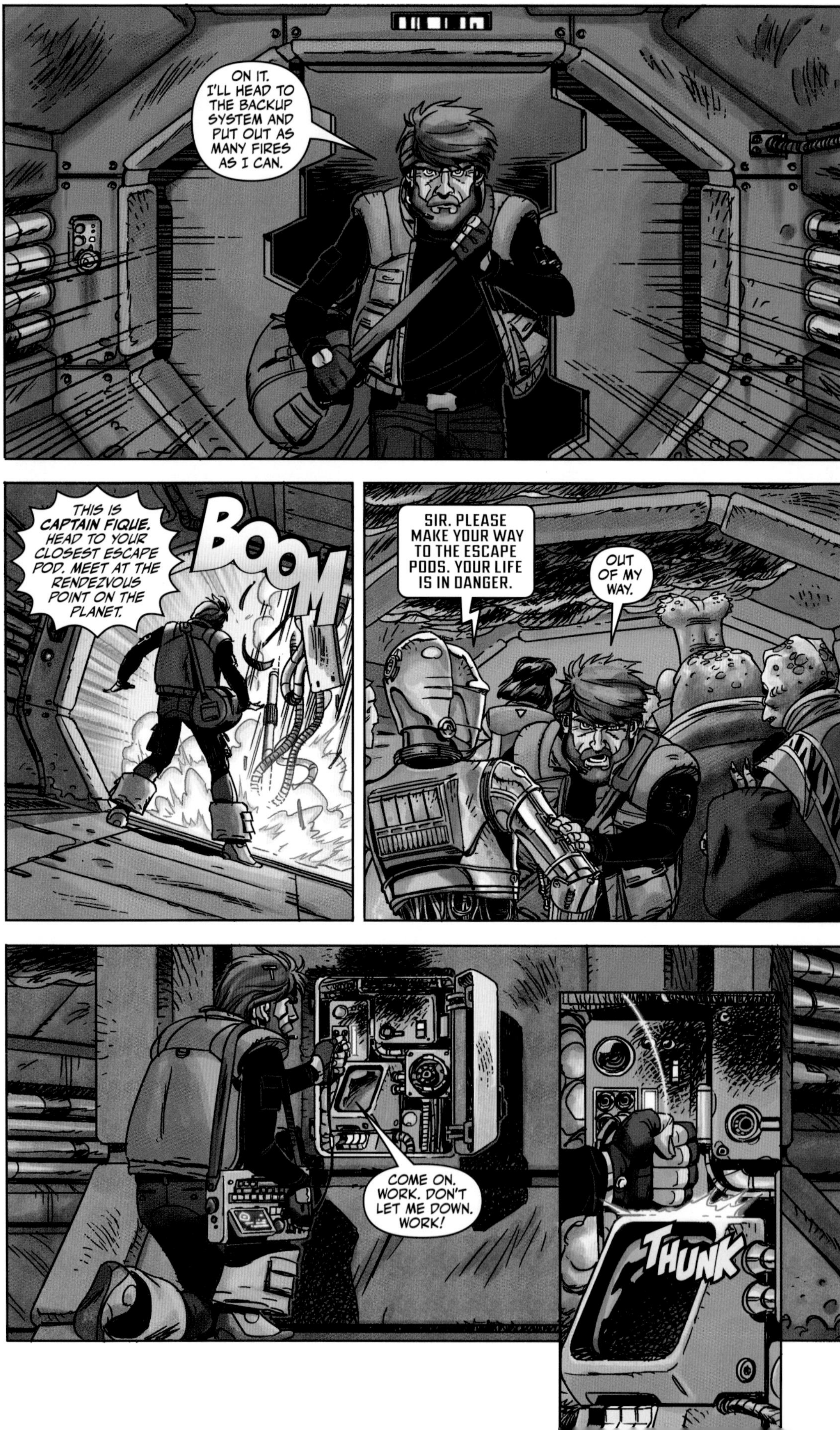
ON IT. I'LL HEAD TO THE BACKUP SYSTEM AND PUT OUT AS MANY FIRES AS I CAN.
THIS IS CAPTAIN FIQUE. HEAD TO YOUR CLOSEST ESCAPE POD. MEET AT THE RENDEZVOUS POINT ON THE PLANET.
BOOM
SIR. PLEASE MAKE YOUR WAY TO THE ESCAPE PODS. YOUR LIFE IS IN DANGER.
OUT OF MY WAY.
COME ON. WORK. DON'T LET ME DOWN. WORK!
THUNK

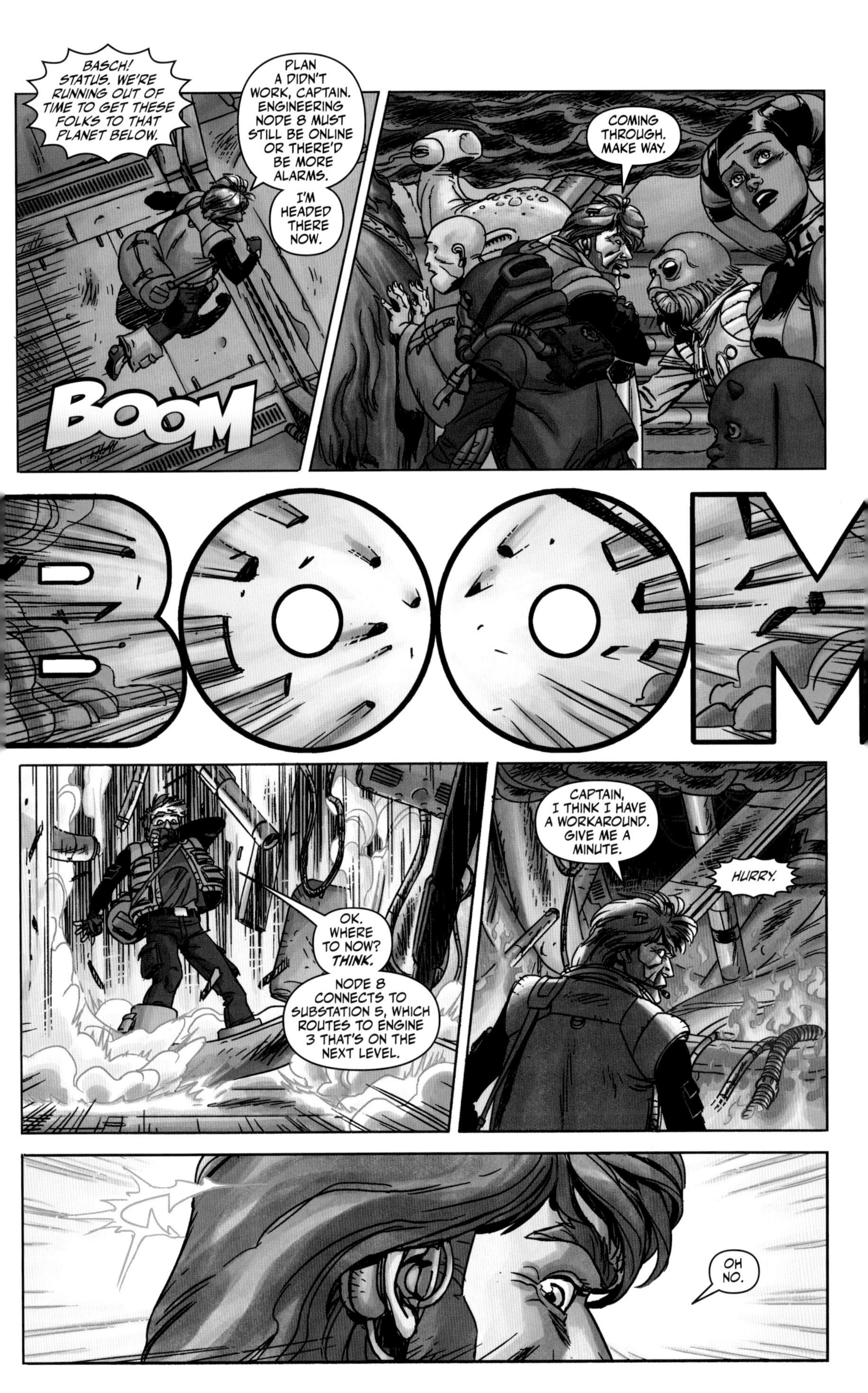
BASCH! STATUS. WE'RE RUNNING OUT OF TIME TO GET THESE FOLKS TO THAT PLANET BELOW.
PLAN A DIDN'T WORK, CAPTAIN. ENGINEERING NODE 8 MUST STILL BE ONLINE OR THERE'D BE MORE ALARMS.
I'M HEADED THERE NOW.
BOOM
COMING THROUGH. MAKE WAY.
BOOM
OK. WHERE TO NOW? THINK.
NODE 8 CONNECTS TO SUBSTATION 5, WHICH ROUTES TO ENGINE 3 THAT'S ON THE NEXT LEVEL.
CAPTAIN, I THINK I HAVE A WORKAROUND. GIVE ME A MINUTE.
HURRY.
OH NO.

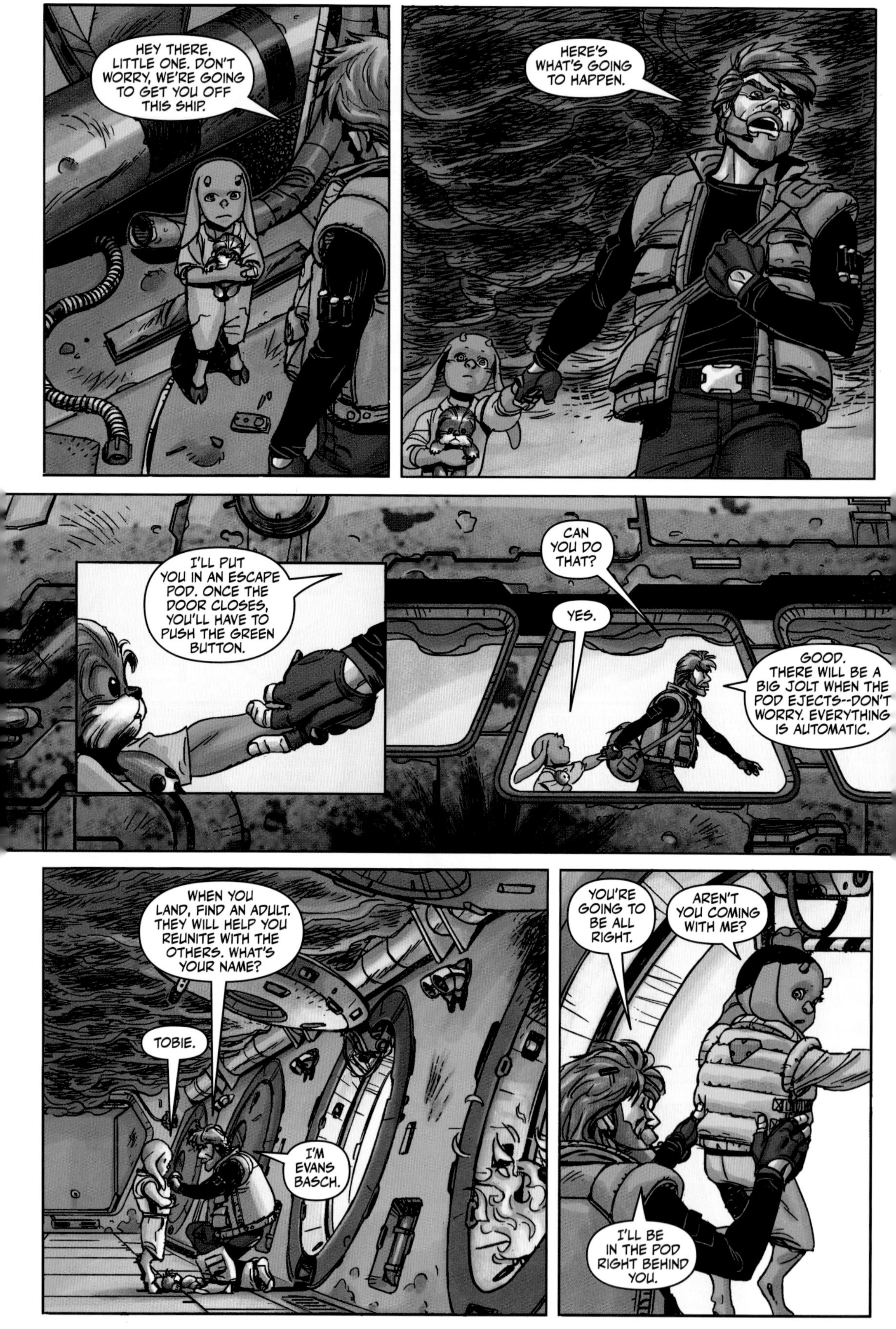
HEY THERE, LITTLE ONE. DON'T WORRY, WE'RE GOING TO GET YOU OFF THIS SHIP.
HERE'S WHAT'S GOING TO HAPPEN.
I'LL PUT YOU IN AN ESCAPE POD. ONCE THE DOOR CLOSES, YOU'LL HAVE TO PUSH THE GREEN BUTTON.
CAN YOU DO THAT?
YES.
GOOD. THERE WILL BE A BIG JOLT WHEN THE POD EJECTS--DON'T WORRY. EVERYTHING IS AUTOMATIC.
WHEN YOU LAND, FIND AN ADULT. THEY WILL HELP YOU REUNITE WITH THE OTHERS. WHAT'S YOUR NAME?
TOBIE.
I'M EVANS BASCH.
YOU'RE GOING TO BE ALL RIGHT.
AREN'T YOU COMING WITH ME?
I'LL BE IN THE POD RIGHT BEHIND YOU.

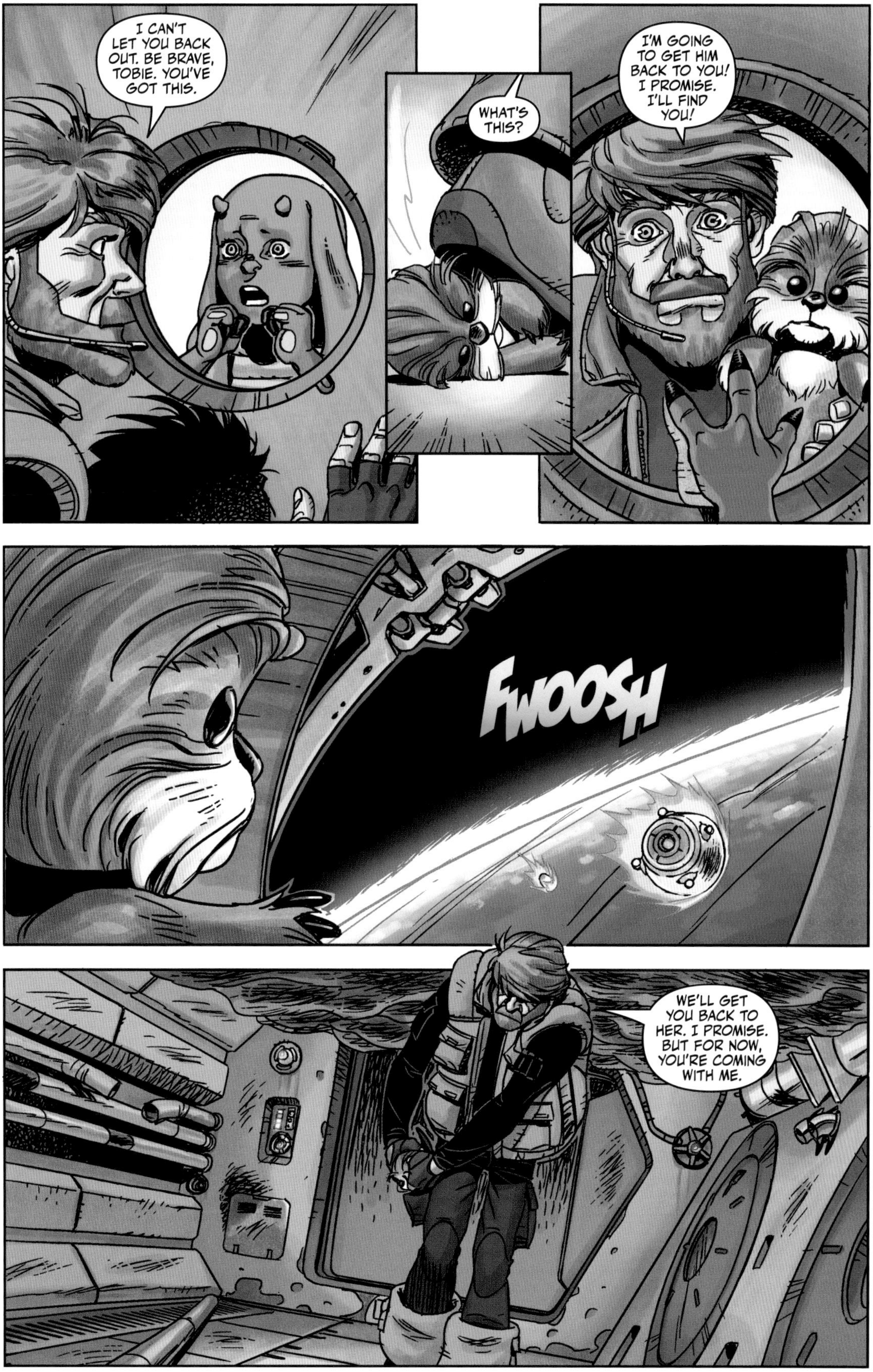
I CAN'T LET YOU BACK OUT. BE BRAVE, TOBIE. YOU'VE GOT THIS.
WHAT'S THIS?
I'M GOING TO GET HIM BACK TO YOU! I PROMISE. I'LL FIND YOU!
FWOOSH
WE'LL GET YOU BACK TO HER. I PROMISE. BUT FOR NOW, YOU'RE COMING WITH ME.

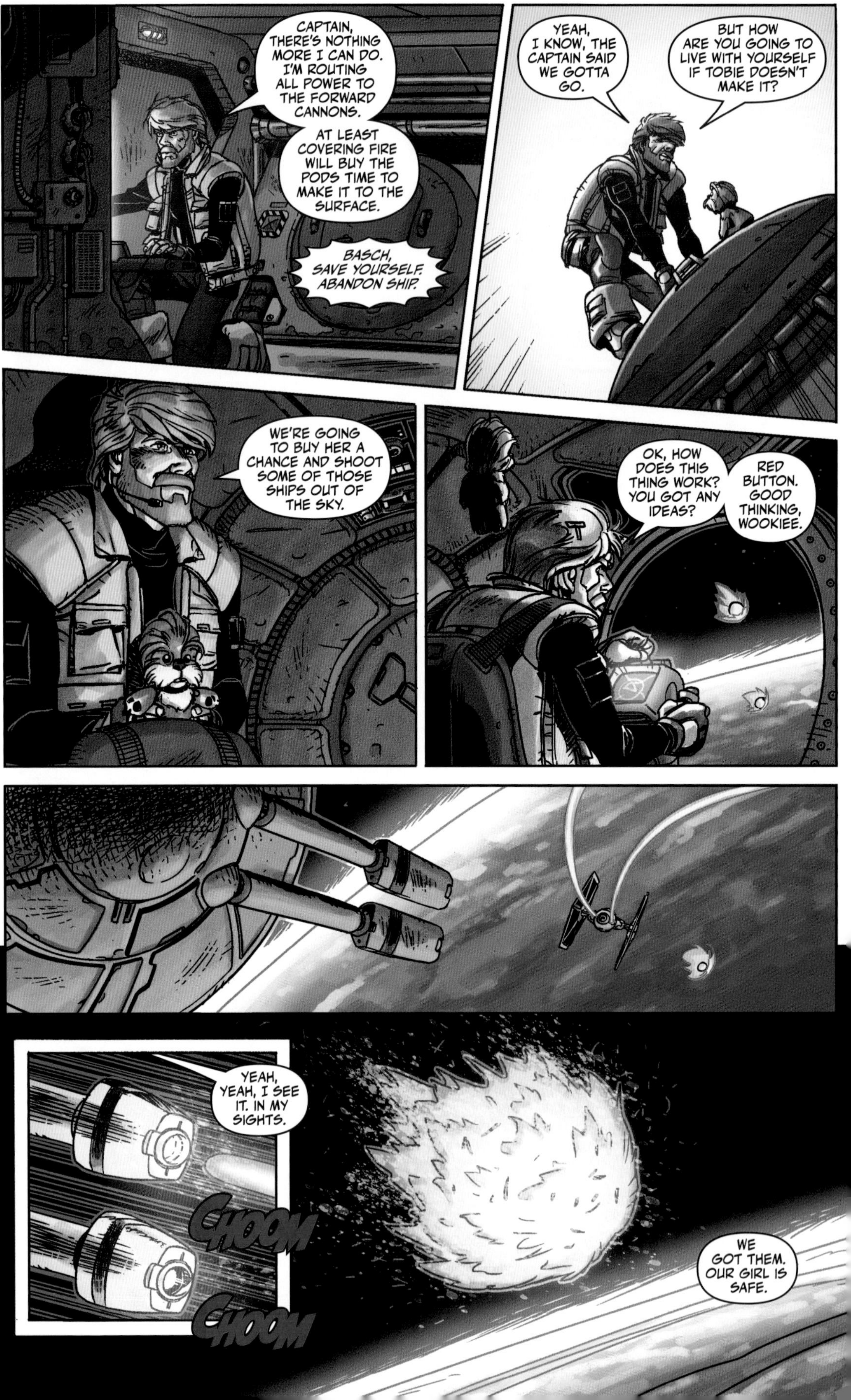
CAPTAIN, THERE'S NOTHING MORE I CAN DO. I'M ROUTING ALL POWER TO THE FORWARD CANNONS.
AT LEAST COVERING FIRE WILL BUY THE PODS TIME TO MAKE IT TO THE SURFACE.
BASCH, SAVE YOURSELF. ABANDON SHIP.
YEAH, I KNOW, THE CAPTAIN SAID WE GOTTA GO.
BUT HOW ARE YOU GOING TO LIVE WITH YOURSELF IF TOBIE DOESN'T MAKE IT?
WE'RE GOING TO BUY HER A CHANCE AND SHOOT SOME OF THOSE SHIPS OUT OF THE SKY.
OK, HOW DOES THIS THING WORK? YOU GOT ANY IDEAS?
RED BUTTON. GOOD THINKING, WOOKIEE.
YEAH, YEAH, I SEE IT. IN MY SIGHTS.
CHOOM
CHOOM
WE GOT THEM. OUR GIRL IS SAFE.

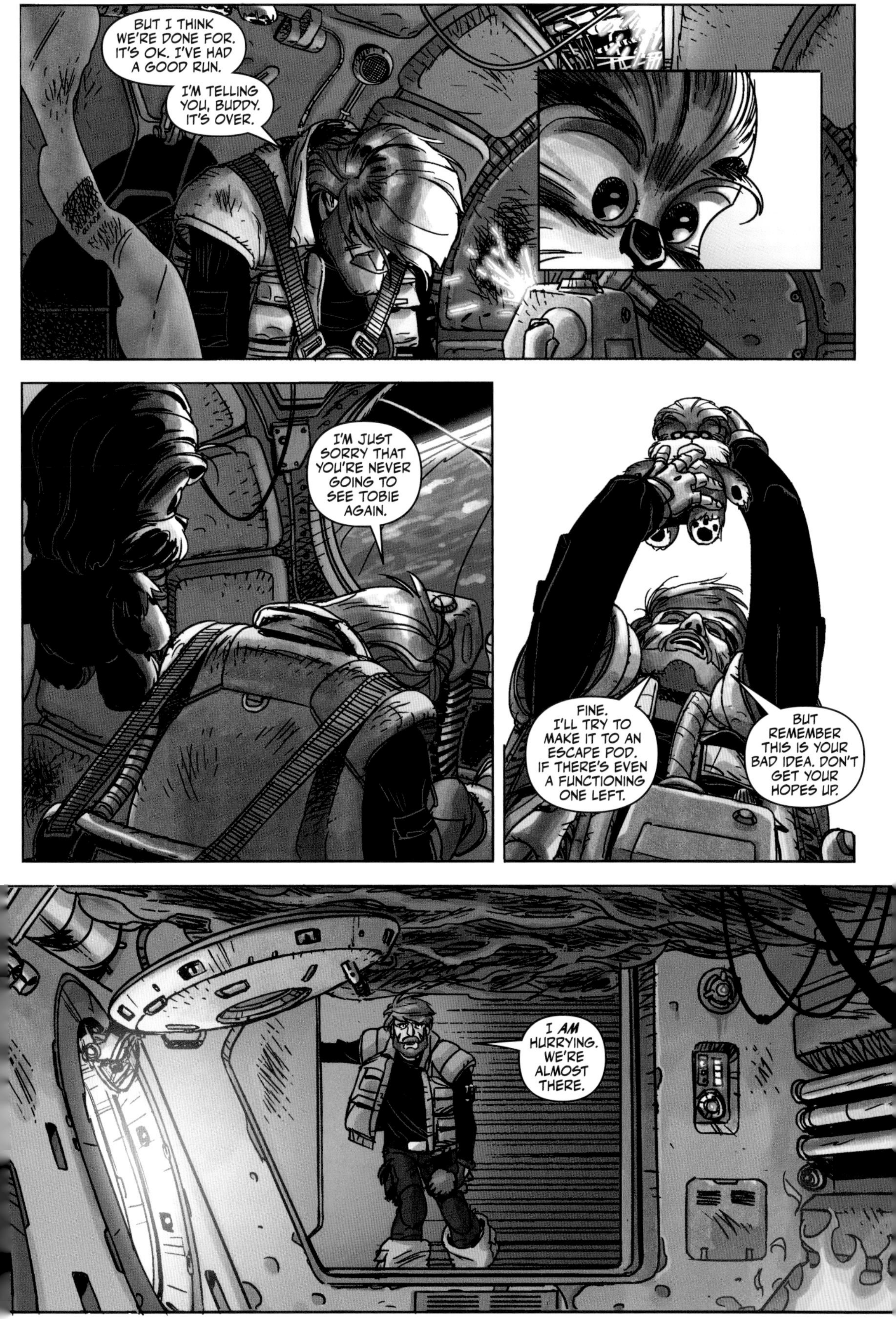
BUT I THINK WE'RE DONE FOR. IT'S OK. I'VE HAD A GOOD RUN.
I'M TELLING YOU, BUDDY. IT'S OVER.
I'M JUST SORRY THAT YOU'RE NEVER GOING TO SEE TOBIE AGAIN.
FINE. I'LL TRY TO MAKE IT TO AN ESCAPE POD. IF THERE'S EVEN A FUNCTIONING ONE LEFT.
BUT REMEMBER THIS IS YOUR BAD IDEA. DON'T GET YOUR HOPES UP.
I *AM* HURRYING. WE'RE ALMOST THERE.

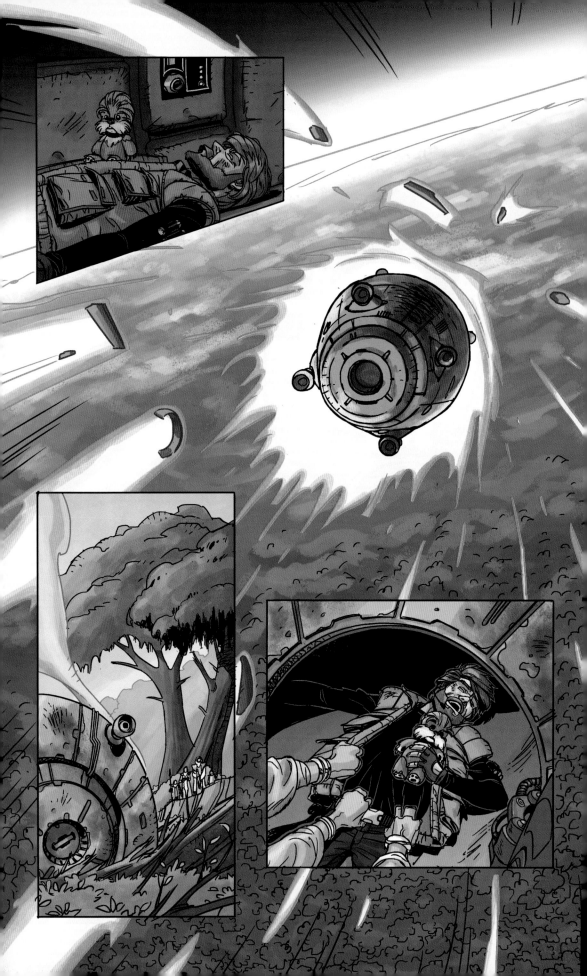

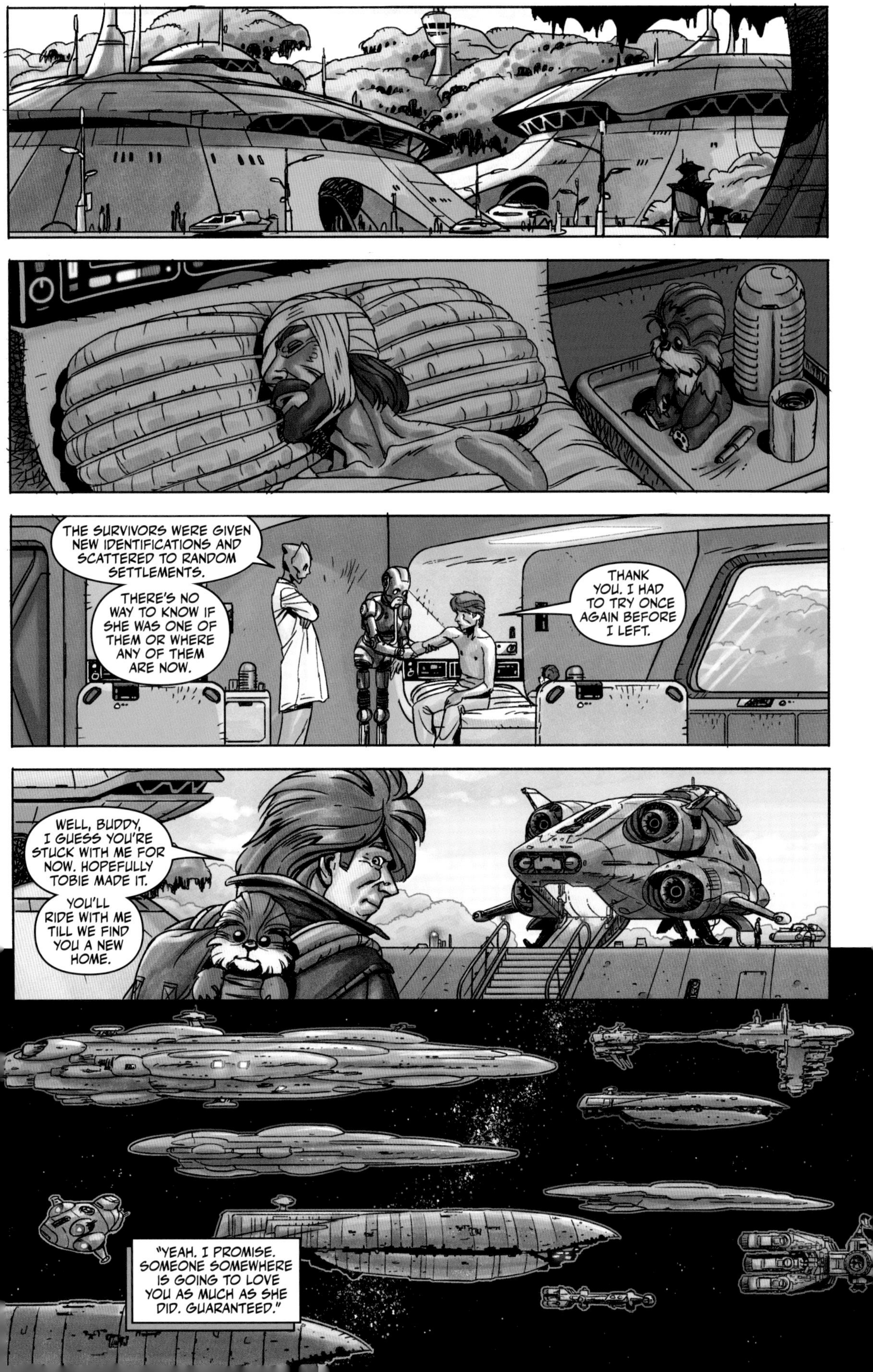
THE SURVIVORS WERE GIVEN NEW IDENTIFICATIONS AND SCATTERED TO RANDOM SETTLEMENTS.
THERE'S NO WAY TO KNOW IF SHE WAS ONE OF THEM OR WHERE ANY OF THEM ARE NOW.
THANK YOU. I HAD TO TRY ONCE AGAIN BEFORE I LEFT.
WELL, BUDDY, I GUESS YOU'RE STUCK WITH ME FOR NOW. HOPEFULLY TOBIE MADE IT.
YOU'LL RIDE WITH ME TILL WE FIND YOU A NEW HOME.
"YEAH. I PROMISE. SOMEONE SOMEWHERE IS GOING TO LOVE YOU AS MUCH AS SHE DID. GUARANTEED."

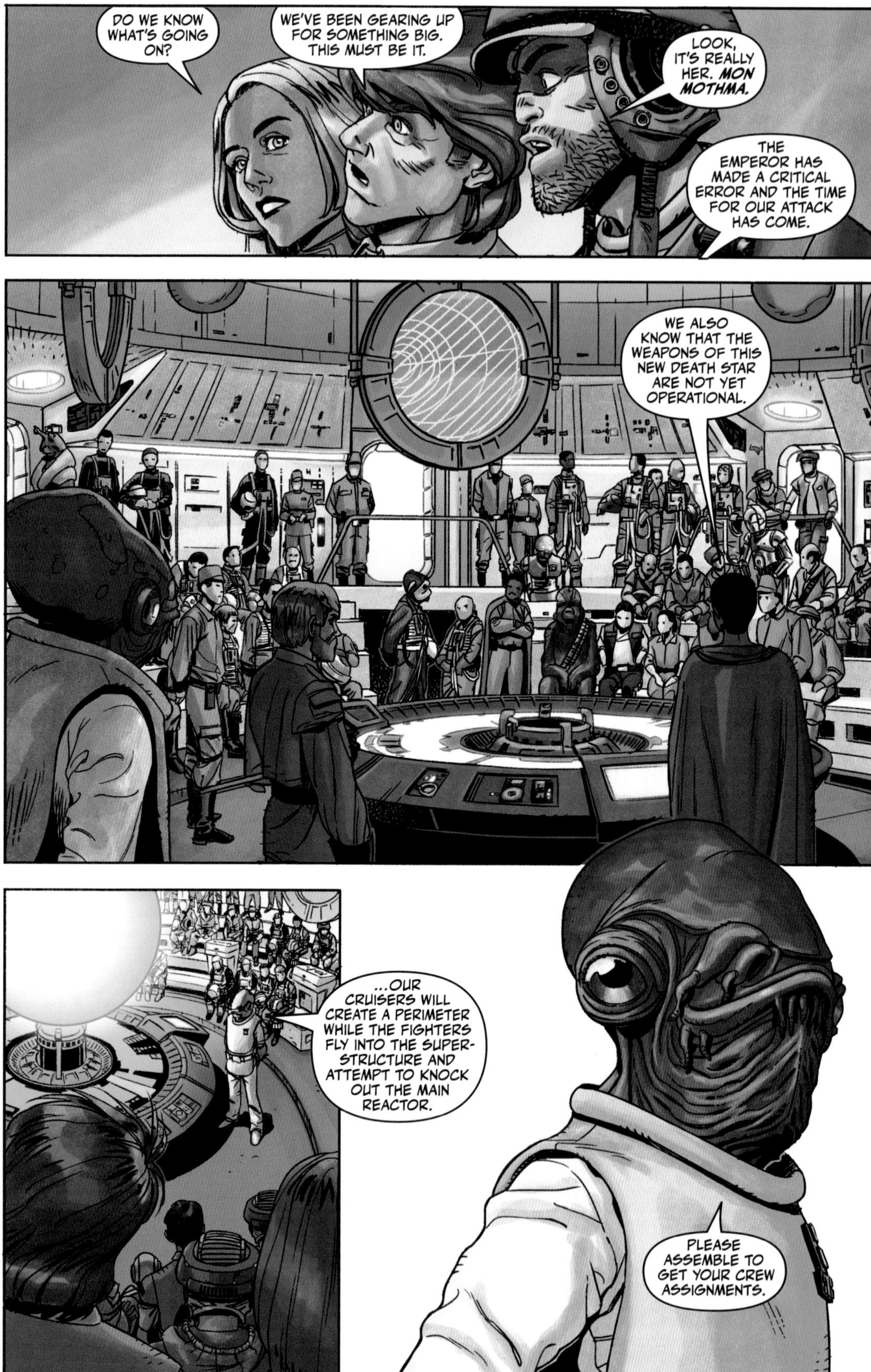
DO WE KNOW WHAT'S GOING ON?
WE'VE BEEN GEARING UP FOR SOMETHING BIG. THIS MUST BE IT.
LOOK, IT'S REALLY HER. MON MOTHMA.
THE EMPEROR HAS MADE A CRITICAL ERROR AND THE TIME FOR OUR ATTACK HAS COME.
WE ALSO KNOW THAT THE WEAPONS OF THIS NEW DEATH STAR ARE NOT YET OPERATIONAL.
...OUR CRUISERS WILL CREATE A PERIMETER WHILE THE FIGHTERS FLY INTO THE SUPER-STRUCTURE AND ATTEMPT TO KNOCK OUT THE MAIN REACTOR.
PLEASE ASSEMBLE TO GET YOUR CREW ASSIGNMENTS.

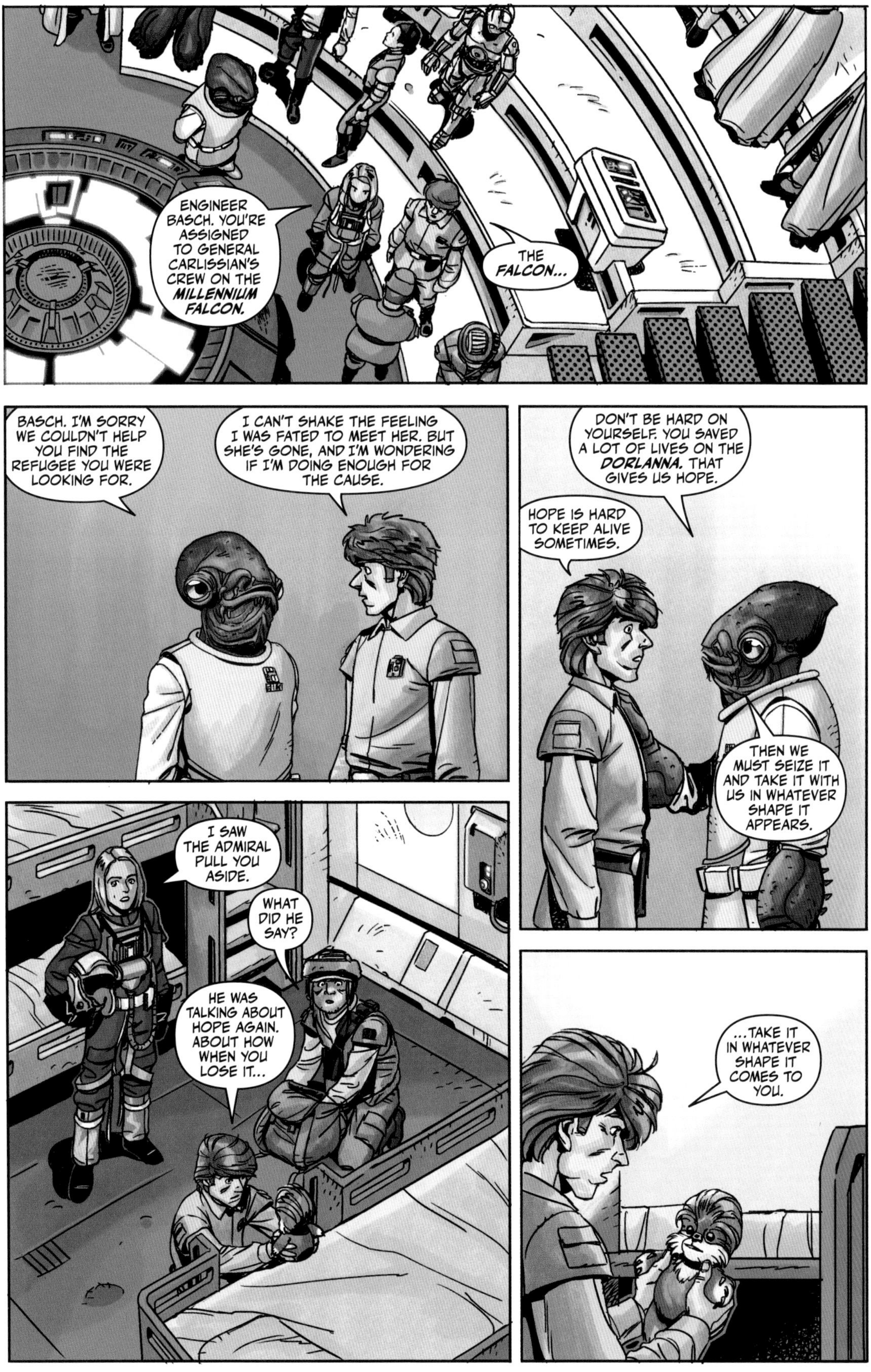
ENGINEER BASCH. YOU'RE ASSIGNED TO GENERAL CARLISSIAN'S CREW ON THE ***MILLENNIUM FALCON.***
THE ***FALCON...***
BASCH. I'M SORRY WE COULDN'T HELP YOU FIND THE REFUGEE YOU WERE LOOKING FOR.
I CAN'T SHAKE THE FEELING I WAS FATED TO MEET HER. BUT SHE'S GONE, AND I'M WONDERING IF I'M DOING ENOUGH FOR THE CAUSE.
DON'T BE HARD ON YOURSELF. YOU SAVED A LOT OF LIVES ON THE ***DORLANNA.*** THAT GIVES US HOPE.
HOPE IS HARD TO KEEP ALIVE SOMETIMES.
THEN WE MUST SEIZE IT AND TAKE IT WITH US IN WHATEVER SHAPE IT APPEARS.
I SAW THE ADMIRAL PULL YOU ASIDE.
WHAT DID HE SAY?
HE WAS TALKING ABOUT HOPE AGAIN. ABOUT HOW WHEN YOU LOSE IT...
...TAKE IT IN WHATEVER SHAPE IT COMES TO YOU.

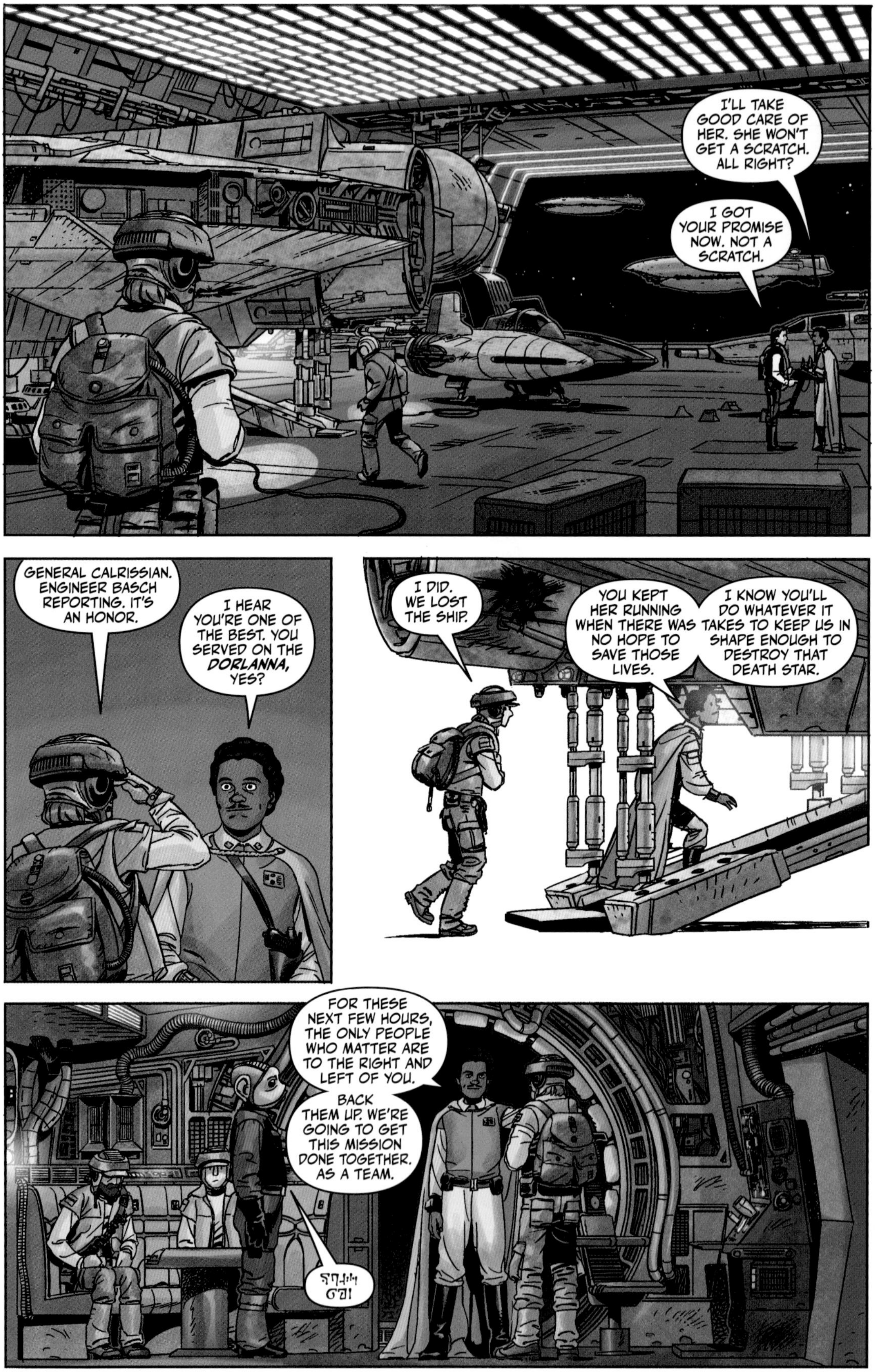
I'LL TAKE GOOD CARE OF HER. SHE WON'T GET A SCRATCH. ALL RIGHT?
I GOT YOUR PROMISE NOW. NOT A SCRATCH.
GENERAL CALRISSIAN. ENGINEER BASCH REPORTING. IT'S AN HONOR.
I HEAR YOU'RE ONE OF THE BEST. YOU SERVED ON THE *DORLANNA,* YES?
I DID. WE LOST THE SHIP.
YOU KEPT HER RUNNING WHEN THERE WAS NO HOPE TO SAVE THOSE LIVES.
I KNOW YOU'LL DO WHATEVER IT TAKES TO KEEP US IN SHAPE ENOUGH TO DESTROY THAT DEATH STAR.
FOR THESE NEXT FEW HOURS, THE ONLY PEOPLE WHO MATTER ARE TO THE RIGHT AND LEFT OF YOU.
BACK THEM UP. WE'RE GOING TO GET THIS MISSION DONE TOGETHER. AS A TEAM.

YOU HEARD WHAT THE GENERAL SAID. BACK ME UP.

WHAT? NO. I'D NEVER LEAVE YOU BEHIND. WE'RE A TEAM, RIGHT? FOR TOBIE.

I DIDN'T REALIZE YOU WERE AN OVERGROWN KID, BASCH.

HE'S NOT GETTING A MEDAL WHEN WE WIN ONE.

I'M GOING TO GET US THROUGH THIS AS BEST I CAN WITH MY LITTLE FRIEND HERE.

FOR THE GIRL WHO OWNED THIS DOLL. IT'S MY GOOD LUCK CHARM AND YOURS TOO NOW.

ENGINEER BASCH? INTERESTING PART OF YOUR ENGINEER TOOL KIT.

I CAN'T IMAGINE THE *FALCON* WITHOUT A WOOKIEE ON BOARD, SIR.

GOOD CALL. WE'LL TAKE ALL THE LUCK WE CAN.

I MADE A PROMISE THAT I'M PLANNING ON KEEPING.

ᐱᎩ ᎩᏛᏑ ᏞᏋᏅᏔᎬᏁᏅ ᏟᎯᏁᏁᎯᏟᏟᎯᎺ ᏻᏛᎯᎩ ᏔᏐᏂᏛ

YOU'RE MORE THAN *CHEWIE'S* SEAT WARMER.

PREPARE TO JUMP INTO HYPERSPACE ON MY MARK.

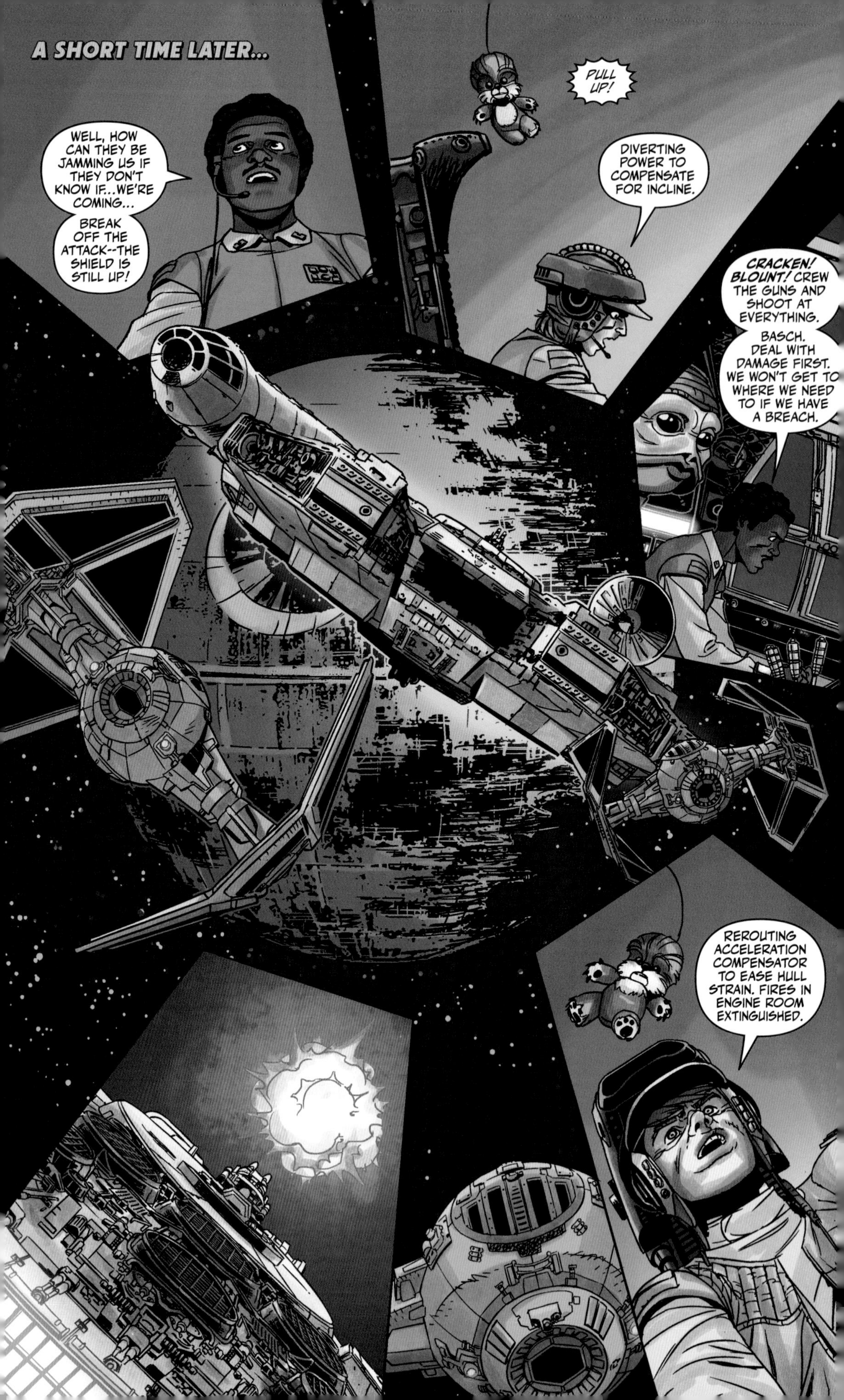
A SHORT TIME LATER...
WELL, HOW CAN THEY BE JAMMING US IF THEY DON'T KNOW IF...WE'RE COMING...
BREAK OFF THE ATTACK--THE SHIELD IS STILL UP!
PULL UP!
DIVERTING POWER TO COMPENSATE FOR INCLINE.
CRACKEN! BLOUNT! CREW THE GUNS AND SHOOT AT EVERYTHING.
BASCH. DEAL WITH DAMAGE FIRST. WE WON'T GET TO WHERE WE NEED TO IF WE HAVE A BREACH.
REROUTING ACCELERATION COMPENSATOR TO EASE HULL STRAIN. FIRES IN ENGINE ROOM EXTINGUISHED.

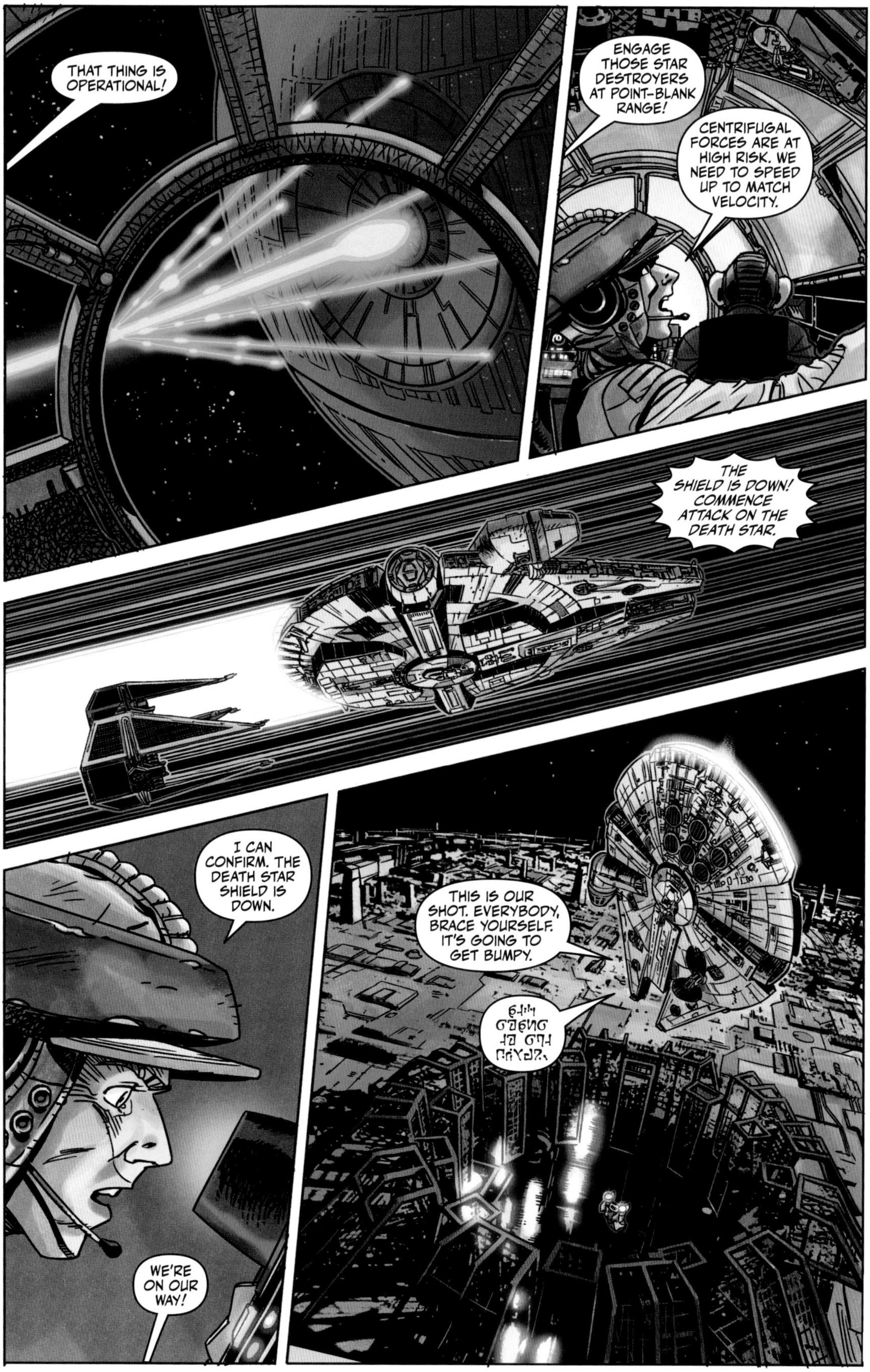
THAT THING IS OPERATIONAL!
ENGAGE THOSE STAR DESTROYERS AT POINT-BLANK RANGE!
CENTRIFUGAL FORCES ARE AT HIGH RISK. WE NEED TO SPEED UP TO MATCH VELOCITY.
THE SHIELD IS DOWN! COMMENCE ATTACK ON THE DEATH STAR.
I CAN CONFIRM. THE DEATH STAR SHIELD IS DOWN.
WE'RE ON OUR WAY!
THIS IS OUR SHOT. EVERYBODY, BRACE YOURSELF. IT'S GOING TO GET BUMPY.

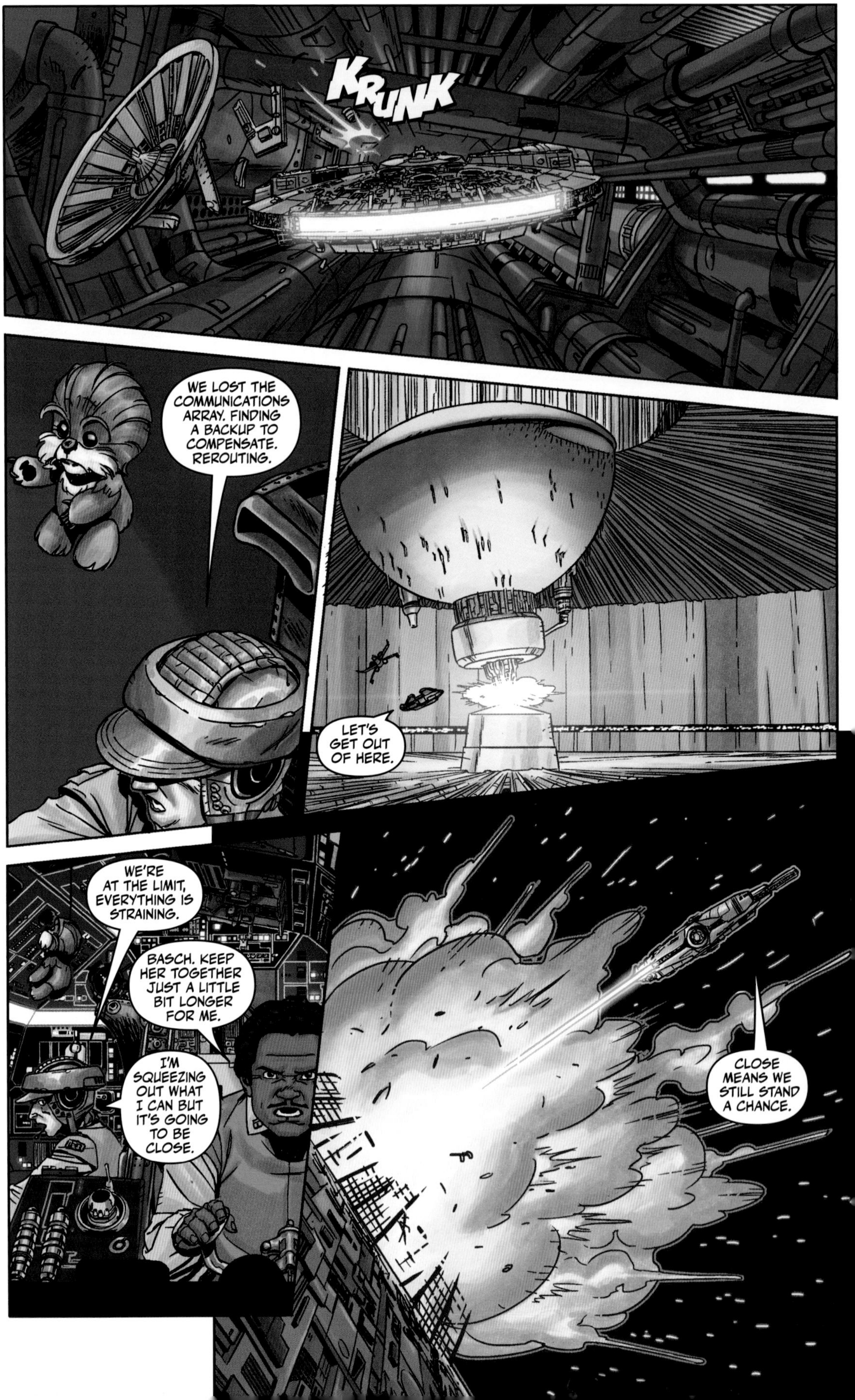
KRUNK
WE LOST THE COMMUNICATIONS ARRAY. FINDING A BACKUP TO COMPENSATE. REROUTING.
LET'S GET OUT OF HERE.
WE'RE AT THE LIMIT, EVERYTHING IS STRAINING.
BASCH. KEEP HER TOGETHER JUST A LITTLE BIT LONGER FOR ME.
I'M SQUEEZING OUT WHAT I CAN BUT IT'S GOING TO BE CLOSE.
CLOSE MEANS WE STILL STAND A CHANCE.

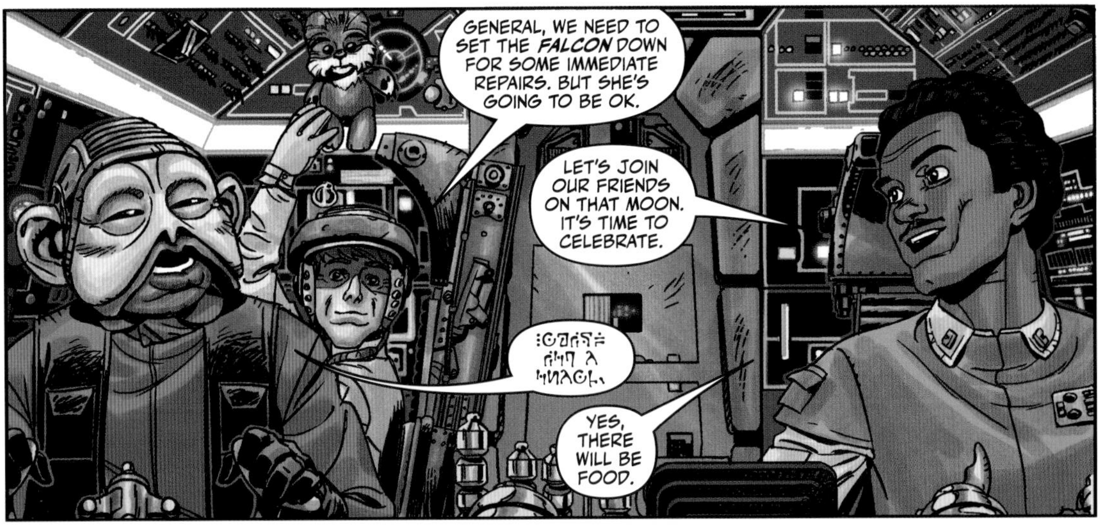
GENERAL, WE NEED TO SET THE *FALCON* DOWN FOR SOME IMMEDIATE REPAIRS. BUT SHE'S GOING TO BE OK.
LET'S JOIN OUR FRIENDS ON THAT MOON. IT'S TIME TO CELEBRATE.
YES, THERE WILL BE FOOD.
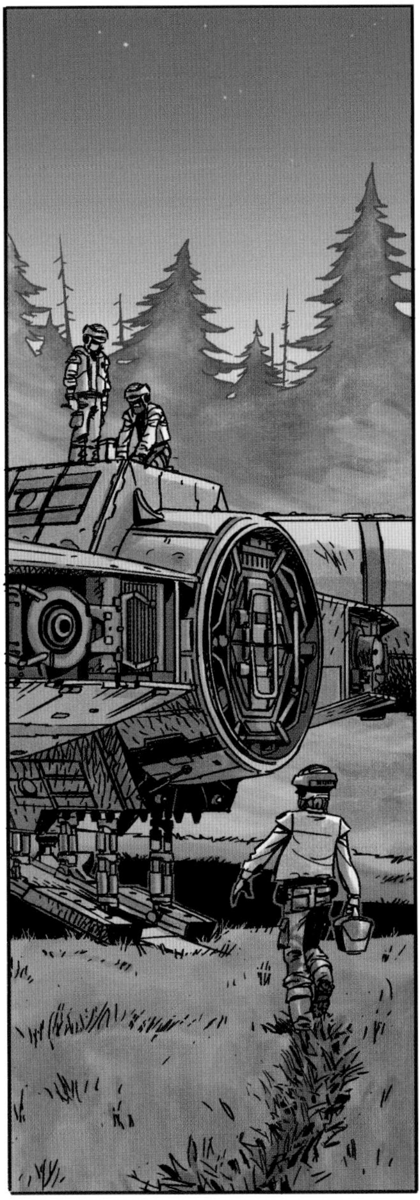
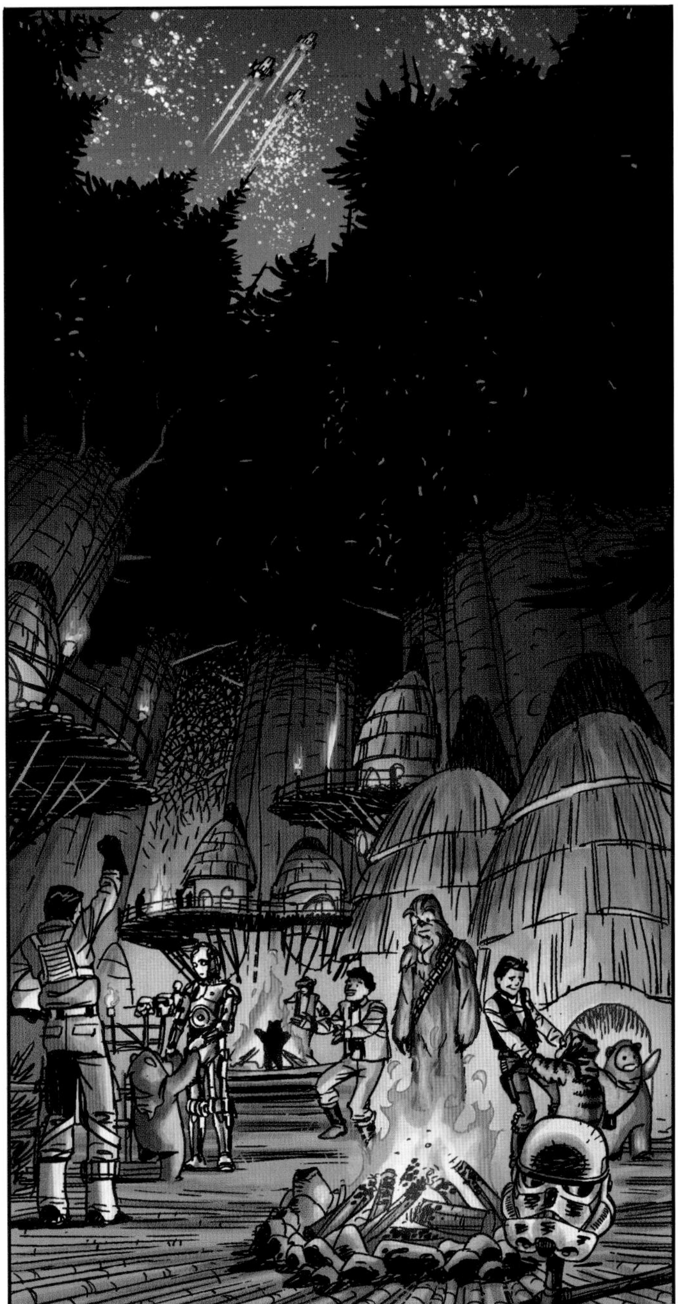

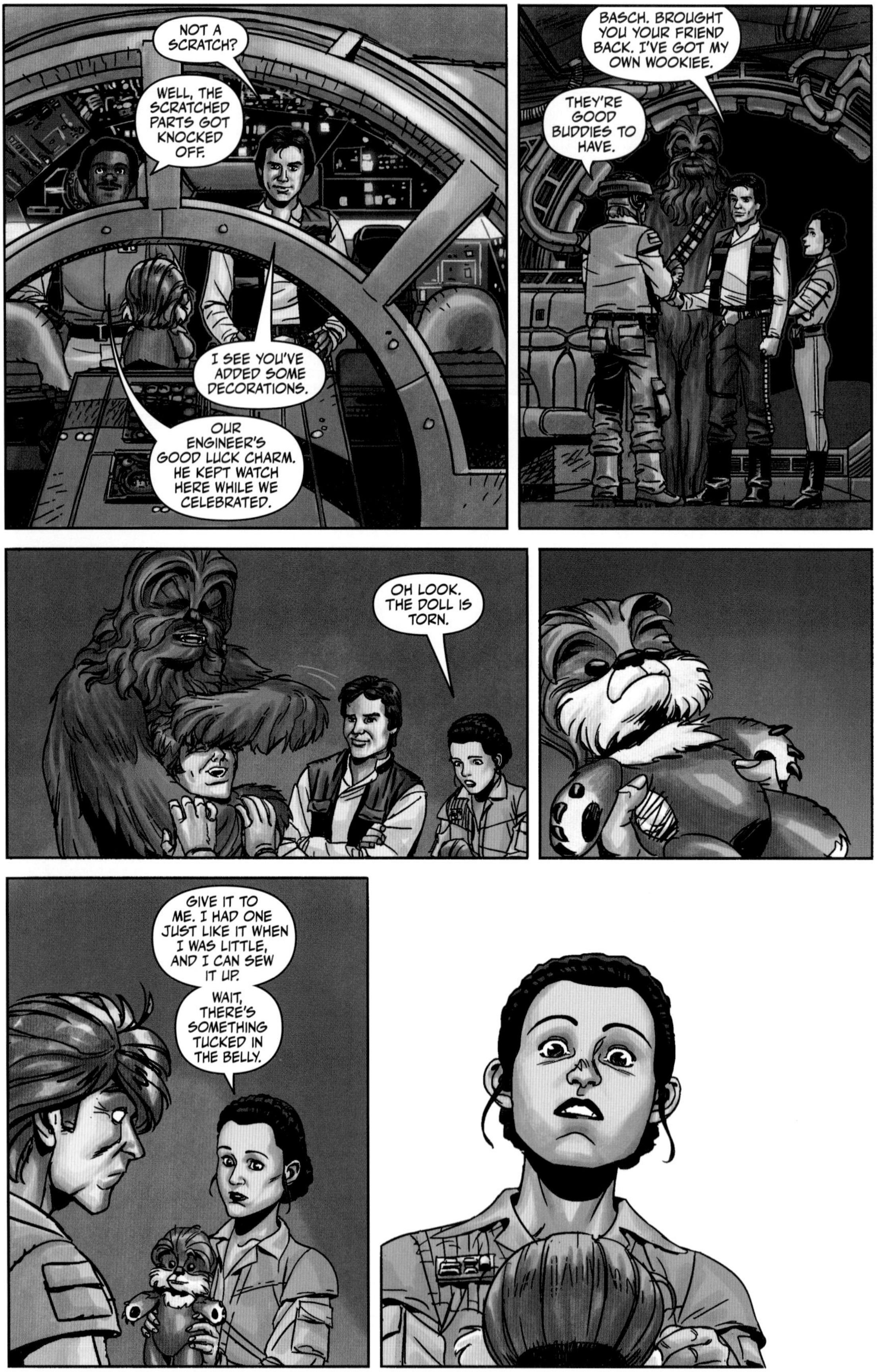
NOT A SCRATCH?
WELL, THE SCRATCHED PARTS GOT KNOCKED OFF.
I SEE YOU'VE ADDED SOME DECORATIONS.
OUR ENGINEER'S GOOD LUCK CHARM. HE KEPT WATCH HERE WHILE WE CELEBRATED.
BASCH. BROUGHT YOU YOUR FRIEND BACK. I'VE GOT MY OWN WOOKIEE.
THEY'RE GOOD BUDDIES TO HAVE.
OH LOOK. THE DOLL IS TORN.
GIVE IT TO ME. I HAD ONE JUST LIKE IT WHEN I WAS LITTLE, AND I CAN SEW IT UP.
WAIT, THERE'S SOMETHING TUCKED IN THE BELLY.

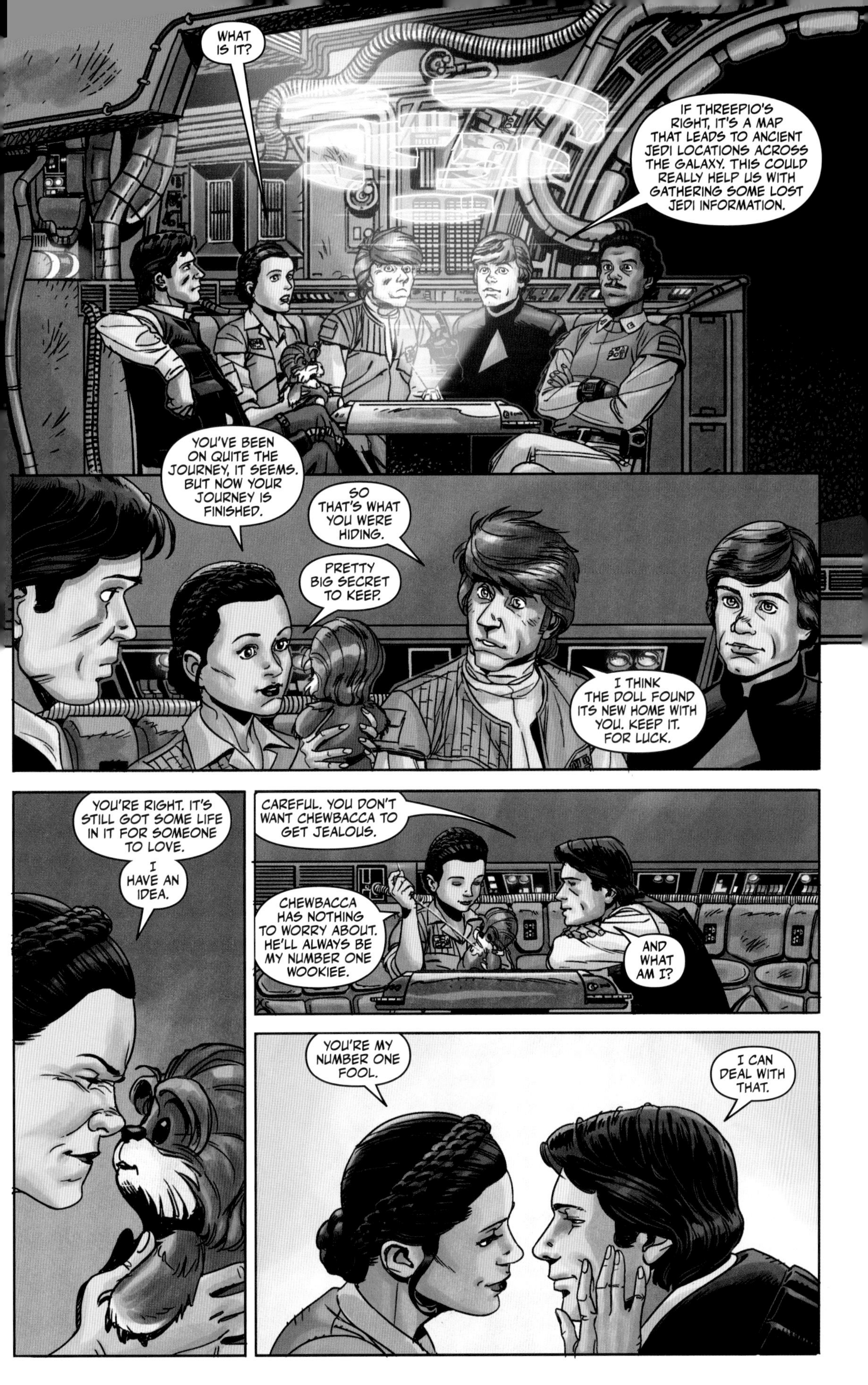
WHAT IS IT?
IF THREEPIO'S RIGHT, IT'S A MAP THAT LEADS TO ANCIENT JEDI LOCATIONS ACROSS THE GALAXY. THIS COULD REALLY HELP US WITH GATHERING SOME LOST JEDI INFORMATION.
YOU'VE BEEN ON QUITE THE JOURNEY, IT SEEMS. BUT NOW YOUR JOURNEY IS FINISHED.
SO THAT'S WHAT YOU WERE HIDING.
PRETTY BIG SECRET TO KEEP.
I THINK THE DOLL FOUND ITS NEW HOME WITH YOU. KEEP IT. FOR LUCK.
YOU'RE RIGHT. IT'S STILL GOT SOME LIFE IN IT FOR SOMEONE TO LOVE.
I HAVE AN IDEA.
CAREFUL. YOU DON'T WANT CHEWBACCA TO GET JEALOUS.
CHEWBACCA HAS NOTHING TO WORRY ABOUT. HE'LL ALWAYS BE MY NUMBER ONE WOOKIEE.
AND WHAT AM I?
YOU'RE MY NUMBER ONE FOOL.
I CAN DEAL WITH THAT.

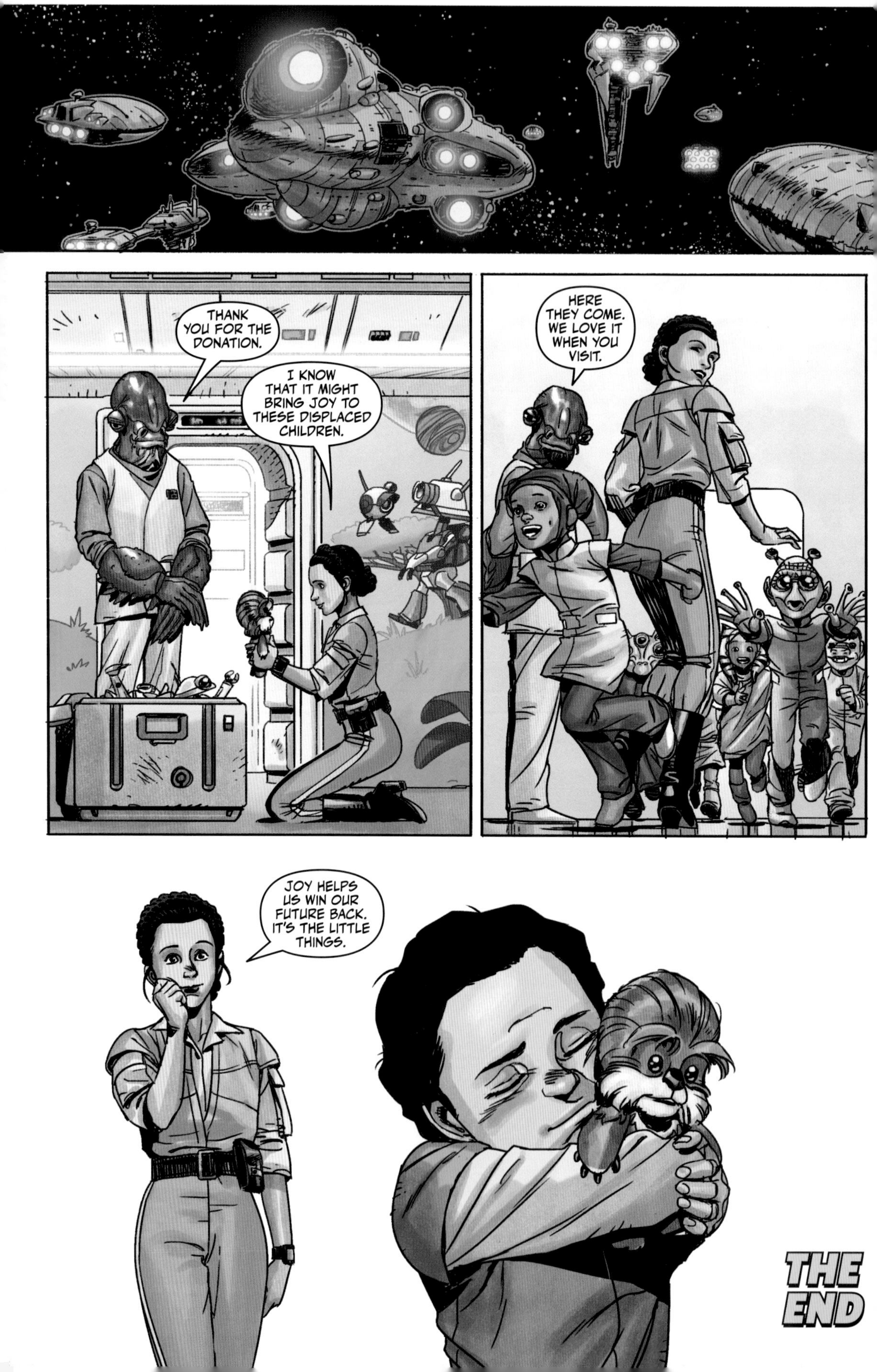
THANK YOU FOR THE DONATION.
I KNOW THAT IT MIGHT BRING JOY TO THESE DISPLACED CHILDREN.
HERE THEY COME. WE LOVE IT WHEN YOU VISIT.
JOY HELPS US WIN OUR FUTURE BACK. IT'S THE LITTLE THINGS.
THE END

COVER GALLERY

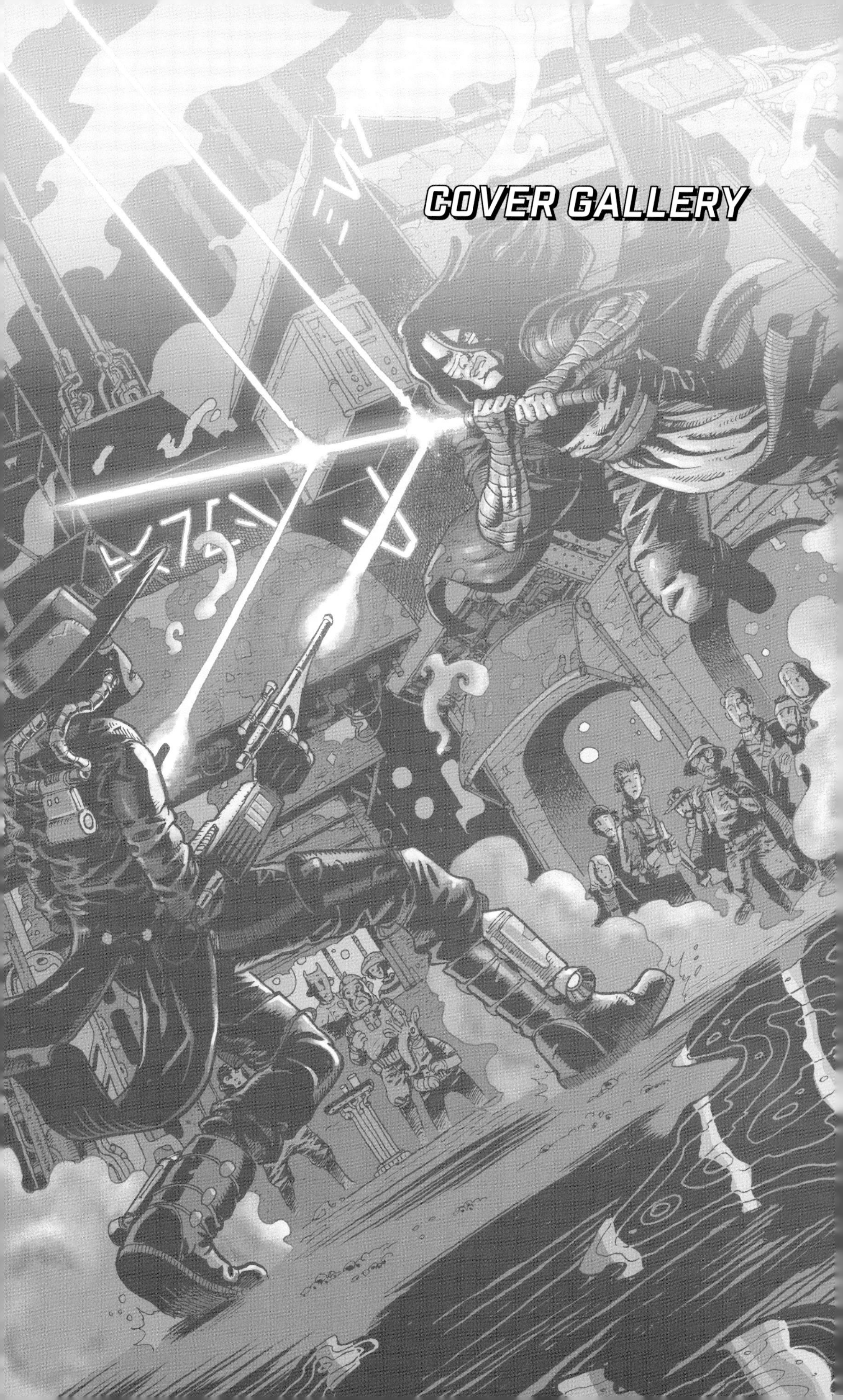

Art by Lucas Marangon

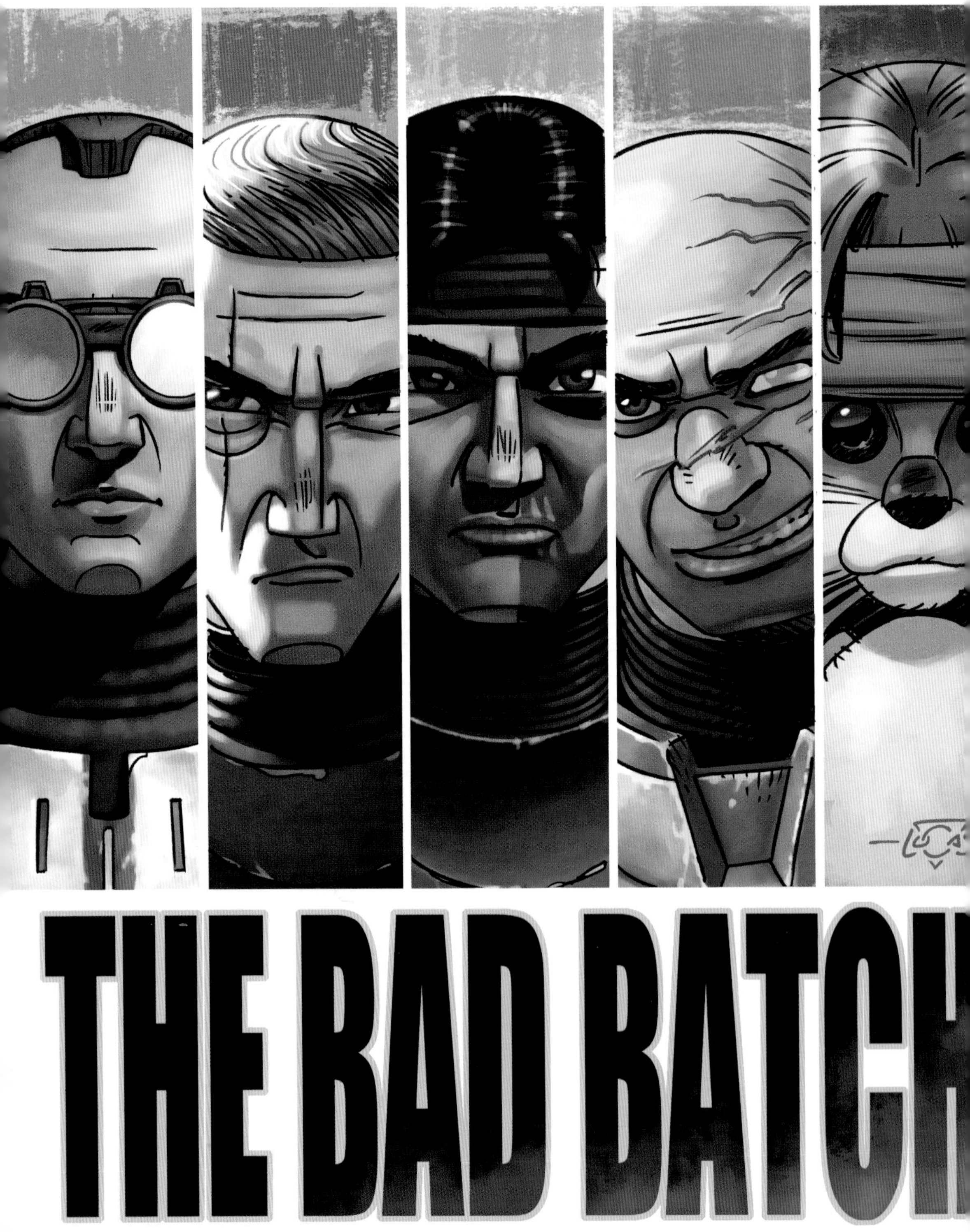

THE BAD BATCH

STAR WARS™

ALSO AVAILABLE

THE ART OF STAR WARS: VISIONS
978-1-50672-851-3 | $49.99

THE ART OF STAR WARS: REBELS
978-1-50671-091-4 | $39.99

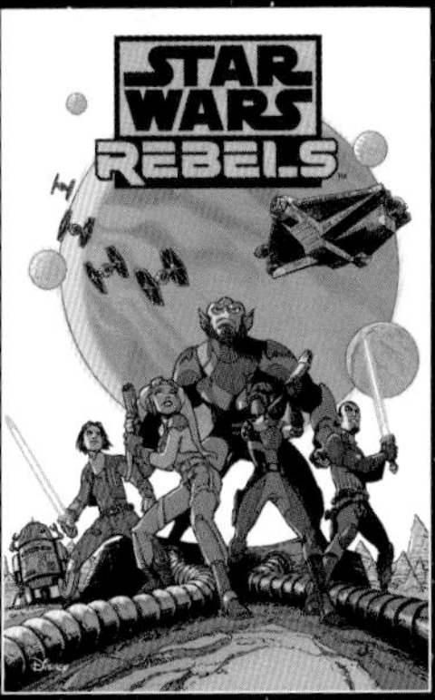

STAR WARS REBELS

STAR WARS: REBELS
978-1-50673-301-2 | $29.99

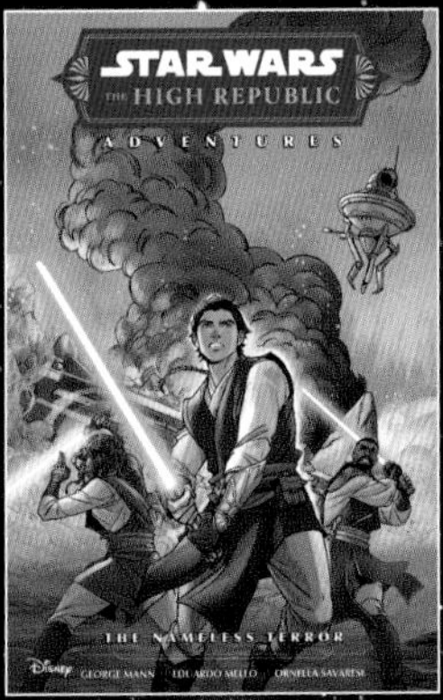

STAR WARS THE HIGH REPUBLIC
ADVENTURES
THE NAMELESS TERROR

STAR WARS: HIGH REPUBLIC ADVENTURES—THE NAMELESS TERROR
978-1-50673-567-2 | $19.99

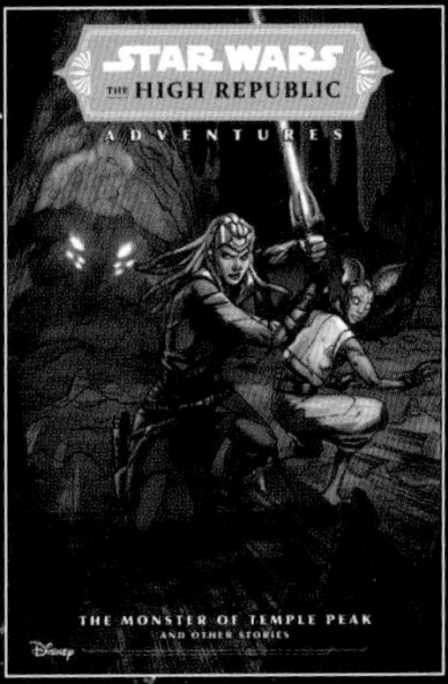

STAR WARS THE HIGH REPUBLIC
ADVENTURES
THE MONSTER OF TEMPLE PEAK

STAR WARS: HIGH REPUBLIC ADVENTURES—THE MONSTER OF TEMPLE PEAK AND OTHER STORIES
978-1-50673-779-9 | $19.99

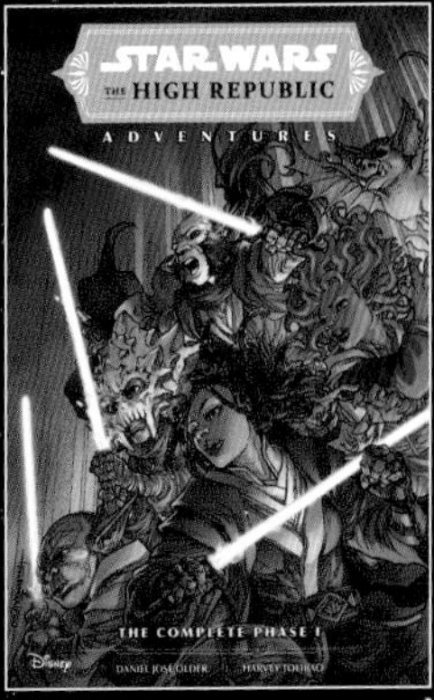

STAR WARS THE HIGH REPUBLIC
ADVENTURES
THE COMPLETE PHASE I

STAR WARS: THE HIGH REPUBLIC ADVENTURES—THE COMPLETE PHASE 1
978-1-50673-780-5 | $29.99

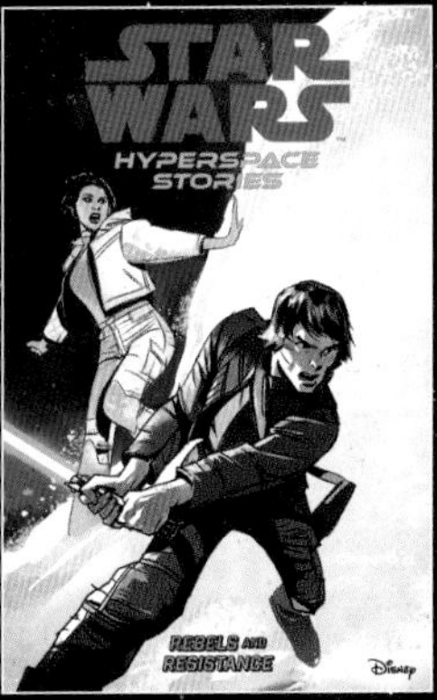

STAR WARS
HYPERSPACE STORIES
REBELS AND RESISTANCE

STAR WARS: HYPERSPACE STORIES—REBELS AND RESISTANCE
978-1-50673-286-2 | $19.99

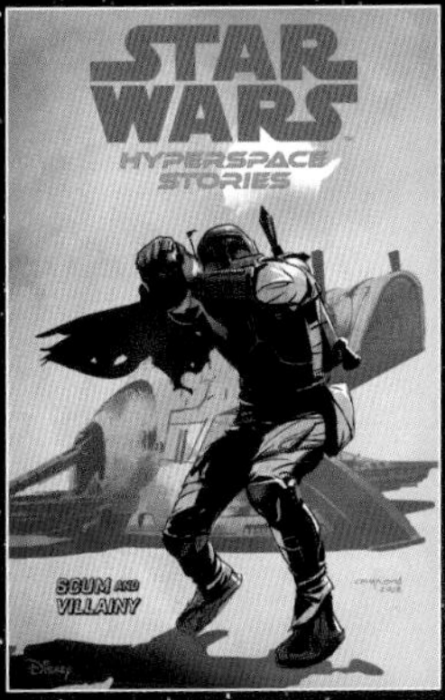

STAR WARS
HYPERSPACE STORIES
SCUM AND VILLAINY

STAR WARS HYPERSPACE STORIES—SCUM AND VILLAINY
978-1-50673-287-9 | $19.99

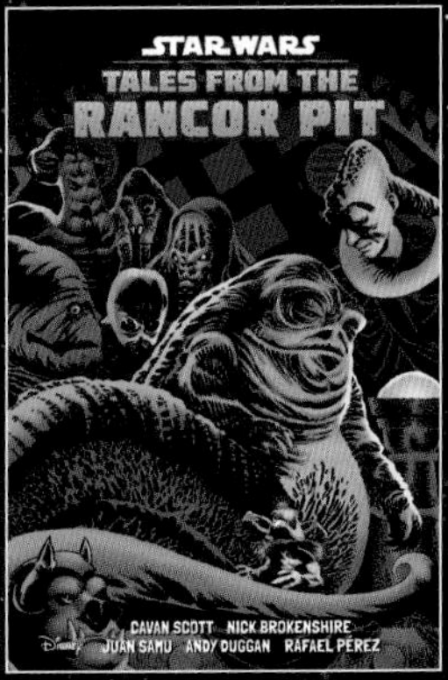

STAR WARS
TALES FROM THE RANCOR PIT
CAVAN SCOTT NICK BROKENSHIRE
JUAN SAMU ANDY DUGGAN RAFAEL PÉREZ

STAR WARS: TALES FROM THE RANCOR PIT
978-1-50673-284-8 | $19.99

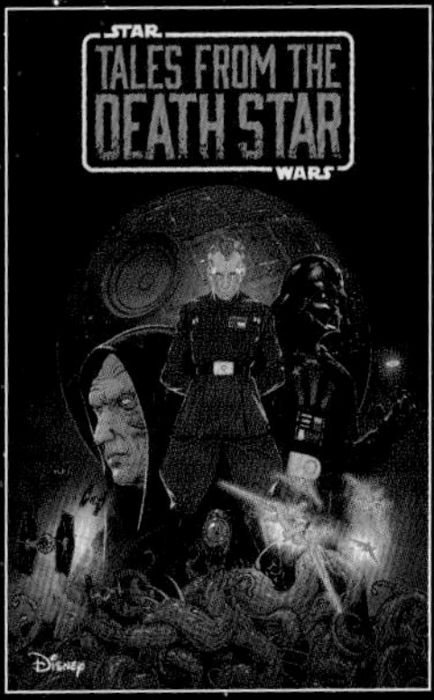

STAR WARS
TALES FROM THE DEATH STAR

STAR WARS: TALES FROM THE DEATH STAR
978-1-50673-829-1 | $24.99

And check out our monthly comics series!

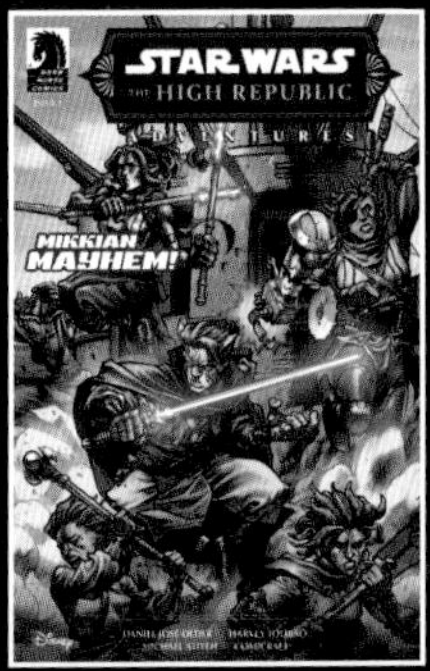

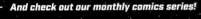

STAR WARS THE HIGH REPUBLIC
MIKKIAN MAYHEM!

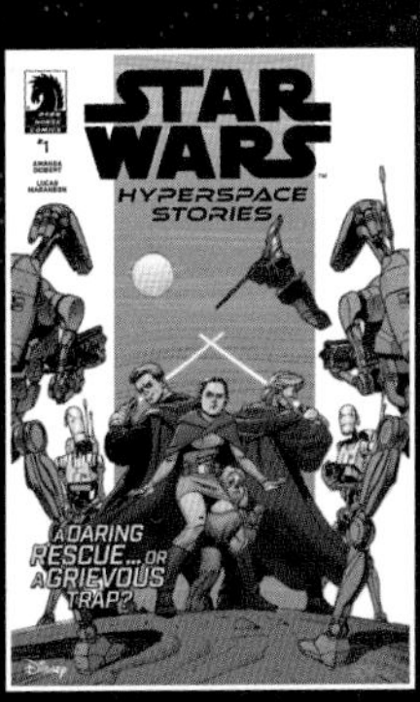

STAR WARS
HYPERSPACE STORIES
A DARING RESCUE... OR AGRIEVOUS TRAP?

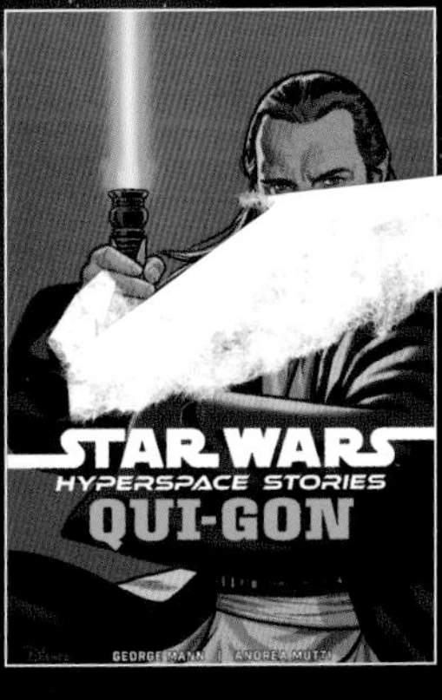

STAR WARS
HYPERSPACE STORIES
QUI-GON

STAR WARS: HYPERSPACE STORIES–QUI-GON
978-1-50673-984-7 | $19.99

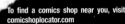

AVAILABLE AT YOUR LOCAL COMICS SHOP OR BOOKSTORE!

To find a comics shop near you, visit comicshoplocator.com

For more information or to order direct, visit darkhorse.com *Prices and availability subject to change without notice.

Art by Cary Nord

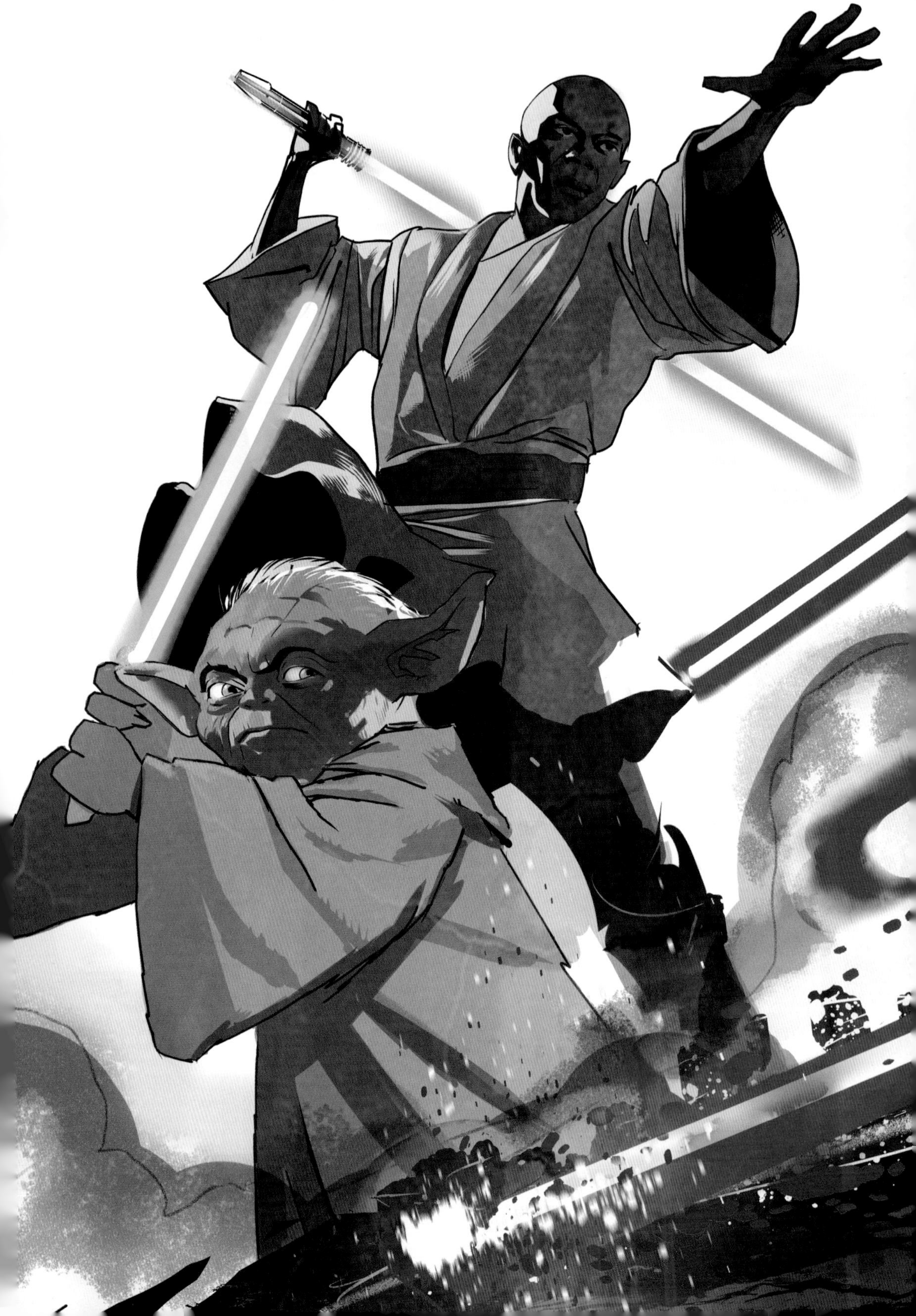